Suite 16

By

Jay Dubya

Suite 16

By

Jay Dubya

Published by
Jay Dubya
Hammonton, NJ 08037
3230_3HC

ISBN 978-1-58909-814-5

Other Books by Jay Dubya

Adult Fiction

Black Leather and Blue Denim, A '50s Novel
The Great Teen Fruit War, A 1960' Novel
Frat' Brats, A '60s Novel
Ron Coyote, Man of La Mangia
So Ya' Wanna' Be A Teacher!
Pieces of Eight
Pieces of Eight, Part II
Pieces of Eight, Part III
Pieces of Eight, Part IV
The Wholly Book of Genesis
The Wholly Book of Exodus
The Wholly Book of Doo-Doo-Rot-on-Me
Thirteen Sick Tasteless Classics
Thirteen Sick Tasteless Classics, Part II
Thirteen Sick Tasteless Classics, Part III
Thirteen Sick Tasteless Classics, Part IV
Thirteen Sick Tasteless Classics, Part V
Nine New Novellas
Nine New Novellas, Part II
Nine New Novellas, Part III
Nine New Novellas, Part IV
Mauled Maimed Mangled Mutilated Mythology
Modern Mythology
Fractured Frazzled Folk Fables and Fairy Farces
FFFF & FF, Part II
One Baker's Dozen
Two Baker's Dozen
Random Articles and Manuscripts
Snake Eyes and Boxcars
Snake Eyes and Boxcars, Part II
Shakespeare: Slammed, Smeared, Savaged and Slaughtered
Shakespeare: S, S, S and S, Part II
O. Henry: Obscenely and Outrageously Obliterated
Twain: Tattered, Trounced, Tortured and Traumatized
London: Lashed, Lacerated, Lampooned and Lambasted
Poe: Pelted, Pounded, Pummeled and Pulverized
Time Travel Tales
UFO: Utterly Fantastic Occurrences

Snake Eyes and Boxcars
Snake Eyes and Boxcars, Part II
Prime-Time Crime Time
The FBI Inspector
The Psychic Dimension
The Psychic Dimension, Part II
First Person Stories
The Arcane Arcade
13 Tantalizing Tales
PLOTS
PLOTS, Part II
THEMES
Hawthorne: Hazed Hooked Hammered & Hijacked
Hathorne Hacked, Shakespeare Sacked, & Thurber Thwacked
Homer's Ill Iliad
Homer's Odd Sea Odyssey
Homer's Ill Iliad & Odd Sea Odyssey
The Timeless Time Machine
War of the Worlds
The Invisible Man
Parody Paradise
Parody Paradise, Part II
Parody Paradise, Part III
Parody Paradise, Part IV
A Christmas Carol
Bee 17, Short Stories
Bee 17, #2, Short Stories
Bee 17, Part III, Short Stories
Bee 17, Part IV, Short Stories
Bee 17, Part V, Short Stories
Bee 17, Part VI, Short Stories

Young Adult Fantasy Novels

Pot of Gold
Enchanta
Space Bugs, Earth Invasion
The Eighteen Story Gingerbread House

Contents

In Memory of William "Billy" Burns, (1967-2009)

"Destiny Beckons"

Cucurbitaceae: the genetic family of all melons and squash including cucumbers, gourds, pumpkins, cantaloupes, watermelons and honeydew.

Jennifer Linda Bozarth, an all-too-curious and attractive brunette farm girl living with her parents in Worcester County was quite familiar with the popular varieties of melons and squashes simply because her father was an accomplished grower who owned an expansive five-hundred-acre plantation near Route 50 in Berlin, Maryland. After graduating from Stephen Decatur High School, Jennifer had attended Salisbury State University where the twenty-three year old had recently earned a bachelor's degree in business accounting. But despite her meritorious academic success, certain vague memories from the young woman's early childhood still occasionally surfaced from her subconscious and bewildered her curiosity, which was not totally satisfied.

"Mom," Jennifer asked Mrs. Martha Bozarth the first Saturday morning in June after *she* had received her important college degree, "don't you remember the small cedar lake that you and Dad had taken me to when I was a mere toddler. All I can recollect is the cold water and I also remember that the lake had been surrounded on two sides by a dense pine tree forest. And also," the daughter stated, "I distinctly recall a small boy near us screaming. The distressed child had been tied by a rope to a sturdy tree while his neglectful parents were preoccupied swimming."

"You must be mistaken Jenn and your imagination is absolutely running amuck," Mrs. Martha Bozarth very politely answered. "There're no such cedar lakes anywhere near Berlin. And if you recall, your father and I would often take you to the boardwalk, to the beach, and then we'd all wade in the surf over in nearby Ocean City. Now please make yourself a peanut butter and jelly sandwich while your father and I get ready to paint the town red in celebration of our thirtieth wedding anniversary."

"That's right Jennifer!" Mr. Judd Bozarth verified. "I believe that your childhood memories are a bit fuzzy. But in regard to your strange cold water cedar lake reference, when you were in kindergarten your mother and I had on several occasions taken you up to Silver Lake in Rehoboth Beach. But Silver Lake is definitely not surrounded by a pine tree forest, and it doesn't have cold cedar water either. If you remember," Judd Bozarth elaborated, "it does have handsome mansions with docks and gingerbread-trimmed gazebos on its shores and the tranquil lake is only a hundred yards or so from the Atlantic."

"But Dad, I still vividly remember the cold water lake that wasn't too far from a huge manor house having a colorful portrait of a beautiful woman hanging above a stone fireplace mantel," Jennifer emphatically insisted. "The lovely woman was dressed in the type of fancy ruffled dress that a sophisticated lady would be wearing just before the Civil War. I don't know why these bizarre thoughts keep recurring in my mind, but they do!" the puzzled daughter expressed. "And the impressive manor house was surrounded by very large cornfields too!"

"Perhaps the little vacation you're planning with your friends over in Ocean City will get your mind focused on much-needed relaxation just before the stress of the melon growing season begins," Judd Bozarth reminded his very intelligent daughter. "As we thoroughly discussed last month, I trust you'll be doing the business's credits and debits' accounting one final time this summer before you try going out on your own to work and live in either Baltimore or Washington."

"Honestly Father, I'm positively bored with Ocean City, Maryland," Jennifer all-too-honestly confessed. "And I'm tired of staying with my girlfriends too up in Rehoboth Beach! I want to spend a few days across Delaware Bay adventuring in Wildwood. I've already made reservations to crash at the Crusader Motor Lodge in Wildwood Crest. From the brochure I had received in the mail, it seems like a decent place to stay. Quite frankly Janice and Lori are looking forward to Wildwood too!"

"Why that's a splendid leisure time idea just before the hectic harvest season," Mrs. Bozarth amiably agreed. "Here's a constructive suggestion. You can also visit the Victorian homes in nearby Cape May and walk the boardwalk in Ocean City, New Jersey. It's quite famous for being a family-friendly resort."

"And perhaps I'll get daring and try my slot machine luck at a glitzy Atlantic City casino," the recent Salisbury State University graduate declared. "I think that the change in vacation venue from Ocean City, Maryland to Wildwood, New Jersey will prove to be most enjoyable for myself and my two girlfriends. And after I return all refreshed and rejuvenated," Jennifer speculated and loyally predicted, "I'll be able to fully handle the tedium of taking care of this farm's summer business stats."

"Sounds mighty copasetic to me," Judd Bozarth acknowledged with a broad smile. "But be careful! Wildwood has a reputation for being a more volatile resort than Ocean City, Maryland and Rehoboth Beach, Delaware do, especially with the late night bar scenes! And don't talk with too many handsome and drunk male strangers! Be sure to stick with your trustworthy girlfriends."

"I won't do anything stupid Daddy," Jennifer promised. "Are you and Mom still going out to supper with the Harrisons tonight?"

"Yes Dear," Mrs. Martha Bozarth confirmed. "We're having dinner over in Ocean City at the Embers. As you know, that's your father's favorite restaurant and I'll bet he'll be ordering his usual surf and turf dinner. He likes the way the Embers' waiters memorize a group's orders without ever writing them down and then deliver the five courses to the table without ever making a mistake."

"Am I that downright predictable?" Judd asked and then reflexively laughed. "Anyway Jennifer, enjoy having the house all to yourself for four precious hours. Big Bob Harrison likes to eat two appetizers before dinner and devour two desserts after the meal, so I've been starving myself all-day-long so that I can stay up with him in regard to total food consumption."

After her parents departed the cozy manor house to drive over to the Harrison residence on the opposite and more rural side of Berlin, Jennifer casually sat on the den's red leather sofa to watch the first several innings of the Baltimore Orioles versus New York Yankees baseball game. 'Perhaps I'll search the On-Demand section of the cable programming to select a romance movie to watch. There's no way that the Orioles are going to overcome a huge five run deficit so early in the baseball game. Oh, no!' the young woman anxiously thought. 'The electricity just went out! Must be a speeding motorist hitting a telephone pole over on Route 50! Yes, there's the siren from downtown wailing away! I believe there's a flashlight in the second cabinet to the left of Dad's desk in case the electricity remains off after dusk.'

Jennifer rose from the sofa, paced to the den's birch wood desk and then stooped down and anxiously rummaged through the second left-side cabinet, finally discovering the sought-after vertical-standing flashlight. Just as she pulled the object out of its remote confinement, much to her emotional relief, the house's power surged on. 'It's a good thing it's still twilight outside because if I had to use this object to shine a light, it just doesn't work! I'll check to see if this old flashlight needs new batteries!'

The battery compartment was skillfully opened and examined, and soon Jennifer was surprised to find a formerly hidden key inserted in a slot situated next to the defunct batteries. 'I'll bet this is the secret key to Dad's personal desk that he always keeps locked. Right now I'm overwhelmed with curiosity and I just have to surrender to the temptation of opening the drawer. Just like Pandora in Greek Mythology, I just have to see what's inside!'

The perceptive daughter slowly removed the aforementioned flashlight compartment key from its lodged position and then gingerly inserted it into the desk's lock. 'A perfect fit!' she reckoned with some nervous satisfaction. 'Every family has a skeleton or two in the closet or a tightly guarded secret concealed in a bank safety deposit box or kept inside a den desk drawer. Let's see if this little investigation of mine yields any family knowledge that I haven't yet been told!'

In the posterior of the desk drawer, Jennifer located an old Manila envelope, which she then very methodically opened. Inside the enclosure the examiner came across a copy of her original birth certificate dated April 3rd, 1987, and her parents were listed as Emanuel and Helen Jennings of Shamong, New Jersey. 'Oh my God!' the astonished girl determined, breaking out in a sweat despite the den's more-than-adequate air-conditioning. 'Mom and Dad aren't my biological parents. How surprisingly bizarre is this! I'm shocked to learn that I've been adopted. Judd and Martha Bozarth aren't my real parents! But what's this stunning mystery all about?'

Other documents found inside the faded tan folder revealed a photocopied check for one million dollars written from the hand of Emanuel Jennings to Judd Bozarth for "Acquisition of Berlin, Maryland Farm" and another Xeroxed check for one million five hundred thousand dollars had been designated for the purpose of "Personal Favor." Jennifer immediately surmised that the "Personal Favor" was money to raise and educate her without the girl possessing any knowledge of her Jennings' family genealogical tree.

'This is not the birth certificate I remember using when I had obtained my Maryland driver's license and my college admission. That document I showed did not have a raised seal and had been obtained from the county clerk's office over in Snow Hill. What a terrible chance cache of information I've stumbled across!' Jennifer angrily realized. 'I'll bet that Judd and Martha claimed that the original birth certificate from New Jersey had been lost and then using their political influence had the county officials make-up a fraudulent one! Now I can't wait to travel up to New Jersey next

4

week with Janice and Lori. I'll temporarily desert them in Wildwood Crest, drive up to Shamong and visit these apparently rich people Emanuel and Helen Jennings to learn more details about my past! I'm going on the Internet right now!' the young lady decided. 'My theory is that Emanuel Jennings is an exceptionally successful melon farmer and that he's the one who got my surrogate father and mother set-up in that same type of prosperous business down here in folksy Berlin, Maryland! Now with a degree of patience,' the distraught girl determined, 'I'll just make the Manila envelope, the birch wood desk drawer and the magic key in the inoperable flashlight appear exactly as they had existed before the brief power failure had initiated this weird chain of events!'

When the elder Bozarths finally returned from having their delicious dinners at the very accommodating Embers Restaurant, immediately the mother astutely noticed an evident change in her daughter's normally placid general demeanor.

"Is everything all right with you Jennifer?" Martha diplomatically asked. "You look a trifle pale."

"Yes, Mother, everything's fine. I guess I'm relieved and I can't disguise my true feelings. We had a minor power failure while you were away and I was quite worried that someone had hit a telephone pole when I had heard the town siren sound," the young lady convincingly explained. "I'm so glad that you weren't involved in a traffic accident."

"It's wonderful having a dependable daughter who is so concerned about our safety and welfare," Judd confidently interrupted. "How long did the power failure last?"

"Only about thirty-seconds," Jennifer replied with a feigned sigh of appreciation. "I suppose that it's hardly anything troubling to ever raise an eyebrow about or to even vaguely remember tomorrow morning!"

* * * * * * * * * * * *

Several monotonous weeks had elapsed, and Jennifer Bozarth accompanied by passengers Janice Ranere and Lori Mitchell drove north from Berlin, Maryland to just outside Rehoboth Beach, Delaware to rendezvous with the nine a.m. ferry that would transport a hundred cars, buses and trucks across scenic Delaware Bay. The seventeen-mile-long Cape May-Lewes Ferry trip to Southern New

Jersey made Janice and Lori anticipate the sights and sounds of spectacular Wildwood.

"This boat ride will be an hour and twenty minutes so we'll have plenty of time to explore all parts of the ship," Janice reported to her voyaging comrades. "But the ferry trip cuts about seventy miles off the normal driving excursion from Maryland to the Jersey Shore, even though time-wise, the total duration will be about the same as if we had motored to Wildwood: that is to say, around three-hours and forty-five minutes."

"Wildwood has a reputation for being an extremely interesting and alluring resort town that really crowds-up during the summer months," Lori added to the generic discussion. "I've vacationed there two years ago with Marge Rafferty and Judy Santora. The three Morey Amusement Piers are pretty terrific, each one having sensational roller coaster rides and as for exciting nightlife," Lori added, "don't forget the rock and roll nightclubs and bars along Schellenger Avenue just off the central part of the honky-tonk boardwalk. Those three ocean amusement piers and the neon-signed bars just off the boardwalk ramps are simply loaded with tons of handsome muscular guys just waiting to make contact with eligible females. I just know we're going to meet three gorgeous hunks."

"I understand that Wildwood and Wildwood Crest have in recent years adopted a retro '50s theme with many of the hotels and motels featuring art deco designs from that nostalgic era," Jennifer informatively contributed to the bland dialogue. "Many '50s rock and roll stars like Bill Haley and the Comets, Bobby Rydell, Fabian and Frankie Avalon got their Show Business starts in Wildwood and also later gaining popularity by performing at the many other hot teen entertainment spots along the Jersey Shore, especially in Somers Point and Atlantic City."

"Let's go inside and enjoy some sodas and snacks," Janice suggested just as the fully loaded ferry's massive departure horns blasted. "What is life without junk food? Then after our leaving the Lewes dock, we could walk around outside on deck and enjoy the June breeze and the radiant sun. Freedom is really a great experience! I say Girls, long live freedom! And may we stay young forever."

"Jenn, why are you so grim-faced and serious?" Lori asked her close friend who appeared deeply engaged in meditation. "Are you homesick already?"

"You might say that I am!" admitted the somewhat aloof, contemplative companion. "Yes, I suppose I'm just a tad homesick,

6

but I promise to soon snap-out of my misery and I hereby firmly vow to enjoy to the hilt our mutual independence from the weight of adult authority. I do declare, let the fun begin!"

The girls' first day at the Crusader Motor Lodge was thoroughly delightful, the trio sunbathing and lounging on towels that afternoon around the pool to gradually develop their initial suntans. That first evening was merrily experienced by strolling the colorful and noisy Wildwood Boardwalk, eating cotton candy and caramel popcorn, browsing about on the three major Moreys Amusement Piers and then checking-out the raucous clubs and bars on Schellenger and Atlantic Avenues.

The second day was used to casually frolic in the surf, to sunbathe on Wildwood's extensive white beach and next to drive back to the Crusader Motor Lodge to shower. Then the activities would culminate by driving back to the vicinity of the boardwalk, parking Jennifer's Honda Civic at a Spencer Avenue lot and regally dining like spoiled princesses being catered to and pampered at the La Piazza Restaurant at the corner of Pacific Avenue and Burk. But Jenn Bozarth disguised her personal thoughts in a rather persuasive statement.

"Since you two fortunate dolls have found eligible guys to share fabulous entertainment with tomorrow," Jennifer shrewdly prefaced her remarks to Janice and Lori, "I want to take a drive alone and explore the back roads through the pristine New Jersey Pinelands. I'm feeling a little melancholy about the negative effects of global warming and I just need to be in harmony with Mother Nature for one afternoon."

"You're punking-out on us!" Janice laughed while gazing at the salad cucumber slice impaled on her fork. "Whatever happened to carnal attraction? Have you lost your interest in the male gender?"

"No, Jan. It's just that you and Lori have been lucky enough to meet-up with Gary and Ken so *that* development allows me to be a lone wolf on the prowl seeking peace-of-mind for a single afternoon," Jenn equivocated and fibbed. "I pledge that I'll become more active on the male-quest circuit when I return to Wildwood late tomorrow afternoon. Honestly, I'm just journeying through a temporary melancholy emotional phase and I need some quality down-time to be by myself."

"Well, what do you say we ask Gary and Ken if the guys can find a suitable male companion for you so that we can scoot-up to one of the Atlantic City casinos Wednesday night and engage in some light gambling?" Janice offered. "If you can't find the King of Hearts

Jenn, then maybe the King of Diamonds will show-up in the form of three sevens on a slot machine jackpot."

"Sounds like a desirable magic formula to me!" Jenn ambitiously smiled as the Italian waiter brought over her hot plate of raviolis and meatballs and from his serving tray the stud placed the steaming dish on the red and white checkerboard pattern tablecloth. "After I get in harmony with the environment, I'll then be fully ready to paint Atlantic City red tomorrow night. Tell Gary and Ken my dilemma and let's see what they can do for me!"

* * * * * * * * * * * *

Jennifer didn't sleep particularly well that evening, her hyperactive mind being mentally disheveled at the prospect of visiting Shamong, New Jersey and then confronting face-to-face her suspected biological parents, Emanuel and Helen Jennings. Early Wednesday morning Janice and Lori had already ventured out to the beach off of Spencer Avenue two blocks north of the Wildwood Convention Hall, so *that* particular circumstance meant that Jenn could conscientiously pursue her own on-a-mission agenda.

After downing a routine continental breakfast in the Crusader Motor Lodge's brightly-lit coffee and snack area, the perplexed female carefully climbed into her silver Honda Civic and soon was heading north on the Garden State Parkway, which thirty miles past Stone Harbor intersected with the Atlantic City Expressway. After speeding west past blueberry farms situated on either side of the busy thoroughfare, a half hour later, the inquisitive-but-determined young lady was soon passing through downtown Hammonton on Route 54, and upon reaching the Route 30 traffic light, *that* unique crossroads marked the beginning of Route 206, which incidentally bisected the Wharton State Forest, better known to ecology-oriented vehicle travelers as the "Southern New Jersey Pinelands."

Seven very straight miles heading up two-lane 206 marked the Hammonton municipal line and the beginning of the Township of Shamong, as the dependable Honda swiftly exited Atlantic and entered Burlington County.

'I'll stop at this small Wagon Wheel breakfast and lunch place, order a doughnut and a cup of coffee and ask the person on duty a few general questions,' Jennifer logically considered. 'Maybe the owner or the waitress will be able to tell me something relevant about Emanuel and Helen Jennings.'

After striking-up a genial verbal exchange with Debbie, who commandeered the Wagon Wheel's counter, the newly inspired researcher felt compelled to get down to brass tacks and inquire about the two prominent area residents.

"Truthfully, Hon. My husband and I just bought the Wagon Wheel two months ago and we haven't met too many of the local yokels yet," the combination waitress/cashier indicated. "We get mostly big rig truckers stopping in here for pancakes, omelets and ham and eggs. Corn farmers and local pineys make up the rest of our mediocre clientele."

"Well, Debbie, have you ever heard of two area residents named Emanuel and Helen Jennings? For you see, I'm an accounting student at Rutgers and am looking for summer employment to help defray my colossal college expenses. I think that working July and August at the Jennings' farm would be a very invaluable and rewarding learning experience. It'll also look good on my college resume."

"I've heard of them, but honestly, Hon, to my knowledge they've never set foot in this establishment," the cooperative proprietor sincerely attested. "According to gossip my ears have heard, they're supposed to be the richest people in these parts, having over a thousand acres of watermelons and cantaloupes I understand. They started out with raisin' corn and then cleverly branched out into growin' other more profitable fruits and vegetables. Now according to other wild scuttlebutt around Indian Mills and around here in Atsion," the waitress confided, "the Jennings are also now respectable thoroughbred racehorse owners, breeding magnificent steeds to compete at Monmouth Race Track with hopes of someday making a big splash winning the high Kentucky Derby stakes at Churchill Downs. It takes money to make money, at least that's what folks more intelligent than me always say!"

"Can you tell me anything else about them?" Jennifer insisted before reaching for a napkin from the nearby counter dispenser. "It's always better to know something about the people who might be interviewing you for a summer job."

"No, Babe. But you could probably find-out more details if you stop at the Pick-A-Lilli Inn about three miles north up 206. All kinds of ornery pineys hang out there," Debbie cautioned her sole customer. "But I warn ya', don't go near there after dark. Motorcycle gangs descend on that tavern den of iniquity and sometimes' brutal fights break out between the obnoxious piney hunters and the ruthless malicious bikers. The cops are over there all the time breaking up mayhem after mayhem."

"Thanks for the sage advice. Where do Mr. and Mrs. Jennings live? Sorry to pester you, but I'm totally unfamiliar with this remote section of Jersey?"

"Well, Doll, since I've taken a liking to your disposition, the Jennings happen to live on a vast estate on Stokes Road, that's County Road 541 that you'll find around a mile on the left past the notorious Pic-A-Lilli. You can't miss that disreputable drinking hole. It has an ancient-but-shiny red fire truck out there boldly advertising the business to all thirsty and brave strangers driving past the premises on their way to and from New York. The building's really a landmark on this highway."

"Thanks for your help, Debbie! Say, this second doughnut is absolutely scrumptious!"

"Thanks, Hon," the garrulous attendant proudly replied. "It's from an old family recipe I've borrowed from my mother! Wish I could reveal the secret to you, but I can't!"

The motivated young woman exited the establishment, re-entered her silver automobile and then eagerly pulled out of the Wagon Wheel's asphalt parking lot. A mile north she honored an urge to stop along the shoulder of the highway to gaze at and admire serene Atsion Lake, which instantly stirred up nostalgic and hurtful memories from her childhood.

'Oh my God! That's the cedar water lake where the little boy had been tethered to the pine tree while his self-indulgent parents were swimming!' Jennifer regretfully realized. 'It looks about the same in shape and dimension except for that small beach and recreation building located a quarter mile down there on the left fringe. I'm certain that this is the same lake that has haunted my psyche ever since I can remember. The tiny arbor near the highway is still there! What an intriguing and marvelous revelation this extraordinary accidental encounter has been! It's like I'm trapped in some sort of surreal time warp!'

After a line of six cars and trucks had sped by, Jennifer adroitly maneuvered her Honda Civic back onto 206 and continued her 'truth expedition.' The young woman's sedan negotiated three consecutive S curves and in a matter of a mere minute she was passing by the infamous Pic-A-Lilli Inn with its easily identifiable red fire engine quite evident while parked on the structure's right hand side.

Just past the Kingfisher's outdoor barbecue grill was Stokes Road, where Jennifer waited in the recently constructed third lane for southbound traffic to zip by before turning left onto tranquil-looking Route 541. Four miles west on the left was fabulous Shadybrook, the majestic farm and country estate of Emanuel and Helen Jennings. The tremendous metal green roofed manor house, which had a very pleasing-to-the-eye expensive exterior that had been re-done in dull yellow stucco, was gracefully complemented by verdant green horse pastures to the left and right of the massive edifice and finally, a mammoth inactive packinghouse and accompanying office were present to the rear of the enormously impressive living quarters. The obstinate not-to-be-denied visitor quietly parked her automobile in the designated "Guest" space, shut off the engine, hastily grabbed a pen and notepad from the glove compartment, exited the silver auto' and then gently rapped her knuckles on the office door.

"May I help you?" the packinghouse manager asked.

"Yes, my name's Sarah Wells, and I'm a freelance reporter, and I write human interest articles for several major national magazines," Jennifer enthusiastically lied. "I'm interested in writing a story about this fantastic farm and having it published."

"Where's your camera?" the alert foreman wondered and suspiciously asked.

"Oh, allow me to explain," the somewhat-startled girl answered, regaining her confidence. "The photographer usually shows-up and takes pictures a week or so after the editors accept the story. That's general procedure now throughout the glossy print publication industry. It's now done that way mostly because of budgetary reasons. The economy's not in the best shape nowadays, as you quite readily know!"

Being satisfied with the prompt and plausible reply, the packinghouse manager immediately became more convivial and accommodating. "Please excuse me for a minute. I'll call Mr. Jennings on the company intercom and see if he feels like being interviewed. He's basically a shy quiet man and is reclusive in many of his ways so don't be disappointed if he stubbornly declines your request. But since his wife Helen is visiting a wealthy friend up in Long Island, the Hamptons I believe," the middle-aged man clarified with a forced grin upon his countenance, "I'll announce to him your presence and purpose. Mr. Jennings seldom turns his back on receiving some good publicity. On the other hand," the foreman stressed, "Mrs. Jennings would probably object to the notion of a magazine article, but her husband would be more likely to go along with the idea."

Several minutes later, the affable manager returned to the Main Office door. "Mr. Jennings says he'll meet you in the manor house den shortly. You're lucky that the spring planting season is over and that the summer melon harvesting time has not yet begun," the foreman articulated. "The boss says he'll only be available for questions for about a half hour before lunch. Sylvia the maid will greet you at the back door and then escort you into the family room where the interview will take place. You'd better be on the up-and-up! Otherwise, I'll have to suffer the verbal abuse consequences."

"Thank you, for your assistance in this matter," Jennifer sincerely said. "You've been most helpful. I'm sure that my visit won't affect you in any harmful way."

Sylvia warmly greeted Jennifer at the back door and led the young lady through the kitchen and then down a maze of corridors into the very copious den. Over the stone fireplace mantel hung a portrait of a rather charming woman, a painting that the enchanted Bozarth girl immediately recollected from her childhood. Jennifer's keen concentration was interrupted by the appearance of a thin elderly gray-haired man who required a cane to amble his frame into the well-appointed room.

"Hello, I'm Emanuel Jennings, the owner of this here horse and melon farm. And you are…?"

"Good morning, Sir. I'm Sarah Wells, a freelance writer for a dozen different national magazines," the guest humbly announced while respectfully extending her right hand. "It's a pleasure making your acquaintance. Before the interview formally begins Mr. Jennings, can you tell me the name of that gorgeous woman in the wall portrait up there."

"Well, you see Young Lady, that wonderful portrait to which you've alluded is a Jennings' family heirloom, and that very special woman was a famous entertainer, a Swedish opera singer way back in the 1830s and '40s several decades before the Civil War. Her name was Jenny Lind and as the fabled story goes," the old man courteously disclosed, "the diva was under the management of the one and only P. T. Barnum when she had successfully toured the United States in the early 1850s."

'Oh, my goodness!' Jennifer perceptively recognized and associated. 'I've connected the dots and everything makes perfectly weird sense now. I'm Jennifer Linda Bozarth and I was probably named after this acclaimed nineteenth century opera star Jenny Lind. But amazingly, I never got the full relationship of Jenny Lind and myself until this very moment.'

Emanuel Jennings failed to interpret Jennifer's instantaneous astonishment so he continued rendering and communicating his historical monologue. "Yes Young Lady," the old decrepit-looking man divulged as he motioned for Jennifer to sit down in a comfortable cloth embroidered green chair, "the founder of this farm eight generations ago was Ephraim Jennings who courageously migrated to America from outside Bristol, England. As the family legend goes," Mr. Jennings continued his account', "my rich ancestor was so infatuated with Jenny Lind after hearing her perform in New York City that the enamored fellow helped develop a cantaloupe named Jenny Lind in her honor. But instead of being orange inside, the Jenny Lind cantaloupe is…"

"Green inside and tastes like a sweet combination of honeydew and cantaloupe flavors!" the knowledgeable Maryland melon farm girl euphorically exclaimed. "Now I get the entire connection!"

"Yes indeed, Miss Wells. But the Jenny Lind cantaloupe isn't all that popular in the New York and Philadelphia wholesale markets and East Coast chain stores because it's shaped like a, pardon the awkward expression for a lack of more appropriate words, it's shaped like a woman's breast with a large knob on its circular appearance, and so," Emanuel Jennings extended his explanation, "it's quite difficult to pack and ship, although the Jenny Lind unmistakably has a delectable taste. We grow ten acres of the fruit here at Shadybrook, but mostly for local farm market consumption. The variety is still quite popular here in South Jersey where it actually had originated under the guidance of old Ephraim Jennings and some of the agricultural professors at Rutgers. But the initial inspiration for the melon was that fantastic woman from Stockholm having her colorful portrait hanging up there, the incomparable Jenny Lind."

After recovering from the powerful shock of learning the identity of the vivacious female represented in the mantel portrait, Jennifer assumed a more professional attitude. The half hour interview transpired rather smoothly and the verbal exchanges eventually concluded with the impostor magazine writer asking, "Mr. Jennings, please forgive the barrage of rather personal questions, but do you have any sons or daughters to carry on your melon and horse breeding enterprises?"

"Well, confidentially, I do have one boy who is not involved in the farm operations, which incidentally started-out with meager corn fields where the lush dual horse pastures now exist. My son Harry Jennings is now twenty-seven years old and currently lives in

Winslow Township, about fifteen-to-twenty miles away from here just west of Hammonton."

"Why thank you for your generous time and patience Mr. Jennings," Jennifer falsely replied, effectively feigning common civility. "I believe I've taken sufficient notes and am sure that I can now organize and author a favorable comprehensive article based on the essential information I've garnered. If the piece is accepted by an editor and subsequently published," the female interviewer prevaricated, "a photographer will be visiting your remarkable plantation in late July to competently capture some artistic images during the height of your melon harvesting season."

"Glad to meet you, Miss Wells, and thank you for stopping by and showing an interest in both me and in Shadybrook Farm!" old feeble Emanuel Jennings genuinely declared. "It was mighty pleasant sharing my property's unique history with such an enchanting and ambitious young lady!"

* * * * * * * * * * * *

Jennifer pulled off of 206 and angled her now-dusty silver Honda into the Pic-A-Lilli Inn parking lot and after shutting off the ignition, next habitually turned on her handheld Blackberry communications' device. 'If I can't get any more useful information about the Jennings' family inside this sometimes rowdy eatery/saloon, then I'll research Jenny Lind on the Internet and learn some more academic trivia about the so-called marvelous Swedish Nightingale.'

The tavern's lunch crowd regulars had mostly evacuated the business and so after entering, Jennifer sat at the bar and ordered a hamburger "medium-well" along with a "cold Pepsi Cola." An old whisker-faced piney stepped out of the Men's Room and clumsily ambled over to his standard position at the bar, which happened to be the stool right next to the recent college graduate.

"Howdy!" the old gent exclaimed in a strikingly friendly tone of voice. "Ain't seen a pretty girl like yourself in this pathetic joint for quite some time!"

"Thank you," the blushing young lady giggled and softly answered. "Do you live around here Mr...."

"Just call me Gus," the weather-worn old geezer replied and then coughed some phlegm into a dirty light blue handkerchief. "Well, ya' see Miss, I used to live nearby over on Atsion Road that parallels the lake up around the bend, but now I reside over in Nesco not far from good old Batsto Village, about five miles outa' Hammonton,"

14

the veteran bearded human being informed. "But for recreation, I still religiously belong to the Antlers Gunning Club and stop around here to chat with some of the old-timers that still take time to fraternize with me. Ya' must be a stranger because I've never seen ya' hangin' around in here before."

"You're correct in your assumption Gus," Jennifer confirmed before sipping a mouthful of cola from her cold glass. "I'm a novice magazine article writer and I'm putting together a story about a farmer in these parts by the name of Emanuel Jennings. Have you ever heard of him?"

"Well, Young Lady, by a wondrous coincidence you're talkin' to the right guy who's an authority on the subject," Gus flirtatiously boasted and then egregiously sneezed into his filthy dark blue hanky. "For ya' see, a couple of decades back I used to work for that tightwad Emanuel Jennings over at his vast thousand-acre Shadybrook Farm; and in truth, I was one of his field foremen but then we got into a bitter quarrel over money matters and bonuses and so the stubborn old codger fired me right there on the spot. And I've held a mild grudge against *that* scoundrel ever since!"

"Do you know if Emanuel and Helen have any children?" Jenn cunningly asked her new acquaintance. "I mean I know that they have a son not affiliated with the farm who lives over in Winslow Township but I don't know of any other siblings. Gus, I would appreciate any basic information you could offer. Could you enlighten me on that aspect?"

"Well, Young Lady," Gus chuckled before imbibing a mouthful of cold beer and then chasing it down with a healthy shot of rye whiskey. "You're right about the son Harry Jennings living over there in Winslow Township, but there's a missing piece to the puzzle you're awkwardly trying to assemble. The son is an emotionally disturbed and mentally challenged unfortunate fella' who's a patient at Ancora State Hospital over in Winslow Township, a mental institution exclusively existing for mostly retarded people. For the record, I know for a fact that little Harry Jennings had been placed there when he was around five or six years old."

'Holy Moses!' Jennifer imagined. 'I have a biological brother who probably has severe mental and emotional issues!' Then, the girl adjusted her senses and asked more emphatically, "Tell me Gus, did this Harry Jennings have any brothers or sisters?"

The old whiskerando leaned over and whispered, his ancient lips disclosing in confidentiality that Emanuel and Helen Jennings had had a daughter too but then transferred all responsibility for raising the girl to an area bad-luck corn and melon farmer with the last name of Bozarth, who had lived on Schoolhouse Lane a quarter of a mile off of Atsion Road. "Speculation has it that Mr. Bozarth owed a lot of money to Mr. Jennings and so the bankrupt grower reluctantly agreed to take Jennings' daughter into his custody and bring her up for the expressed purpose of erasing the enormous debts and then be able to start a new life somewhere down in Eastern Shore Maryland, I believe. It was actually an arrangement of convenience for both parties. What did ya' say your name was Miss?"

"Er, Sarah, Sarah Wells from Edison, New Jersey over near New Brunswick. I had transferred from Seton Hall two years ago," Jennifer evasively exaggerated. "Now please relate to me Gus, why would Mr. and Mrs. Jennings have Mr. and Mrs. Bozarth raise and take care of *their* only daughter?"

"Because the Jennings already had a retarded son and feared that the daughter would possibly be mentally handicapped too, since she apparently displayed lots of stubbornness as a toddler," Gus shared. "Mental illness is said to run in the Jennings' family tree. I remember all of this background quite clearly since it all happened about the same time when that no good greedy creep Emanuel and I had our little argument out there in the north-side watermelon patch. Another rampant rumor at *that* time had it that amorous Helen Jennings had twice gotten pregnant out of wedlock!"

The waitress behind the bar sauntered out of the kitchen's swinging paneled doors and cheerfully delivered Jennifer's hamburger platter and a second glass of ice cold Pepsi Cola. The stunned girl sipped her soda through a straw and silently pondered her actionable alternatives.

'This is some serious stuff that I have to mull over and think about,' Jennifer plausibly reasoned. 'That little boy tied to the tree over at Atsion Lake must've been my older brother Harry. How cruel and inappropriate I had always thought *that* despicable ugly misdeed was! Now I fathom everything more lucidly. I was at the lake with the Bozarths, who were really sort of my adopted foster parents at the time. Harry was at the lake with the Jennings while the final settlement for my personal disposition was being arranged,' Jennifer intelligently conjectured. 'I must take proper loving care of poor Harry in the future!'

Then, the angry girl evaluated several other salient ideas. 'And my supposed biological parents Emanuel and Helen Jennings probably still have my original birth certificate in their possession and I strongly suspect that it's secretly stashed away somewhere. I'm

16

certain that a good lawyer can excavate the chronological truth and easily locate my original birth document at the Burlington County clerk's office or at the Shamong Township Municipal Building that I had just passed on Route 541 on my way to and from illustrious Shadybrook Farm.'

"Say there Sarah, ya' seem to have become awfully quiet ever since that hamburger and second soda arrived at the counter," Gus verbally conveyed to his wandering-mind listener. "Forgive me for pryin', but ya' must be awfully hungry!"

"I sure am pretty-well famished Gus!" Jennifer quickly concurred, mechanically nodding her head. "It's not polite to speak with food in my mouth but I wanna' thank you for giving me some vital background I needed. I think that I now have a new prism from which I can view and approach my organization of the magazine article. Your graphic details filled-in the missing sections."

"Glad I could be of service," Gus genuinely commented. "Ya' wouldn't be embarrassed if I told ya' that if I was fifty years younger I'd surely ask you out on a date! Ha, ha, ha!"

'Now, I know precisely what I plan to do,' Jennifer concluded, skillfully ignoring Gus's boisterous jocularity. 'Why should I struggle for thirty-five years as an aspiring accountant starting-out only making a diminutive beginner's level salary? I've made up my mind. I'm going to drive down to Hammonton, find myself a championship quality lawyer and then get my ultimate revenge by suing my original parents Emanuel and Helen Jennings for my denied birthright and for my assorted lost inheritance privileges. Then after I eventually acquire ownership of Shadybrook up here in the Jersey Pinelands,' Jennifer hypothesized with a broad self-indulgent smile on her countenance, 'and after I fully inherit the very successful Bozarth seven hundred acre melon plantation down in Berlin, Maryland, I oughta' be one of the premier fruit and vegetable growers operating along the entire Eastern Seaboard. Not a bad business career destination for a possible illegitimate child!'

A momentary silence reigned supreme at the Pic-A-Lilli Inn counter. The old weather-worn wrinkled-faced deer hunter desired to resume his verbal exchanges with the cute pert young lady seated next to him.

"Do ya' want another hamburger Sarah?" Gus innocently inquired. "I'll treat ya' to one before those belligerent motorcycle gangs start pilin' into this place and causin' all sorts of havoc!"

"No thanks, Gus!" Jennifer amply laughed. "I think that I have enough on my plate already!"

"Fantasy Book Land"

Frank and Betsy Lanier were glad that the busy and hectic summer season was over at their well-established sixty-year-old South Jersey family business going by the all-too-familiar trade name of Fantasy Book Land. Finally it was time for the couple to enjoy a well deserved and relaxing fall hiatus, a getaway Columbus Day weekend. In South Jersey, the deciduous tree leaves were resplendently beginning to transform into their autumnal hues and to the needed-to-be-rejuvenated Laniers, a much-anticipated tour bus trip up to New Hampshire's White Mountains represented a most welcome departure from the continuous daily grind of adult responsibility.

"I'm glad we're again going with Ralph's Bus Tours up to New England," Betsy said to Frank as the husband pulled his black Mercedes into the Cape May Senior Citizens' Tour Bus Terminal parking lot. "The change in scenery will be most appreciated. We'll be able to forget our identities and duties for the next four days and be just two ordinary anonymous vacationers seeking asylum from grueling drudgery and accountability."

The Laniers were indeed rather fatigued from operating the thriving fifty-acre family business that catered mostly to young children ages four-to-twelve along with the kids' ever-doting parents. "Didn't we just go up to the Beacon Resort two years ago?" Frank grumpily asked Betsy as he pulled a heavy suitcase from the car's trunk. "On second thought, if my memory serves me correctly I did savor our last bus excursion up there. The food was excellent and I think we also got to see a baby moose entering a mountain pine forest. It's amazing that my mind is still functioning at 6 a.m."

"Yes Dear," Betsy calmly answered her jittery soul mate. "The fall foliage was simply spectacular! And as you've already recalled, so was the Beacon's irresistible food. But according to the latest brochure we had received in the mail, the resort's suites have been totally renovated with inviting Jacuzzis large enough to accommodate two weary loungers like ourselves. And on the menu at the lodge's Dad's Restaurant is prime rib au jus the first night, filet mignon for the second evening's meal and lobster tail will be feasted on for the third night's farewell dinner. Really Frank, I could almost taste the scrumptious food already. I'll just have to abandon my austere diet. All you can eat plus salad, the soup de jour and finally, a variety of tantalizing desserts too!"

"Not to mention three fantastic hardy breakfasts. Suddenly I've acquired a tremendous appetite!" Frank laughed and then beamed a broad smile upon his countenance. "Yes Betsy, my stomach is now demanding instant gratification!"

The anxious forty-eight passengers' patiently waited in a straight line and then slowly ascended the semi-spiral staircase into the luxurious Cape May tour bus where they were individually greeted by their cordial driver Mike. An hour later the excited-but-carefree adventurers were chatting and motoring past Asbury Park heading north on the Garden State Parkway, and sixty minutes later the mostly elder explorers would be stopping at a rest and snack station at Montvale. Frank's emotions had significantly transformed into a much more civil mood as the chronic worrier finally got his mind off of the family's Fantasy Book Land enterprise, which now was a distant memory, geographically a full hundred miles behind.

"I hope we're going to see some new and different New Hampshire attractions this second time around," Frank indicated to his devoted spouse, who was sitting closer to the aisle. "Somehow, I do remember the last time up there visiting a religious shrine near Dixville Notch."

"Yes Frank, that was the Our Lady of Grace Shrine up in Colbrook, and then of course right afterwards we had a fine lunch later that day at the classy Balsams Resort, which if you recall reminded us of the magnificent Hotel Del Coronado out in San Diego," the wife recollected and emphasized to her husband. "And if you remember Frank, the Balsams up in Dixville Notch is where the first votes are cast during each Presidential Election. They even had a special balloting room set aside to allow for the famous voting process. And only around thirteen citizens participate in the event."

"True Honey, that unique hotel is not too far from the Canadian Border," the South Jersey entrepreneur elaborated. "And then during that last trip we also went onto a pontoon boat and toured that decent-sized lake where the movie *On Golden Pond* had been filmed. I believe that it was called...."

"Squam Lake and the 1981 film you just mentioned starred Katherine Hepburn and Henry Fonda," Betsy Lanier politely lectured and informed. "But on this particular trip we'll be taking a ferry ride across huge Lake Winnipesaukee and then the bus will meet us at the other side to take us to see the incredible Castle in the Sky mansion. And the numerous mansions built along Lake Winny along with the incomparable Castle in the Sky will be terrific attractions that'll make this a very memorable fall vacation. I'm glad that we brought along our video camera to document everything. It's your special duty not to lose it!"

"Montvale!" Mike loudly-but-courteously announced over the ultra-modern bus's intercom. "Now Folks, this is only a brief rest and snack stop so please be back inside the vehicle in thirty minutes. We aren't that far from the Tappan Zee Bridge going across the Hudson River, and then we'll be in New York State for less than an hour before eventually hitting Connecticut. And don't swallow-down too much junk food here at Montvale. Lunch will be served in approximately three hours at a pretty nifty Cracker Barrel near the Connecticut/Massachusetts Line."

After downing several tasty Dunkin' Donuts and big cups of much-desired coffee, Frank and Betsy re-entered the four-hundred-and-fifty-thousand-dollar, well-equipped motor coach and promptly resumed their propensity for civil marital conversation. Soon the bus and its occupants were zipping across the Tappan Zee Bridge into historic Tarrytown, New York, the site of famed American author Washington Irving's mansion Sunnyside, which was located on the north bank of the regal Hudson. And then fifteen minutes later the forty-eight riders were viewing and marveling at the impressive skyscrapers emblematic of White Plains, which indeed confirmed the fact that the wide-eyed riders were on the perimeter of the New York City metropolitan area.

"We're right on schedule," Frank confirmed to his wife and business partner, pointing to his Rolex. "I gotta' admit, Mike is a really skilled driver! He's the same guy we had two years ago."

"Yes Dear, and if there aren't any accidents or lengthy traffic snags along the way, we'll be having bacon and eggs at the Cracker Barrel in just two hours or so. And Frank," Betsy coyly added in a low tone of voice, "now that your father is turning full control of the business over to you as the newly appointed CEO, don't forget your chief assignment that you've been officially delegated. Pop wants you to be on the lookout for..."

"For a dynamic new attraction to add to Fantasy Book Land for the upcoming spring season," the husband astutely finished his wife's sentence. "And Pop's been quite generous in his expense allotment. Once the project's been approved, I'm allowed to spend up to a million dollars on the imaginative amusement park improvement, at least that's what the corporation has initially budgeted. I sure hope I get a miraculous inspiration while meandering through the lackluster tourist traps up in the White Mountains. Holy Toledo Betsy!" the husband exclaimed. "What in the blessed world am I saying?" Frank chuckled and then reluctantly grinned. "Am I a hypocrite or what? I myself manage and operate a prosperous tourist trap just outside Atlantic City!"

As the thoroughly modern motorbus rumbled through the center of Hartford, Connecticut, Frank pointed out the shiny golden dome of the State Capitol Building and then Betsy pontificated that the last time they had journeyed on bus up to the Beacon Resort that three state capitol edifices had been observed: the first in Hartford, the second in Springfield, Massachusetts and the third one in Concord, New Hampshire.

"You must be a good buddy of the Sandman because you were sleeping both ways back and forth to and from New Hampshire," the wife mildly stated and complained. "Downtown Hartford I've seen before despite your incessant snoring. I even had to jab you in the ribs a dozen or so times to quiet you down. But getting back on subject," Betsy persisted in her harmless jabbering, "maybe you'd like to put miniature models of the three state capitol buildings inside Fantasy Book Land," the woman casually joked. "Or perhaps a small version of Mark Twain's famous steamboat-shaped home that had been built right here in Hartford."

"No Betsy, but I really need to come-up with a novel ride or exhibit for older kids and adults to experience," the more serious-minded and emotionally pressured husband replied. "I mean the Three Billy Goats Gruff and Troll Bridge scene is adequate, the Goldie Locks/Three Bears House is okay situated next to the fairly decent Three Pigs and Big Bad Wolf venue, the Giant and the Jack and the Beanstalk castle has been a hit ever since our amusement park was initially built back in the early 1950s' but I have to admit," Frank Lanier confessed, "the Hansel and Gretel Gingerbread House is getting a little old and obsolete-looking although it's still quite popular with the youngsters."

"I totally agree and think that we definitely need another transportation ride to go along with the train that makes a figure eight passage from one side of Fantasy Book Land to the station platform at the other end," Betsy constructively suggested. "I mean, don't get me wrong Frank! We have a merry-go-round, a small whip, a nursery rhyme haunted house, a small Ferris Wheel along with seven other moving kiddy rides, not to mention lively calliope music being played all over the park, but as you've stated, we don't really have something dynamic and intriguing to entertain and satisfy the twelve-year-olds and up."

"It's always far easier to borrow an idea than to actually invent a new one," Frank verbally conveyed. "This winter I plan to visit at least a dozen entertainment theme parks across the USA just to obtain and achieve that one special brainstorm I need. My glorious new structure will not be a pure plagiarism, but instead it'll be some cost-effective inventive modification of a functional ride that already exists somewhere else. All I have to do is discover the thought-evasive thing, but I assure you Betsy," the under-duress spouse emphasized, "I'll readily recognize the evasive object I'm contemplating the minute my alert eyes perceive it!"

"What about a roller coaster, or mechanical horses on a track or perhaps a challenging miniature parachute jump ride!" Betsy Lanier diplomatically recommended. "Those types of sensational features helped get the Coney Island and Atlantic City boardwalks started back in their heyday. Or perhaps we could have a Swiss-style gondola skyway cable ride installed going north and south across the park while our current figure-eight train transports our customers east and west."

"A cable-driven Swiss sky ride? That's an excellent possibility," Frank sincerely maintained while scratching his head. "It's certainly worthy of consideration! Perhaps we can call it the Mother Goose Aerial Freeway and each gondola could have a different children's theme painted on it like Tom Thumb, Little Miss Muffet or Little Jack Horner."

The scheduled "brunch" at the Connecticut Cracker Barrel was delectable and after using the restaurant's lavatory facilities, Frank and Betsy sat on convenient-but-sturdy white rocking chairs on the establishment's front porch until an overhead speaker announcement was made that the "Cape May, New Jersey Senior Citizens' bus is now available for boarding."

"We're less than three hours away from gorgeous Lincoln, New Hampshire and the Beacon Resort," the wife reminded the husband. "I can't wait to sink my fork into the advertised four-course supper, and then later see the comedy show in the theater, sip some Merlot and then finish-off this evening's activities by stepping into the soothing warm water of our deluxe Jacuzzi."

Frank Lanier's mind was suddenly stimulated with his wife mentioning the utilization of a Jacuzzi bath. "Maybe my new incredible attraction will feature a terrific water park theme with huge cascading falls and an assortment of massive flume tubes for the older kids and adults to cavort around in and bravely zoom through," the husband imagined and expounded. "No Dear, on second thought such a wild and dangerous monstrosity would be an absolute insurance nightmare. We need to consider something less exotic and much more mundane, something more practical. Have any solutions?"

"Well, Hubby, sometimes an idea enters your mind when you're least expecting it," Betsy encouraged and supportively expressed. "That's exactly how many important discoveries have been made throughout history, many of them by sheer accident, chance or coincidence. Here's my theory for all that it's worth!" the wife enthusiastically exclaimed. "Just keep an open mind and have perceptive eyes and ears. I'm certain that the answer to your little dilemma will come when you least expect it!"

After arriving at the rather ordinary-looking Beacon Resort, room keys were distributed and then Mike the bus driver and two lodge employees delivered the passengers' luggage to their respective suites. Everyone arriving enjoyed the following two hours freshening-up, reading room literature and area guides and preparing for the highly anticipated dinner extravaganza, "The Prime Rib Luau." The comedy show that followed the extensive feast was especially hilarious, despite the abundance of slapstick comedy routines provided by the four principal entertainers, who in reality seemed old enough to be former Vaudeville stage performers.

The next morning the Laniers partook of the "New England *You Serve* Buffet Breakfast," and at nine a.m. the couple was again ascending the semi-circle stairway onto the "kneeling bus," which when stationary was lowered several inches by air hydraulics to allow riders to more easily board.

"What's on our itinerary today?" Frank inquisitively and curiously asked his lady companion. "Are we going to see Mt. Washington or Franconia Notch again?"

"No, Dear. We're going to travel through the ultra-modern resort community of Meredith en route to a popular ferry landing known as Weirs Beach. Then we'll go up the gangplank onto a two hundred and thirty foot long ferry, the Mount Washington, named in honor of the highest and coldest peak in New Hampshire that you just mentioned," Betsy explicitly narrated as if she were the official bus tour moderator. "We'll have a delightful one and a half hour scenic cruise across famous Lake Winnipesaukee and we'll view myriad fantastic homes erected along the banks. I understand that some of the mansions have three door boat ports in addition to standard three door car garages."

"And are we having lunch on the boat too?" Frank innocently inquired. "Lately it seems that my stomach has been ruling my brain. I really should put off my next physical with Dr. Carver for a whole month after we return back to Jersey following this grueling vacation. My nasty cholesterol reading will be invading into diabetes warning territory!"

"Don't be so pessimistic Frank! You'll be able to relax and view the various sights after you consume, or should I say after you 'devour' some Italian stuffed shells, baby back ribs, boiled potatoes, green salad and apple pie that's listed on the ship's menu," Betsy reminded and related. "Unfortunately, it's all just what Dr. Carver didn't order!"

"The Mount Washington is coming around the bend right now," Frank said, pointing west with his index finger. "Listen to the whistle blasts! Why it's shaped sort of like a Mark Twain era Mississippi steamboat."

"Yes, and it's even older than Fantasy Book Land," the wife observed and elucidated. "Your grandfather borrowed money from banks, friends and relatives and began constructing the original twelve frame-house exhibits right after he had left the Army in 1947. Four years later, after much labor and aggravation, and after near bankruptcy, with admirable perseverance, your Grand-pop Tony finally got the park open to the public."

"I still remember what grand-pop always used to say," the husband nostalgically rehashed and shared. "He volunteered to go up against the Nazis to defend the world from Hitler's insanity and *his* private goal was to protect America in order to preserve democracy and to safeguard free enterprise. And Grand-pop Tony's strong American dream was to design and build Fantasy Book Land for young kids and for interested adults still young at heart. I feel that it's my obligation to continue the tradition!"

"And now we're both carrying on your family's wonderful business heritage," Betsy contributed to the dialogue as the Mount Washington slowly approached the crowded docking pier. "Oh well, the passengers are preparing to disembark and Mike has already given us our tickets. But we're not going to be returning to Weirs Beach," Betsy reminded Frank, who was still oblivious to the basic itinerary. "Instead Mike will be driving the bus over to Wolfeboro, a colonial town on the opposite side of Lake Winnipesaukee. We'll reunite with him and his bus there."

"Well Betsy, when we finally retire from operating Fantasy Book Land, you can be my personal tour guide when we eventually get to be elderly jet setters flying all around the world and staying at spectacular exclusive European, Asian and South American resorts. Say Honey, how big is this prodigious lake anyway?"

"The pamphlet I had read back at the Beacon described it as being seventy-two square miles and for your information, the article indicated that your favorite body of water, Squam Lake feeds directly into Winnipesaukee."

"It looks like you've done your homework and that you're already beginning your illustrious tour guide career right here and now in beautiful autumnal New Hampshire," Frank laughed and commended. "And Betsy, you'll probably point out and identify every singular island in this mammoth lake along with every canoe, every dock, every native bird and every fishing boat visible in the entire environment."

After the recently painted Mount Washington docked in Wolfeboro, the forty-eight chattering New Jersey travelers again boarded Mike's very comfortable bus and within ten minutes the driver was pleasantly on his way upland into Moultonborough. After ascending a second steep spiral grade, the wide-eyed riders were treated to a heavenly sight. High on a majestic mountain ridge was an exceptionally breathtaking view of Lake Winnipesaukee gleaming like a gigantic stretch of terrestrial splendor below, the calm fresh water sparkling like assorted diamonds in the radiant sunshine.

Then, after the enchanted passengers were politely instructed to remain in their seats, Mike gave his riders a brief impromptu background description of the sensational Castle in the Clouds. "Construction on this eighteen room stone palace had begun in 1913 and it was financed and solidly built by a multimillionaire shoe manufacturer named Thomas Plant, who incidentally was a close friend of Theodore Roosevelt. The two pals often accompanied each other on hunting expeditions both here in New Hampshire and also out West. Anyway," Mike continued his thoroughly memorized oratory, "Mr. Plant had a fascination, or should I say 'a fixation' with the number five and only pentagon-shaped stones were used in the mansion's external facades," Mike further explained into his hand-held microphone.

"How many men worked on the project?" an old male passenger in the first seat second row opposite the bus driver asked.

"A thousand stonemasons were hired to complete the structure, the job finally terminating in 1915," Mike authoritatively answered. "This extraordinary estate consists of five thousand acres of mountain land purchased by Mr. Plant, who was a very shy and

26

introverted fellow that obviously valued his privacy. The Castle in the Clouds mansion was one of the first homes in America to have electricity, running water for sinks, toilets and showers along with telephone communications. Before you leave, be sure to visit and inspect the two octagon rooms that were deliberately built one on top of the other."

"Was Mr. Plant married?" a woman occupying a fourth row left side seat asked the standing narrator. "He seems to have been a very eccentric man for a woman to have to live with!"

"Yes, he was married, but physically speaking, bashful Mr. Thomas Plant happened to be a very short fellow who probably suffered from a mild inferiority complex, if not a Napoleon complex. But when it came down to managing his noteworthy business accomplishments, Mr. Plant was an industrial giant, an economic wizard of sorts. Ironically though, he did have a tall wife, over six foot in height I believe. And at one time the short-in-stature gentleman had owned the largest shoe factory in the entire United States. And finally," Mike suavely and astutely summarized, "Mr. Plant possessed and frequently utilized a secret room, a sort of library/study strategically situated directly off of the living room where he often sought leisurely isolation from other humans dwelling or staying inside his handsome residence. But Folks, inside the mansion you'll have to stoop down low to fit through the opened portal wall panel to be able to enter the 'Secret Room.' If you frequently go to a chiropractor for back adjustments, I urge you not to bend down and enter the low portal."

"And I thought I had some annoying psychological hang-ups to deal with!" Frank giggled to his very perceptive wife. "Mr. Thomas Plant sounds like he required the full-time services of a trained psychiatrist. But Betsy," the amusement park tycoon added, "you have to admire somebody like this early twentieth century business genius Thomas Plant. The risk-taking capitalist overcame his beleaguering emotional phobias and throughout his life's ordeal, and despite his diminutive stature, the shoe mogul still managed to amass a sizable fortune."

'That's precisely what I always tell our three grandchildren," Betsy answered tongue-in-cheek. "If you can't act your age, then kindly act your' cotton-pickin' shoe size!"

* * * * * * * * * * * *

That evening the variety show in the Beacon Resort Theater was rather mediocre and the late-night Jacuzzi seemed like veritable paradise to the Laniers' aching joints and muscles. After sunrise, a wake-up call from the main office aroused the resort guests and in half an hour the bleary-eyed New Jersey tourists obediently assembled inside Dad's Restaurant, and then swallowed-down a "Hefty Country Breakfast", which featured a tall stack pancakes with New Hampshire maple syrup, and after returning to their rooms for bus trip preparation, Frank and Betsy descended the lodge's wooden steps and slowly ambled over toward the awaiting bus.

"What's first on the agenda?" Frank energetically asked Mike. "I hope it doesn't involve too much walking. After yesterday, I think I'm developing a bad case of flat feet, not to mention aggravating my chronic arthritis and rheumatism."

"Well, Mr. Lanier, first thing we'll be heading over to Cannon Mountain in nearby Franconia Notch, a popular ski area," Mike informed. "But the Old Man's face and head, the famous symbols of New Hampshire's White Mountain history, regrettably fell off down the mountainside several years ago." After *that* academic description, Mike adroitly changed his' subject matter. "Next I'll be taking you to a scenic and rustic local nature preserve. You'll walk down a winding trail and explore a forest creek and then enter the main building to browse through a gift shop and at the very end, you'll see a film about the area's geographic features and historic past."

"Are we then going to visit Loon Mountain?" Betsy asked Mike. "It's really pretty active during the winter. My sister Marge always comes up here with her family every January to ski and ice skate. Of course," Mrs. Lanier garrulously clarified, "they habitually stay at the Beacon while doing so!"

"Unfortunately, the Loon Mountain Ski attraction is temporarily closed because of scheduled repairs and improvements, so *that* part of the tour has been scratched," Mike reported, much to the disappointment of Betsy Lanier. "That mountain as you might know was named after the local bird that can only land on lake water during the summer months. Its legs are too fragile to impact on ice during the colder months December through March."

"Well, Mike, what have you planned as a replacement activity?" Betsy Lanier asked as a small crowd of concerned gossipy bus passengers gathered around the two conducting the dialogue. "I'm not looking for a refund but Loon Mountain was supposed to be one of the highlights of this trip!"

"Well, Mrs. Lanier, I've contacted my boss back in Cape May and he's already arranged for us to zip over to DeClerk's Trading Post. It started out as a small general store but over the past thirty years the owners have expanded the property into a very impressive recreational facility. You'll notice exactly what I mean when we arrive there. I think you'll be quite surprised by what you'll see."

"Well Mike, sometimes it pays to be upbeat and expect the worse, only to be gratefully satisfied later on," Betsy optimistically answered. "Now Frank, let's clamber up the steps before our perpetual questions cause a scene. As you know, I happen to abhor arguments and conflict."

Indeed, Cannon Mountain was not the same spectacle without the Old Man's Face protruding from its summit but a half hour later the late morning trek along the prescribed Franconia Notch babbling brook proved very invigorating to the opinionated and chatty bus tour patrons. After enduring (on soft cushion seats) the well-produced New Hampshire film in the nature center's vast recreation building, Betsy took several still pictures of Frank standing next to a family of giant stuffed brown bears, snapshots of him posing beside a ponderous-looking moose and close to a standard-sized deer, animals all indigenous to the serene White Mountains.

"Now, we're off to DeClerk's Trading Post," Frank reminded his always-vigilant wife. "Quite honestly Dear, I want it to be better than it sounds. Now Bet, I don't desire to spend the rest of the day examining a bevy of key chains, souvenirs and knick-knacks. And Honey," the husband haughtily jested, "I don't wish to sound like a bragging wet blanket pest but *we* do have our own comprehensive New Jersey gift shop back at Fantasy Book Land."

"On our modified itinerary agenda, it states that Mike will be distributing box lunches for us to eat at a designated picnic table pavilion," Betsy answered to allay her husband's negative attitude. "Who knows? Maybe DeClerk's Trading Post will be a marvelous substitute for Loon Mountain after all."

Situated only several-miles south of the popular Beacon Resort, DeClerk's Trading Post had over the decades been expanded from a typical general store into a full-fledged family recreation/amusement facility. A dynamic steam locomotive was situated at the "Main Entrance" and was ready to take interested visitors on a circular train track adventure through a pine tree forest that surrounded the core entertainment area on three sides.

A village of small cute early 1900s-style houses, stores and municipal buildings had been constructed along a paved street.

Parents, children and guests could saunter around and enter any of the very clean-looking "O. Henry era" places and experience the novelty of a turn-of-the-century firehouse, a nickelodeon-style silent cinema theater presently showing a classic Charlie Chaplin movie, a "Gay '90s" horse and carriage depot, a livery stable, an impeccable brick façade town hall, an archaic candy store selling all sorts of sweets including red and black licorice, a post-colonial apothecary shop, a mom and pop grocery store and finally an old-fashioned ice cream parlor.

An announcement was made over the park's loud speakers for all recently arrived guests to advance to the south end of the immaculately kept facility, in order to enjoy the hourly "Trained Bear Show" that was slated to commence in ten-minutes.

"After the circus-style bear performances, we'll go over to the shaded picnic tables and enjoy our box lunches," Betsy dictated to Frank as was her annoying habit. "Not to engage in plagiarism, but have you gotten any useful ideas from this novel park about how to improve Fantasy Book Land?"

"Well, Bet. The Main Street sector was pretty neat but my conclusion is that it was too much like the Main Street district down in Disney World," Frank Lanier mildly criticized. "But overall, it's something for me to consider if we don't somehow stumble upon a more satisfactory utilitarian idea. I'm hungry and my stomach's growling for some peculiar reason. Remind me to swallow-down a hot fudge sundae at the Professor Harold Hill Ice Cream Parlor before we head back to the Beacon at 2 p.m."

"Didn't you tell me that it's a lot easier to borrow than to invent?" Betsy characteristically challenged. "I don't know how a bear entertainment show would fit into *our* plans but I do think that an early 1900s Main Street theme addition would be a definite plus for our aging Fantasy Book Land Park."

"It's something to consider and it's certainly within the realm of possibility," the predictably skeptical husband maintained, "but it's still not the million-dollar panacea that I'm searching for! Oh well," the frustrated entrepreneur compromised, "let's sit through the bear show upon those hard metal bleacher seats. I'm glad that the animals are caged-in by that circular Cyclone Fence. And I suspect that the corpulent bears are muzzled and probably de-clawed too! I don't need to be viciously mauled and maimed five hundred and thirty miles from home!"

"Stop being so cynical, just because you can't think of a new tremendous attraction for Fantasy Book Land!" Betsy balked. "I think that you're just envious that this DeClerk Trading Post rivals our Jersey theme park."

Much to the Laniers' delight, the bears and their trainers put on a very entertaining tricks' program, and next, the box lunches at the picnic pavilion were quite substantial and nutritious, and now it was time for the tourists to hop aboard an open-air carriage car (located behind the steam locomotive) and take a breezy ride through the dense pine tree forest.

"We do have the extra twenty-acre pine tree woods behind the amusement ride sector of our park," Betsy said, comparing the present DeClerk scenario to a potential Fantasy Book Land upgrade. "Maybe *this* well-maintained railroad feature will provide you with the ideal solution you've been searching for."

"We'll see what transpires during the train ride," Frank stubbornly declared, disguising his eagerness. "If it's just a standard passage through the woods, then it'll be a little too mundane and commonplace. Let's look for anything in the 'unique department realm' that might have been cleverly improvised."

The train whistle sounded, signaling for everyone to "Climb aboard!" as the uniformed conductor bellowed and commanded. The noisy locomotive produced six puffs of steam and the loud machine slowly chugged away from the station platform. Soon the entourage aboard was being conducted over an enclosed New England bridge and the vehicle was now progressing into the interior of the dense pine forest.

A loud antagonistic and threatening male voice was quickly discerned by everyone's ears and from out of a "Gold Prospector's Mine Cave" stepped a bellicose-looking bearded and hairy mountain degenerate who boisterously introduced himself to the startled train passengers as "the Wolf Man."

"Betsy, capture all of this with our video camera," Frank demanded. "I like the hostile demeanor of *that* petulant barbaric fellow! By sheer pot luck I think we've just hit upon the magic answer that I've been pursuing."

"How do we hear the Wolf Man's bass voice inside the train?" the wife wondered and asked as she continued aiming her video camera. "It's really quite powerful and at first his ornery nasty tone was actually startling!"

"It's really a wireless remote microphone transmitting his voice from his location directly *here* into the overhead carriage car speakers," the husband explained. "Now the bellicose fellow is warning us not to trespass into *his* territory or else we'll have to face the dire consequences! I wonder if this bad-tempered Wolf Man lives over in Wolfeboro!" Frank facetiously joked as Betsy continued filming without ever breaking her concentration. "Look! Now the uncouth insulting guy is shooting his loud shotgun at us! I hope that thing's firing blanks! Ha, ha, ha!"

The steam locomotive and its trailing carriage cars then speedily passed through a woods' clearing on one side and the ubiquitous Wolf Man was now driving an old rusty and tarnished Model-T roadster and aggressively yelling new epithets and unflattering remarks at the thoroughly amused "trespassing" train passengers. This particular sequence lasted for a full minute until the pretentiously aggravated Wolf Man stepped on the accelerator and swiftly sped ahead while seated inside his remarkable jalopy convertible.

And just when the train (along with its harassed and amused passengers) exited another patch of woods, there stood the verbally taunting Wolf Man again firing his imitation shotgun and vociferously screaming a flurry of derogatory remarks and unsavory insinuations at the apparently thrilled riders, many of whom were documenting the series of incidents with their various cameras.

"That whole sequence of events was positively rich!" Frank euphorically exclaimed. "That's the miracle idea I couldn't seem to envision on my own!"

"It's always easier to borrow than to invent!" Betsy hollered back from behind her still-raised video camera. "It appears that the DeClerk Trading Post's wonderful Wolf Man creation has been the brilliant God-send you've been trying so hard to discover!"

* * * * * * * * * * * *

Upon returning back to all-too-familiar southern New Jersey, out of family courtesy and professional ethics, Frank Lanier presented the idea of a Fantasy Book Land train ride through the property's rear pine woods to his father, the outgoing corporation CEO, and Mr. Joseph Lanier eagerly put his stamp of approval on the "most excellent proposal," which was then a week later unanimously endorsed at a hastily announced board of directors' meeting.

The necessary building permits were quickly acquired and an extremely competent and reputable job foreman was hired to oversee the intricate "architectural project phases" from beginning to end. Contracts were swiftly signed with major carpenter, plumbing, electrical and mason unions, the acquisition of materials was rapidly initiated and construction on 'Phase One' of the colossal "train and rail project" was begun in early March with the final rendition to be completed and subsequently open to the general public a full calendar year later.

"We came in just two hundred thousand dollars over our original budget," Frank ecstatically told Betsy Lanier on the long-awaited morning of the grand opening of the Fantasy Book Land Overland Express. "And guess what Honey?" the exuberant husband rhetorically asked. "I've managed to get the real Wolf Man from up there in Lincoln, New Hampshire to come down to South Jersey and play the role of Piney Jack terrorizing *our* prospective about-to-be-mesmerized train passengers."

"How did you manage to pull that fantastic deal off?" the wife curiously asked. "Have you been studying hypnotism, black magic or voodoo without my knowledge?"

"I made the former Wolf Man a very tempting overture that he couldn't refuse. I offered the talented bearded fellow a ten-month contract worth twenty-five thousand bucks more than he was making petrifying people way up there in the White Mountains, and I also guaranteed Piney Jack, alias Wolf Man, an additional two months employment and an extra salary bonus with full benefits to labor as a maintenance worker from January to the end of February when the park is closed."

"Well, Dear, I must confess that you've always been a shrewd businessman," the wife reluctantly congratulated her very successful spouse. "Maybe things won't be so nondescript around here in the future. Oh my!" Betsy exclaimed, pensively staring at her diamond wristwatch. "The park's going to open for the new season at noon and it's about ten a.m., time for the Overland Express to have its first official run through the pine woods."

"Piney Jack's already in his Pig Iron Bog Lair, or should I say 'Cave Hideout,' and here comes Pop now ready to help us commission this ceremonial train trip."

Soon, all invited family members and dedicated park employees climbed into the first open-air carriage and then Sam the Engineer strongly blasted the steam whistle three times. Seconds later the brand new shiny black locomotive tugged the trailing cars out of the recently built and colorfully painted "Victorian Train Station."

"This fine train was a really terrific addition Son," Joseph Lanier amply complimented his chief heir and descendant. "I'm quite proud of your creativity Frank, and I'm happy to note you having the wherewithal of conceiving a superb attraction like this very desirable

Overland Express. I assure you that it'll be the envy of all amusement venues within seventy miles of Atlantic City."

"Well, Dad, I did spend plenty of cerebral time taxing my brain and I finally settled on the Overland Express idea," the red-faced son less-than-modestly answered. "Indeed Pop', this ride will be a tribute to the Lanier name for many decades to come. But just wait until you see the stunning surprise that Betsy and I have planned and arranged! I just know you'll be getting a grand kick out of it!"

The blustery locomotive picked up speed and advanced down the tracks, gracefully rounded a bend, traversed across a wooden covered bridge and then soon entered the posterior thick pinewoods. From out of his Pig Iron Bog Works Foundry Building came Piney Jack, a frightful-looking New Jersey facsimile of the New Hampshire backwoods Wolf Man. Much to the riders' emotional delight and excitement, a very antagonistic and hysterical Piney Jack articulated a series of threats and complaints directed at the fascinated passing train passengers.

"That fellow's absolutely terrific! Very animated and hilarious too!" Joseph Lanier hollered and clapped his gloved hands. "I must say that he looks mighty vindictive, mendacious and dangerous, even though we all know that he's harmless and only acting!"

"I knew you'd absolutely love his routine!" Frank confidently replied. "It's loaded with exaggerated histrionics! I know that I did relish the whole melodramatic routine when I had first seen the guy perform up in New Hampshire!"

"This whole scenario is totally captivating!" Betsy aptly agreed. "Even our usually bored grandchildren are enthralled with the wild man's crazy antics!"

Piney Jack rapidly fired six rounds of blanks from his signature shotgun as the maiden-run train completed its semi-circular pass through a clearing and then resumed its journey on the rails that bisected the thick coniferous forest. At the next break in the woods Piney Jack's voice was clearly discernible as he drove his customized dump truck convertible out of the Pine Barrens Saloon's swinging doors and then the souped-up vehicle followed a dirt and gravel path that intentionally was designed to parallel the train tracks. All of the cheering passengers stood up to catch a full glimpse of Piney Jack's frantic gestures and to attentively listen to his booming barrage of barbs and preposterous denigrations.

"This has got to be the ultimate in family fun entertainment!" Joseph Lanier marveled and exclaimed. "Bravo Frankie! Bravo I say!" the elderly man hooted as he removed his felt hat from his noggin and then wildly waved the object above his head.

Before Frank could organize a plausible and grateful response, a second vehicle was detected speeding out of the pine tree thicket and ambitiously pursuing directly behind the fleeing Piney Jack's chopped-off-roof dump truck, and seated inside the modified Corvette convertible was a dark red-faced hideous-looking figure dressed in the exact appearance of the notorious Jersey Devil, who was persistently and intensively chasing the panic-stricken nefarious personage currently disguised as Piney Jack.

"Why this is really most bizarre and extraordinary!" Joseph Lanier instinctively praised his pallid-faced son. "Frank, you're a first-class impresario, that's what you are! A veritable genius I say!"

"Betsy!" an excessively shocked Frank Lanier uttered to his equally perplexed and horrified wife as the thrilled grandchildren jumped about, screaming and shrieking with unbridled satisfaction. "Is this some kind of bizarre hallucination I'm witnessing? Did you by any chance hire a costumed Jersey Devil performer behind my back for the expressed purpose of scaring the living daylights out of Piney Jack!"

"No Frank!" the still-awed wife uttered in total disbelief. "It obviously appears that the real Jersey Devil doesn't at all like the now-cowardly Piney Jack encroaching and trespassing onto *his* sacred pine barren territory!"

"Accidental Coincidence"

It was April Fools' Day and Hammonton, New Jersey CPA Troy Rogers was extremely stressed. The April 15th IRS tax deadline was looming only two weeks away and the conscientious accountant's phone was constantly ringing with worried clients inquiring about their estimated or already tallied income tax burdens. 'I should run away to the South Pacific for the rest of my life or else join the French Foreign Legion if the organization still exists!' the harried "numbers' cruncher" lamented and fantasized. 'It's a good thing I have a trusty secretary/assistant to help me through these especially rough times. Mrs. Cheryl Penza's a terrific aide and I can't afford to lose her steadfast allegiance. In fact, in appreciation of her loyalty I've decided I'm going to offer her a two thousand dollar raise effective May 1st!'

The phone rang inside the anterior office and Cheryl put the caller on hold and immediately relayed the message to the overwhelmed tax law authority, who was disgustedly staring at a stack of alphabetical order folders that had been accumulating over the past week upon his cluttered desk.

"Troy, it's Phil Caruso on Line 1," Cheryl announced in her normal pleasant tone of voice. "What should I tell him? He insists on talking to you."

"Tell that neurotic insurance salesman I just stepped out of the office to mail some important tax returns at the post office," the fatigued CPA instructed. "Tell Phil his tax return will be done within two days and that I'll get on the horn to personally convey the dreaded bottom line to him. That feasible explanation ought to stave off that annoying worry wart's incessant curiosity for at least forty-eight hours."

"Okay Boss," the cooperative office assistant concurred, "but I've also just got paranoid Hector Russo on Line 2. This time he's a little over the top, insisting that he's one of your biggest accounts and he's demanding that I get through to you or else he's going to take his coveted business elsewhere."

"Put the petulant maniac through Cheryl!" the assets and debits expert directed. "I can't afford to lose that nutcase fanatic as a customer even though his nasty mercurial temper is undeniably on the reprehensible side."

Cheryl Penza immediately honored her employer's command and transferred the call to *his* desk.

"Hello Hector! How's your seven hundred acre blueberry crop looking for this coming season?" Troy Rogers greeted his significant account subscriber. "I'll bet that pretty soon the honey bees will be buzzing around doing their vital field thing!"

"Don't try soft soaping me!" the vitriolic and volatile blueberry farm mogul yelled. "I've got a seven million dollar a year fruit operation going for me and if I need to scrape-up more than a quarter million bucks in a hurry to pay off that legal crook Uncle Sam, I have to know how much I owe the greedy thief pretty damned soon so that I can sell stocks in my UBS cash management account, which incidentally isn't performing too well because of the terrible economic recession that's currently plaguing the country."

"Hector, I'm working diligently on your complex statistics and I promise you I'll have the ballpark data in your possession by noon tomorrow," the numbers guru committed and vowed. "Now my preliminary evaluation is that you won't have to pay a penny over three hundred thousand! But truthfully," Troy Rogers qualified, "I'll be able to provide a more thorough and comprehensive analysis of your tax liability situation no later than four p.m. tomorrow, Greenwich, England time!"

"Stop being such a really dumb, preposterous sanctimonious Ignoramus!" prominent blueberry grower Hector Russo squawked and protested. "If I was standing next to you right now I'd be inclined to beat the living daylights out of you after first making you swallow your front teeth! I used to be a middleweight boxer in the Navy before I inherited my father's fifty acre farm and expanded it to over fourteen times its original size!" the blueberry empire agriculturalist egotistically bragged. "Now then Mr. Rogers, CPA, get my tax information to me by noon tomorrow or else I'm gonna' find myself a more reliable and less difficult tax accountant to handle my personal money affairs! Ya' know Troy, it's wise guys like you that really get my dander up and make the world a rather lousy place to live in!" Click.

'I think that the inimitable Hector Russo should read the book *How to Win Friends and Influence People*!' Accountant Troy Rogers concluded as he gently placed his land-line phone back into its charging cradle. 'It's amazing how that belligerent Idiot could've ever become a successful influential businessman! Market conditions of supply and demand I suppose, especially when the great demand for fresh-picked New Jersey blueberries tremendously exceeds the available supply.'

38

Cheryl Penza again buzzed her perturbed Boss. "Troy, it's Cynthia Harper on the line and she wants to speak with you about her upcoming social event."

"Alright," the beleaguered financial genius answered, shaking his head. "But from here on out, I'm not taking any additional calls today. Fact is Cheryl, I'm literally drowning in a sea of responsibility. Oh, hello Cynthia!"

"Troy, I just want to remind you that you've been invited to my masquerade party that's slated for this coming Saturday night but I haven't yet received your RSVP," the vivacious tanned blonde-haired hostess stated. "Are you attending my affair or aren't you? I assure you it'll be a real gala happening that you'll definitely regret missing!"

"Why Cindy, of course I'm going to be there! I wouldn't miss it for all the gold bullion in Fort Knox!" Troy communicated and exaggerated. "But honestly Cynthia, I've been deluged with a colossal workload this tax season and I must've inadvertently forgotten to contact you. Please accept my genuine excuse! I sincerely apologize for the grievous oversight."

"Well Troy, I just want you to know that Rita Maimone is going to be a special guest at my party and I've picked-up gossip around town that she has her eyes on you and I've also heard through the local grapevine that you've taken more than a casual interest in her," Cynthia Harper confided and then giggled. "That luscious revelation alone oughta' be sufficient motivation for you to get your rear end in gear. Exactly what costume are you going to be wearing? As a personal policy I really don't like having any costume duplications at a masquerade party, you can understand my position, don't you?"

"Wow, Cindy! I'm more than thrilled that Rita will be there, fancy mask and all I presume," Troy "Buck" Rogers gleefully exclaimed. "And by the way, thanks for the confidential information! I'll treasure it and promise to keep my intel' source a secret!"

"Well, Troy. Here's a bit of indispensable news you can count on. She'll be wearing an exquisite Marie Antoinette outfit and won't be hard for you to identify!" Cynthia Harper voluntarily revealed. "But the big question is, what will *you* have as a suitable disguise so that I'll be able to recognize you when you enter?"

"I plan to arrive as a distinguished Egyptian pharaoh so that you'll easily be able to confirm my attendance," the CPA disclosed and joked. "Possibly Ramses II or King Tut!"

"Great! I don't have any pharaohs on my list!" the talkative party-giver enthusiastically divulged. "And Troy, don't forget to have your vizard on Saturday night!"

"What's a vizard?" the bewildered accountant asked.

"It's a type of mask Silly! William Shakespeare himself often used *that* cool word 'vizard' in many of his comedy plays! See you at my place Saturday at eight!" Click.

Troy Rogers placed the phone into its cradle a little harder than usual. 'Oh, mercy me!' the CPA mentally anguished and languished, holding his aching head. 'It's Monday and I forgot to order a King Tut or Ramses II outfit for Cindy's big masquerade party. I know what I'll do! There's a historical costume rental store over in Mays Landing inside the Hamilton Mall and it's only twenty miles away. Cheryl's not yet meltdown material and definitely not too argumentative during the all-too-vexing tax season! And besides, my Girl Friday is very dependable and can keep her calm composure even during a major crisis!' Troy Rogers determined. 'I'll temporarily put her in charge of the office and let her diplomatically contend with all of the relentless mounting duress while I'm out of the vicinity preoccupied on my weird in-quest-of-a-disguise shopping expedition!'

* * * * * * * * * * * *

Troy Rogers pulled his dark blue Lexus out of the Vine Street parking lot located next to Columbus Park and then made a left turn onto Egg Harbor Road. Soon he passed by Hammonton Lake Park and the Little League and Babe Ruth League baseball complexes. Several miles later on his all-too-familiar route was the blinking Red Traffic Light. After stopping at the four-way signal, a right was made onto County Road 559, better known to local motorists as Weymouth Road, and after the Lexus ascended the Atlantic City Expressway overpass, the two-lane highway meandered in a snake-like fashion left and right past the 1,300 acre Atlantic Blueberry Plantation, the largest cultivated blue fruit farm in the world. 'In five more minutes I'll be heading east on Route 322, the Black Horse Pike and I'll be halfway to my destination,' Rogers reckoned.

The Alpha-minded CPA had his immediate itinerary already sketched-out in his belabored mind, for ever since his childhood days Troy had always been a stickler for honoring minutia and enacting details. 'I'll park my car in the Hamilton Mall lot, take the center mall escalator up to the food court for a couple of slices of pizza and a Coke and then hasten over to the Acme Costume and Tuxedo Rental Store to obtain my gaudy pharaoh's garb for Cindy Harper's posh party.'

Fifteen minutes later, the stressed-out man was sitting at a Food Court table staring at his rather mediocre lunch. 'Not exactly an Epicurean banquet but nevertheless these two tomato and cheese slices are adequate junk food substitutes,' Troy imagined as he began gobbling-down his fast food meal. After downing his two savory pizza slices and his medium-sized cola, the pressed-for-time accountant took the convenient escalator downstairs to the mall's main corridor. A right hand side amble soon had Troy Rogers stepping into the desired retail rental place of business.

"Hello," a tall thin mustached clerk behind the counter amiably greeted the new arrival. "I'll bet you know exactly what you want without browsing around. May I help you?"

"Yes, I've been invited to a very special masquerade party extravaganza and I'd like to go as an ancient Egyptian pharaoh, possibly either King Tut or Ramses II," Rogers concisely stipulated. "Ever since I was in middle school I've been fascinated by ancient Egyptian culture, the Nile River, the pyramids and especially Cleopatra. You seem to have a vast inventory here on your racks. I believe that I've come to the right place!"

"Yes, you have Sir, but regrettably, our only pharaoh ensemble has already been rented and will not be returned until late Thursday morning," the suave store employee informed his disappointed visitor. "But Sir, I promise you that our dry cleaner can get the pharaoh getup spruced-up and shipped to your door via UPS no later than Friday afternoon, that is to say, if you luckily live in either Atlantic or Cape May County."

"Well now, I do live in Hammonton, Atlantic County," Troy stated, his overall demeanor suddenly reflecting mild relief. "But how can I be certain if the pharaoh outfit will fit me if I don't have the opportunity of trying it on for size."

"That's quite easy to explain Sir," the pleasant store attendant insisted in a mellow tone of voice. "It states right hear in the company catalog that the pharaoh costume is specifically tailored to fit any man ranging between the heights of five foot eight inches and six foot two and who weighs anywhere between one hundred seventy and two hundred and ten pounds," the salesman indicated. "Here is a glossy representation of the particular item on this page presented in vivid color. Notice Sir that the handsome black mask accompanies the exotic-looking apparel and headdress. And if I may add Sir, it's

at no additional charge. Now then, after viewing this color photo'
what do you think about you impersonating Ramses II? Isn't the
costume rather intriguing?"

"It's very outstanding, extremely top notch!" Rogers commended
the persuasive salesperson. "That's my personal opinion. Exactly
how much will it cost me to rent all of the Ramses II paraphernalia
Friday through Sunday."

"A real bargain Sir. Only a hundred bucks plus ten dollars to
cover the UPS express delivery," the clerk recited. "I say only a
hundred smackers simply because the costume was not in stock
when you had stepped through the store's main entrance to make
your inquiry. I'm proud to say that *that's* our strict company discount
policy. What's your pleasure Sir?"

"Okay, here's the hundred dollars up front," the convinced
customer said, handing the clerk a crisp Ben Franklin note. "And
here's an Alexander Hamilton to cover the express freight delivery
charge. I believe you'll now need my residential address and phone
numbers, both landline and cell."

"Yes, Sir. I'll gladly take down that pertinent information and
give you a copy to keep as a receipt. Now I only have one further
question. Is your girlfriend or wife going to the grandiose party as
Cleopatra?"

"No," Troy laughed and grinned, shaking his head in mild
amusement. "She's actually going to the shindig as Marie
Antoinette."

"Sounds like a definite conflict in historical eras to me," the
congenial fellow behind the counter chuckled. "Oh well Mr. Rogers,
I guess it could've been even more problematic like Adolph Hitler
and Dolly Madison or diabolical Ivan the Terrible escorting
dangerous Lucrezia Borgia, ha, ha, ha!"

At six p.m. Friday evening, a brown UPS truck pulled into the
CPA's Walnut Street ranch home's asphalt driveway and the carrier
delivered a large package from the Acme Costume and Tuxedo
Rental Store, Hamilton Mall, Mays Landing, NJ. Five minutes later
the excited recipient quickly unwrapped and opened the string-tied
cardboard box but was highly upset upon discovering and examining
its mistaken contents.

'Oh no!' the disappointed resident thought. 'Those incompetent
imbeciles sent me an ancient Greek warrior's regalia instead of the
elaborate Ramses II getup.' The man's frustration was heightened
upon him calling the Hamilton Mall store.

"Sir, we're sorry for the unusual mix-up!" an apologetic voice on the other end stated. "Wilhelm, the fellow who had rented you the pharaoh's costume is away on vacation in St. Thomas, Virgin Islands so obviously he's not available to speak with you about the matter. But from what I can determine," the sympathetic Acme employee related, "three costumes had been simultaneously sent to the wrong customers, your pharaoh outfit to someone else, the Greek warrior one that you've accidentally recently received and a third one inadvertently addressed to an altogether separate party. I'll speak to the owner and arrange an appropriate refund for you because of the oddball shipping error."

"Never mind the trivial explanations!" Troy angrily and vehemently protested. "I'll wear the pathetic Greek thing you've sent me, bronze sword, helmet, sandals and all to the masquerade party tomorrow night, but with truth as my witness, I'm never going to recommend or do any further business with your irresponsible company ever again!" Click.

Slowly regaining his emotional composure, the Walnut Street resident sat at his computer desk and typed in "Greek heroes" into the Google search box. After perusing the faces of battle uniformed Odysseus, Hercules, Agamemnon, Menelaus and Ajax, Troy Rogers eyes eventually focused upon the graphic color illustration of the magnificent champion Achilles.

'This is without a doubt the exact guy I'm going to impersonate!' Rogers concluded. 'It says here that Achilles was the mightiest of Greek warriors during the Trojan War, a ten year conflict that happened around 1184 BC as chronicled by the supposedly blind poet Homer in his narrative epic poem the *Iliad*.' Rogers reflected for a moment and then continued reading the language presented on his desktop computer screen. 'And this tragic hero figure Achilles in spiteful revenge had killed Hector, the King of Troy's son because Hector had previously killed Achilles' best friend Patroclus. But,' Rogers paused and gasped before resuming his remarkable reading session, 'later in the adventure tale saga King Priam's younger son Paris accurately shot an arrow and killed Achilles by hitting him in his most vulnerable area, the heel of his foot. Hence, that part of the human anatomy is now called the Achilles tendon. Oh my God!' Troy Rogers realized. 'The Trojan King Priam's son Hector in the *Iliad* bears the same name as Hector Russo, my unsavory nemesis in real life!' the superstitious CPA keenly evaluated. 'What a truly oddball set of coincidences with the names Troy, Hector and Achilles all seeming to spontaneously be intersecting.'

* * * * * * * * * * * *

Saturday evening eventually arrived, and after admiring his newfound appearance in the living room mirror, Achilles (alias Troy Rogers) climbed into his dark blue Lexus, meticulously exited his circular driveway onto Walnut Street and then proceeded to turn left onto Third. The driver's mind was still troubled and distracted by the peculiar shipping error. The disgruntled motorist was heading his 'chariot' toward downtown Hammonton and soon Troy had to slam on his brakes when a huge dump truck going south on Fairview Avenue rumbled through a yellow traffic signal. Instantly Rogers' automobile was then unexpectedly and violently rear-ended by a shiny black Mercedes.

Immediately, two cursing masked men, one dressed as a Greek warrior and the second aggressive fellow as a Trojan Prince swiftly evacuated their respective vehicles. The enraged pair soon confronted one another.

"See here you arrogant, clumsy Fool!" Troy wildly screamed at the Prince Paris impersonator. "You were recklessly speeding and smashed into the back of my car. 'If you weren't going so damned fast you rambunctious Fool, and also speeding recklessly and deliberately tailgating me, then this unnecessary collision would've never occurred!"

"Don't give me any stupid crap or I'll decapitate you with your own sword!" the infuriated man regally dressed in the Trojan apparel bellowed as he pointed to Troy's bronze weapon. Then getting an impulsive evil inspiration, the incensed maniac removed an arrow from his quiver, inserted it into his bow and aimed the primitive weapon at an astonished and suddenly intimidated Troy Rogers, who instantaneously turned and frantically fled onto a North Third Street home's front lawn.

The truly out-of-control and greatly irritated Prince Paris pretender/ shot his arrow, which accurately pierced the back of Troy Rogers right foot. The victim fell to the turf with a thud, agonizing, crying and then writhing about in excruciating pain as the arrow recipient futilely held his wounded lower right appendage.

* * * * * * * * * * * *

Hammonton Chief-of-Police Henry Passarella sat behind his town hall office desk and was in the process of seriously reviewing and assessing the report of the outlandish Saturday evening traffic accident at the corner of Third Street and Fairview Avenue. The Chief was conversing with Sergeant Fred Ingemi, the equally confounded on-duty investigating officer handling the case. The two guardians of the peace were putting together the complicated pieces of the strange sociological puzzle.

"Fred, you've written here in your report that Hector Russo, oddly dressed as Prince Paris of Troy, shot and wounded Troy Rogers in the right heel using a primitive-looking bow and arrow, and you've also indicated that Mr. Rogers at the time of the incident was dressed as the Greek hero Achilles. And," Chief-of-Police Passarella proceeded with his oral analysis and interpretation, "a witness to the accident/crime, blueberry farmer Skeeter Bertino had been traveling as a passenger in Hector Russo's black Mercedes and Officer Ingemi, your strange report states that the third party had been dressed as an Egyptian pharaoh named Ramses II! What kind of an insane anachronism is this incident Sergeant?" Chief Passarella bellowed. "The peculiar set of events will easily make national tabloid journalism news along with cable chatter once the ravenous Philly' newspapers and TV stations grab a-hold of this thoroughly demented story! Don't *you* get it? Our respectable town will become the laughing stock of the entire nation!"

"At least the two principal participants were driving cars and not riding in ancient war chariots!" Sergeant Ingemi humorously articulated, much to his superior's chagrin. "It seems Chief that all three subjects were en route to a masquerade party down on Central Avenue given by that blonde knockout dame Cindy Harper. I surmise that since all three men were wearing masks," Ingemi hypothesized and nervously stated, "I believe that Troy Rogers and Hector Russo didn't recognize one another even though they actually knew one another in real life!"

"And also, Fred, the corresponding hospital report explicitly states that Mr. Rogers injury is only minor and that the doctors in the Atlantic Care Emergency Room have determined that the arrow wound is only superficial," the Chief read. "Thank God for *that* minor miracle!"

"That's right, Hank!" Sergeant Ingemi confirmed in a more personal tone of voice. "Troy Rogers will not be hobbling around for long, and fortunately, he won't be a cripple for life. He'll be able to make a full recovery and be back on his feet without crutches in less than a week," the officer disclosed to his boss. "I've also learned from interviewing Troy Rogers in his hospital room that he plans on suing that detestable bully Hector Russo for attempted manslaughter.

And once the shrewd accountant wins the accident civil case in the local municipal court," Sergeant Ingemi predicted, "then Troy will be filing a felony criminal lawsuit at the county level, and if he wins that particular litigation," the policeman elucidated, "Rogers will be awarded a gigantic settlement by an empathetic jury and will possibly wind-up with perhaps half of Russo's prosperous blueberry farm empire. Being wounded by a non-poisonous arrow might actually be a blessing in disguise," Fred Ingemi divulged and punned.

"What incredible irony!" Chief Passarella exclaimed. "Hector Russo should've stopped his rage at shooting-off his big mouth! Now he's in real deep hot water for thinking that he was Prince Paris of Troy shooting-off an arrow at his avowed ancient Greek foe Achilles, alias Troy Rogers, coincidentally wounding him in *his* right heel. Now Fred," Chief Henry Passarella emphasized to his loyal and obedient subordinate, "I hope that you don't think that you're almighty Zeus and then angrily hurl a million volt lightning bolt in my direction just two weeks before I can enjoy my long-awaited retirement from the Hammonton Police Force!"

"Repro' Man"

On the second Saturday in November of 2009, five Hammonton, New Jersey volunteer firemen were comfortably sitting upon cushioned chairs at a round table in the lounge of Firehouse #2, playing poker and discussing current events, along with sharing sundry local gossip. Bill Ryan, Tom Morano, Ken Parkhurst, Steve Kowalski, and bachelor Charlie Heggan were good friends, who often bowled together; attended Philadelphia Phillies baseball games; frequented the exciting gambling tables at Atlantic City casinos as a group, and the five comrades were the proud executive officers of the very popular fifty-member Boot Hill Deer Gunning Club.

"How was the apple crop this fall?" garrulous car dealer Bill Ryan asked equally-talkative farmer Tom Morano. "You've got the last five Jonathan and Red Delicious orchards in Hammonton, now that blueberries have taken-over most of the local farm acreage from lowly peaches and apples."

"A few guys still grow tomatoes, squash, corn, and peppers," Morano grimly answered Ryan as *he* closely scrutinized his five dealt cards to determine which two "bummers" he intended to discard for substitutes. "But the amazing blues bring the best value and yield per acre of any other area fruit or vegetable, and the Blue Crop and Duke varieties command the best prices in the rough and tumble East Coast supply and demand fruit and produce markets. In fact, Bill," the industrious farmer expounded, "I'm planning to remove my less-profitable apple trees after next year, and plant another hundred-acres of Dukes."

"Is there any serious downside to solely growing blueberries?" successful plumber Ken Parkhurst asked Tom Morano. "It's more than obvious that Hammonton has an abundance of self-made millionaires, and I would venture to guess that three-quarters of them are ambitious blueberry farmers. It seems that everybody in the local agricultural arena with an iota of good judgment is getting heavily into blueberries."

"The only problem that I foresee with the luscious blue fruit is the issue of labor," Tom Morano promptly replied as the flush holder further scrutinized his strong, card-playing hand. "A mere hundred men could easily keep a huge thousand-acre peach or apple farm going, but blueberries are much more labor intensive, and it would require at least a thousand migrant pickers to harvest a thousand-acres of blues over the course of the brief eight-week summer growing season. But here's every blueberry farmer's major fear," Tom Morano confided. "Someday, there might be a shortage of Mexicans, Haitians, and Guatemalans around South Jersey, and then the fresh pick summer crop couldn't be adequately harvested."

"Well, Tom, what about using those giant picking machines I see on all the major blueberry farms?" house builder Steve Kowalski wanted to know. "I'll bet that one of those blueberry picking mechanisms could easily do the work of a hundred migrants."

"You would think so from general appearance, however, things underneath often aren't as they might appear on the surface," Tom Morano stated with a stern face. "Unfortunately, all of the blueberries don't get ripe at the same time, and as I've already mentioned, the delicate crop is extremely labor intensive. That's the nature of that very perishable fruit. Generally speaking," Morano lectured as his eyes surveyed his cards and his mouth's words further informed his captivated listeners, "each blueberry field is handpicked four times at eight-day intervals. And then the machines are sent-in for two additional pickings to get the remainder of the blue fruit off the bushes. The handpicked berries are targeted for the chain and grocery store fresh markets, while the machine-picked berries are used for jam and syrup, and are later processed for those specific purposes in local bulk-houses. The machine-picked berries are not of the in-demand, superior quality as the handpicked ones are, and many of the bulk-house blues are incidentally damaged by the harvesting machines. If the source of migrant workers ever dries-up, well then …."

"Then, quite possibly, the blueberry farmers will lose most of their crop for a lack of labor should the hard-working migrant Mexicans ever stop coming in droves to New Jersey," house building contractor Steve Kowalski finished Morano's sentence, as the momentarily happy fellow keenly examined *his* full house of three nines and two queens. "But Tom, thanks for the general education you've just explained about the risk of growing blueberries as opposed to the other area crops like peaches and apples, that used to dominate the Hammonton farm scene. Now tell me," Steve Kowalski resumed his probing commentary. "How adversely has the recent economic recession affected you guys? If things don't improve soon, I'm afraid that my ailing business will be in trouble with state, county, and local contracts drying-up from the lack of available government tax money. I mean to say that banks won't loan me money unless I can show the loans department some bona fide home construction contracts."

"I'll tell you guys *straight,*" car dealer Bill Ryan impulsively remarked as the auto salesman held his *hearts' flush* closer to his vest. "I'm fairly satisfied that I'm selling Toyotas and Fords with General Motors and Chrysler currently being in such dire straits. But with fresh cash being scarce, and with unemployment rising," Ryan emphasized to his fellow volunteer firefighters, "it's damned difficult being in the car business, or in any other vulnerable business during these very drastic hard times. If things don't change for the better soon, then we're all going to go down the tubes, and I hereby predict that it'll be 1929 and Depression Time all over again."

"I agree with Bill's general assessment of the country's financial situation," plumber Ken Parkhurst opined. "People all over town are hoarding their money and putting-off certain home improvement projects, like new additions or installing new toilets, bathtubs, and vanities. At least those lucky folks still have savings left in their dwindling bank and stock market accounts and can do some home improvements, but those town residents are in the minority," pipe-installer Parkhurst seriously maintained. "About the only calls I now get are emergencies, where faucets are broken, or where water pumps or septic systems shut-down, and automatically require my immediate attention."

"Ken's is absolutely right," Steve Kowalski chimed-in a second time. "My good buddy home builder Hank Perna has only erected three houses so far this year, and the homes were all low-end structures, around in the two-hundred-and-fifty-thousand-dollar range. The banks aren't granting loans like they used to be doing before the housing and real estate crash happened," the despondent businessman disclosed. "I mean, Guys, three years ago, Hank was constructing a full dozen half-million-dollar and up mansions in developments all over South Jersey. But now, he's barely meeting his basic expenses, and Hank Perna had to lay-off four of his best carpenters. If this ugly recession continues much longer," Fireman Kowalski continued in a melancholy tone of voice, "then I'm afraid that guys like Hank Perna and me will have to give-up our independent companies. Then, I'll have to become an average-salaried union tradesman again, doing random circuit breaker and ordinary wiring work, or dangerously climbing telephone poles for Atlantic City Electric."

"I feel guilty discussing the economic crisis with you depressed Fellas', because the national recession hasn't hit me quite as hard this summer, despite the mediocre crop and weak prices in the New York and Philly' food distribution networks," blueberry bush and apple tree mogul Tom Morano contributed to the ongoing dialogue. "What about you, Chuck?" Tom casually inquired of Charlie Heggan. "You have that cake state gig, and are pretty secure with your seniority status. Your sacred cow government job isn't in jeopardy, is it?"

"I don't think so!" Charlie Heggan self-consciously indicated. "And my pension seems to be safe if the greedy governor doesn't keep raiding the employees' fund to transfer the accumulated assets somewhere else in his fragile state budget."

"Guess what, Guys!" Bill Ryan remembered and declared. "It's nearly deer hunting season, and according to tradition and past practice, one' of us Boot Hill club executives needs to be selected to go-out into the woods to the log cabin and clean-up the place for the other members. Now, Steve Kowalski here has five straws in his shirt pocket, and whoever draws the shortest one is designated to drive-out to the Wharton Forest tract on *Route 206* and get the old clubhouse in order."

The five firemen sitting around the table's circumference laid their card hands face-down, and then each Boot Hill member very methodically chose a separate, partially-concealed straw from Steve Kowalski's clenched right fist.

"Not again!" Charlie Heggan hollered in disgust, much to the amusement and delight of his four companions. "I had to clean-up the filthy lodge last year! I think that this questionable straw-selection process is maliciously rigged against me!"

"Thank Lady Luck for frowning on your unlucky fate, Heggan!" Ken Parkhurst exclaimed, and then loudly laughed. "Now Charlie, destiny dictates that you have to pay some price for being favorably insulated from the ongoing recession by simply luckily and securely working in Trenton for the tax-hungry State of New Jersey!"

"But the union has already gone along with the governor's budgetary request, and the leadership has foolishly consented to a salary freeze for next year," Charlie futilely objected and argued as his four colleagues chuckled and smirked. "And now, Gentlemen, because of my union's stupid blunder, I have to contribute even more dough out of my pay to cover my pension benefits and my health insurance, too!"

"Welcome to the real world of American capitalism!" Bill Ryan bellowed, momentarily feigning contempt for Charlie Heggan's guaranteed state employment security. "There're always winners and losers in the competitive U.S. free enterprise system."

"But just remember one important axiom of life in America, Charlie," Tom Morano added with a very evident poker face. "The true definition of the word *job* happens to be the letters j.o.b., which translated from the three-letter abbreviation, stands for the gloomy expression 'just over broke'."

* * * * * * * * * * * *

Charlie Heggan drove his two-year-old white Toyota Tundra (that he had loyally purchased from Bill Ryan) out of Hammonton Fire House #2's parking lot, turning the recently washed vehicle *right* onto busy *Route 30,* the White Horse Pike. A half a mile west, just past Ace Hardware, the recently appointed and assigned gunning club janitor made a right onto Basin Road, and proceeded north until he came to Union, a mile ahead. A quick right onto Union Road, and then a thousand-feet after the sharp curve (through well-maintained blueberry fields on either side) was two-lane *Route 206,* where the shiny white Tundra came to a gradual halt.

'I'm not going to procrastinate cleaning-up the Boot Hill log cabin like I did last year,' Charlie decided before pulling-out onto the highway and again heading north. 'I put-up with a lot of guff from the fellas' last fall, and the verbal tormenting was agonizing. The cabin's electricity was switched on last week,' the driver recalled. 'So I know I'll have power to run the vacuum cleaner and to get well water from the kitchen faucets. I'll bet the dual sinks are greasy, and the toilets grimy, too,' Heggan speculated in disgust. 'I wonder if the other four conniving guys back at the firehouse card table know a slick trick that I'm unaware of about how to avoid choosing the short straw. I smell a rat, with *me* again being designated for *this* rather lousy, unsavory duty.'

Five-miles up the two-lane highway (just after the abandoned old cranberry bogs and just before the Wagon Wheel Restaurant) was a dirt road that snaked into the eastern section of the Wharton State Forest. After negotiating the right-hand turn, Charlie Heggan carefully drove his dependable truck a half-a-mile into the interior, finally realizing that the trail dust from his tires was churning-up and dirtying his formerly immaculate white truck's exterior. Reaching his drab cabin's destination, the disgruntled fireman hit the brakes and halted his dust-laden vehicle.

Inside the unkempt cabin, "the Boot Hill custodian" busied himself: first cleaning the corroded kitchen counter where deer meat was often butchered, and upon which all varieties of whiskey and beer had been wildly-poured (the past December) into plastic cups and old glasses. The two crusty porcelain sink basins were then intensively scoured with detergent and coarse Brillo soap pads, until the drains magically glistened. And after the wood on the antiquated furniture had been rag-polished, and the front and rear windows given the 'Merlin Windex treatment', Charlie Heggan determined that the rugs in all four rooms had to be vacuumed at least thrice.

Upon removing the ultra-loud 1960s' vintage cleaning apparatus from the musty-smelling utility closet, the recently appointed lodge custodian suddenly noticed a dark shadow blocking-out the sun's rays, and thus, preventing afternoon November light from refracting through the rear kitchen window.

'That's awfully strange!' Heggan impulsively considered. 'Is there some sort of solar eclipse in progress that I haven't read about in the morning paper, or hadn't seen reported on TV cable news?'

Upon stepping-over to the now crystal-clear window, situated above the now-spotless kitchen sinks, the baffled lodge-cleaner reflexively stared-up at the outside shadow's source. 'Holy cow! I think it's a wobbling UFO hovering overhead. Now the alien object's drifting slowly over that weed field patch behind the cabin, and the saucer appears to be landing in front of the woods,' Charlie nervously marveled and gasped.

Seconds later, the awed deer hunter considered his plan of action. 'I'll take a shotgun from the gun rack, go outside, hide behind a wide tree, and investigate this phenomenon more in detail. Boy, I wish one of the guys had come along to verify this close encounter of the first kind! Maybe I can make a breakthrough contact with the space voyagers, assuming they're friendly cosmic travelers in need of my personal assistance!'

Feeling anxious with a palpitating heart fiercely beating inside his chest, and with his normally steady hands shaking, Charlie used his personal access key to open the paneled gun cabinet; removed a 22 caliber from the storage case, and next quickly loaded a pair of shells that the shooter then obtained from the locked ammunition drawer. Skulking-down, Heggan stealthily exited the front door like a burglar on the prowl, and then the intrigued searcher meandered and slinked his way into the clustered forest pines, crouching-down and then eventually crawling forward like a Parris Island Marine basic training recruit, clumsily advancing his chubby body, another thirty-feet to the trunk of an enormous oak.

Without any palpable evidence of being detected, the courageous fireman was startled when a silent-but-powerful laser beam sheared-
52

off an overhead limb, which instantly separated from the tall broad deciduous tree, and soon a part of the descending branch grazed Heggan's face.

'I'm bleeding a little bit, but still alive!' Charlie neurotically recognized. 'These particular space aliens might have advanced technology at their disposal, but the trespassers seem to be honoring their basic primitive survival instincts. I'll take a few shots at the hostile invaders to try and scare them off, but if the science fiction movies I've seen are correct, the humanoids probably have some kind of fantastic force field shields around them, that'll protect their bug eyes and their skinny butts from shotgun pellets and the like. On second thought, I'd better avoid contact with them if I could!'

Charlie's mind imagined that he was a greenhorn soldier at nearby Fort Dix, about to engage in a life-or-death target practice session, so out of desperate fear, the skilled hunter revised his survival strategy. Heggan mechanically rolled-over, holding his shotgun; carefully took aim at two gray-skinned figures standing at the side of the landed spacecraft, and then intrepidly fired a loud blast. The surprised space creatures swiftly scurried-up an entrance ramp that quickly closed behind their entrance, and within a matter of ten-seconds, the out-of-this-world saucer was ascending above the forest tree canopy, and moments later, the circular craft zoomed out of sight, zipping across the sky at an incredible velocity, veering westward in the direction of Philadelphia.

Still feeling befuddled and in a state of shock, Charlie cautiously rose to his feet and gingerly walked-over to the weed-infested field where the interstellar spaceship had landed. The perplexed and rattled UFO investigator alertly noticed that all evidence of earth vegetation had been mysteriously scorched-away. But nearby the aforementioned saucer landing area, Heggan detected a shimmering metallic device, which he hesitantly stooped-down to further inspect and touch.

'It's some type of weird, three-inch by four-inch, wing-shaped gizmo, probably originating from another planet!' the now-paranoid deer hunter theorized. 'There're two indentations, and I presume that the tiny crater on the left is for the left thumb, and the small one on the right is for the opposite thumb. And there also appears to be three distinct symbols that look somewhat like ancient Egyptian hieroglyphics, and now I see a slightly raised dial indicator directly below the three odd figures, probably indicating three setting modes. This totally foreign thing's made from some strange yellow metal alloy that I've never seen or felt before.'

Overwhelmed by intense curiosity, Charlie pressed-down on the singular instrument's left thumb 'hollow button', which apparently was designed to activate the device. And when Heggan mustered sufficient daring to firmly touch the right-side counterpart raised impression, instantaneously, ten identical reproductions of himself' materialized, each newly created entity standing absolutely erect and evidently at attention.

'This is truly unbelievable!' Charlie Heggan concluded. 'That really in-genius right side setting has effectively duplicated my physical existence tenfold. Now, I'll try pushing the right-side indentation twice, and objectively observe what kind of unearthly extraterrestrial cause-and-effect situation develops.'

After attempting his second novel experiment, the tenacious initiator was astounded to perceive that the ten counterparts of himself' had quickly vanished into thin air, and then in a heartbeat, a hundred three-dimensional replicas of himself had 'miraculously' formed in their place.

'Great Caesar's Ghost. I wonder what the third and final symbol setting will accomplish,' Charlie's brain intrepidly-but-hesitantly hypothesized. 'If exponential mathematics is in play here, which I think it is, ten-times-ten-times-ten is ten cubed. I'll bet that I can form an awesome army of a thousand Charlie Heggans' by simply applying my right thumb to this remarkable contraption three consecutive times,' the astonished possessor of the ultimate reproduction machine euphorically imagined.

Heggan's mind suddenly turned greedy. 'I'll bet I could easily sell this superior device to the United States military and make an astronomical fortune. I've heard of the dreaded Repo' Man, repossessing automobiles while working for demanding creditors. But I now believe that I'm destined to be the first *Repro' Man,* capable of multiplying myself at my whim, and I'll easily battle and defeat any evil-minded culprit attempting to abuse or harass me.'

The very thrilled discoverer didn't have any spare time to evaluate whether a thousand Charlie Heggans' could be generated, because at that very moment, a Jeep carrying three rambunctious hell-bent-for-leather pineys came speeding-down the dirt trail from the direction of *Highway 206.*

'Oh no!' Charlie thought and regretted as the human multiplier quickly erased his 'obedient army' and promptly concealed his new-found human duplicator inside a pocket of his green fall windbreaker. 'I'll furtively keep the fabulous reproduction appliance ready for immediate use, just in case I need it in a hurry.'

54

* * * * * * * * * * * *

"Well now, looky here, Boys," Theodore "the Hammer" Griffin announced to his two Big Buck Hunting Club associates, Jake "the Coyote" Billings and Vince "the Outlaw" Hawkins. "It's a bona fide, in the flesh, member of one of our rival gun clubs, the wimpy Boot Hill creeps! Now tell me, Knucklehead!" scar-faced Ted Griffin yelled at Charlie. "What's the big idea of shootin' off your shotgun a full month before deer huntin' season begins. We heard the blast echoes in the woods, way on the other side of *206*. Ain't ya' got no kitchen calendar in your house? It's not even bow and arrow buck season yet. That week comes along just before Thanksgiving, you screwed-up, nutjob nincompoop."

"Didn't you guys just see a flying saucer whisk-by around five-minutes-ago? It was definitely heading west toward Philly'!" Charlie stammered. "No kidding! I saw the UFO with my own two eyes, and then I took a shot at the fleeing gray-skinned aliens!"

"Ha, ha, ha! Was that what ya' was shootin' at, a freakin' imaginary UFO!" Jake Billings cackled, much to the elation of his criminal-minded, villainous pals. "Was you aimin' at the flying saucer, or was ya' pointin' your shotgun at the aliens ridin' inside it! Ha, ha, ha!"

"We don't believe your phony story, and think it's a ridiculous attempt at creatin' a hoax, so that *we* don't beat the stuffing out of ya'!" ruthless-looking Vince "the Outlaw" Hawkins very strongly insinuated. "Now, what should we do with this spineless scumbag, Ted? Let's teach this freak a lesson in honesty, that's what the heck I think we three wild-ass pineys oughta' do!"

"Okay, you yellow-bellied Punk, you asked for it by intentionally lyin' to us about why you were firing-off your gun like some sort of idiotic moron!" Ted "the Hammer" Griffin threatened, as the brute and his two muscle-bound cohorts moved forward to ostensibly grab and physically punish poor Charlie Heggan. "What do ya' say we toss this pea-brain Hammonton Fool up onto the roof of his Boot Hill clubhouse; that is, after we first provide him with a little bodily and emotional duress! Let's teach this wimpy liar a lesson he'll never forget!"

Responding to his dire need for self-preservation, Charlie quickly removed his secret handheld reproduction machine from the right pocket of his green jacket; firmly pressed the right-side indentation, and amazingly, ten magnificent representations of himself' appeared

55

with clenched fists. Being outnumbered nearly four to one, and not comprehending exactly how the uncanny human multiplication had occurred, the three piney roughnecks became intimidated, and suddenly turned craven. Then, the frightened trio frantically hustled inside their dilapidated Jeep.

Ted "the Hammer" Griffin frenetically turned the ignition key; put the gearshift into reverse; popped the clutch, and his decrepit three-tone vehicle performed a crude semi-circle going backwards. And then, in the blink of an eye, the three petrified barbarians sped-off from the remote forest road, fleeing west towards *Route 206,* eagerly seeking the security and the comforts associated with benign and predictable lawful civilization.

'I'm still a little flustered from experiencing that ugly ordeal encounter, and cleverly implementing this incomparable, miraculous human body duplicator,' Charlie reckoned with a deep breath. 'The refrigerator inside the cabin is empty, and I think I need some heavy-duty alcohol in my system. I'll first go inside the cabin and wash the dried-up blood from my cheek. Then, I'll drive my Toyota over to the Pic-A-Lilli Inn up on *206.* It's only a few miles away from here, just past Atsion Lake. I'll swallow-down a cold draft beer or two, and contemplate what I plan to do with *this* truly outrageous but quite functional human body duplicator.'

The reckless and treacherous Zombies Motorcycle Gang had just arrived at the infamous Pic-A-Lilli Inn, and the gruesome members were assiduously polishing the exposed chrome parts of their expensive bikes. Seeing meek-looking Charlie Heggan appear in his white Toyota Tundra, Big "Boss" Jenkins, the chief Zombies' 'hog', decided that it would be good sport (consistent with his vile reputation) to deliberately confront and wickedly bother and taunt the new elderly arrival. The Zombies leader initiated a conversation with the frail-looking, but now-omnipotent Repro' Man.

"What are ya' doin' drivin' around in a lousy foreign Japanese truck?" Boss Jenkins yelled at Heggan as the peace-loving fireman approached the Pic-A-Lilli's main entrance. "Don't ya' know, Pal, what a made in the USA Ford, Chevy, or Dodge truck looks like? Your choice of vehicle upsets me and my friends greatly!"

"Look, Sir. I don't want any trouble!" Charlie apologetically replied as twenty ferocious-looking, tattooed, skinhead hoods stood behind their antagonistic and bellicose leader. "I only stopped in at this tavern to down a beer or two, and get my mind off my problems, before hitting the road again."

"Well, Jerk, it looks like you're on the brink of having some new *troubles* in your dull life, like huge hospital bills and massive doctors' fees!" Boss Jenkins boasted while his aggregate of supporters egged the gang's honcho on by boisterously uttering a plethora of background derisions. "And don't worry, Mack!" Jenkins continued his obnoxious berating. "The Pic-A-Lilli owner ain't gonna' call the cops, because both the bar owner and the fuzz are pretty-damned scared of me and my clan!"

Just as Boss Jenkins was reaching-out for a set of brass knuckles being supplied to him by a loyal gang confederate, Charlie quickly located *his* incomparable reproduction tool, and then very deliberately pressed the right-side thumb depression two times. A full second elapsed, and much to the incredulous twenty-one bikers' alarm and chagrin, a hundred angry-looking Charlie Heggan' facsimiles crystallized directly behind the now-haughty and fearless fellow. The formidable, notorious motorcycle gang's brazenness soon transformed into obvious cowardice.

"What the frig' is this crap all about!" Boss Jenkins shrieked like an authentic ninety-eight-pound weakling. "Come on, men! Let's get the hell out of here before the miserable world comes to an end! I feel like vomiting up my intestines, along with all the putrid, slimy digested food inside my guts!"

The twenty-one terrified bullies hopped onto their respective Harley hogs; fired-up their engines, and frantically skidded and hightailed their bikes out of the Pic-A-Lilli parking lot, acting like a family of scared rabbits. Charlie Heggan, feeling nobly invincible, keenly gazed at and admired his new-found 'supernatural device'.

'I just have to satisfy my curiosity! Let's find out what this third right-hand dial setting achieves!' Heggan confidently thought as the device's possessor fully accepted his new public prowess. 'I know I can form ten re-creations of myself by hitting the first symbol by pressing my right thumb once, and I know that I can materialize a hundred duplications of myself by pushing the second symbol and then the right indentation twice. I'll touch the third symbol and the right-side depression three times, and see if I can actually generate a thousand physical renditions of myself.'

Charlie Heggan bravely and confidently enacted his latest fantasy, but instead of a thousand carbon copies of himself' inexplicably manifesting around his presence, the adventurous experimenter spontaneously vaporized into the atmosphere, and then amazingly disappeared from sight.

* * * * * * * * * * * *

Immediately stunned and fully flabbergasted, Charles Richard Heggan endeavored interpreting his alien, surreal, metallic environment, which was characterized by pulsating and alternating shades of purple, violet, and indigo-colored light. The confused captive's concentration was abruptly interrupted by the appearance of two tall, thin, pale-faced, bug-eyed, gray-skinned figures that the new arrival automatically perceived to be super-intelligent space travelers. Instantly, the immensely petrified fireman fathomed that he had become a helpless prisoner inside a flying saucer that was speedily exiting the earth's atmosphere. And the incarcerated hostage quickly comprehended that his two silent, foreign, alien observers possessed the unique capacity to telepathically communicate with his human brain.

'Greetings, pathetic Earth Creature!' the first space voyager mentally transmitted, as the humanoid amazingly held and opened Heggan's wallet to locate vital identification credentials. 'I'm Dr. Zancor, and this is *our* competent pilot/navigator, Lieutenant Eutak. We're from a planet known to our race as Xanton, in what your inferior civilizations call Constellation Virgo. I suppose that your lackluster, inferior mind has a few rudimentary questions that you'd desire to have answered.'

'Yes, Dr. Zancor!' Heggan mentally and neurotically stuttered. 'I'd like to know exactly what happened to me after I pressed the right-hand-side indentation three times and then...'

'Hand me the Universal Duplicator/Teleporter Device that's still in your feeble possession!' Dr. Zancor imperatively and mentally commanded. 'You haven't quite yet mastered its usage completely, and if you're not careful, you might stupidly teleport yourself outside our speeding ship, and then accidentally disintegrate in the coldness of black outer space, and consequently, be lost and erased from existence forever.'

Charlie very hesitantly and meticulously transferred control of the extraordinary computer mechanism to his no-nonsense captor. The eminent Planet Xanton scientist, Dr. Zancor, then cerebrally explained and defined Heggan's new reality to the still-puzzled and trembling earthling.

'I perceive and fathom that you're still wondering about the nature of my latest invention that I'm currently field-testing all over the galaxy. This advanced appliance I'm holding is the prototype model of the Universal Duplicator/Teleporter and,' Dr. Zancor

58

paused for a moment to study Charlie Heggan's pallid face, 'I've recently applied for exclusive patent rights to market the device back home on Xanton. Confidentially, Mr. Heggan, I intend for the apparatus to make me the wealthiest person on my planet.'

'Well, Dr. Zancor, exactly what does it do that I don't already know?' the now-paranoid space detainee nervously asked. 'I mean, from *your* advanced perspective, what does it do?'

'My complicated invention has two basic functions that you've already tampered with,' emotionless and callous Dr. Zancor objectively communicated without ever moving his ashen-looking lips. 'As you've already learned, Earthling Charles Richard Heggan, the dial setting numbers one and two on the machine's right-side will multiply your existence ten-fold, and a hundred-fold respectively. But I managed to trick your inadequate judgment, along with your extraordinary propensity for curiosity with the third setting, which automatically....'

'Teleported me into this spacecraft, instead of multiplying me a thousand-fold!' Charlie finally understood the alien ruse. 'But for what purpose?'

The eminent Dr. Zancor deferred further telepathic exposition about *his* versatile invention to the more-reticent Lieutenant Eutak, who upon his superior's explicit approval, voluntarily provided the appropriate explanation to *their* now physically immobilized 'guest prisoner'. The no-nonsense Xanton military officer was firmly blunt, precise, and directly descriptive in the graphic presentation of his enlightening narrative.

'All of our citizens on Xanton are exceptionally rich, so we have to import servants from all over this sector of our galaxy to accommodate our many societal needs,' the Lieutenant's mind mentally transmitted. 'And so, Dr. Zancor had shrewdly exploited your human egotistical need for power, and took advantage of your psychological need to fully demonstrate your self-centered prowess to your fellow Earthlings, even to those socially dysfunctional motorcycle gang deviates, having malevolent narcissistic intentions. And so, Mr. Charles Richard Heggan, for that's *your* authentic identification as indicated inside your wallet cards,' Eutak reiterated, 'for the remainder of your life, you'll be...'

'You'll be a humble and grateful servant to *me* on Xanton, and you'll be obediently attending to my every personal demand,' Dr. Zancor sternly divulged to his newly-acquired, totally horrified human slave. 'And now that my revolutionary experiment has been a tremendous success, I can easily duplicate you a hundred-fold, and sell your facsimiles to other Xanton natives, who are perfectly willing to pay a rather handsome stipend for your reproductions' indispensable services.'

'I was duped and victimized!' the slave UFO hostage assessed and realized. 'You're an absolute scoundrel, Dr. Zancor!'

'Quite true, and I do detect an element of wisdom originating from the weak mind of this rather inferior being!' Dr. Zancor mentally answered his appalled space hostage. 'And the most wonderful element of this entire experiment is the fact that you have thought that you could create a thousand copies of yourself by employing the third dial setting! This strange interview has been quite revealing to me, and it represents about the closest that *our* Xanton species can truly come to feeling fun and amusement, right, Lieutenant Eutak?' Dr. Zancor mentally conveyed to his colleague as defeated and disconsolate Charlie Heggan sorrowfully listened to the scientist's flagrant and arrogant braggadocio.

'Yes, Dr.,' Lieutenant Eutak mentally returned without ever cracking a brief smile or a mere momentary grin. 'This incompetent, ludicrous, captured Idiot tried duplicating himself a thousand times outside the primitive tavern, but instead, the Imbecile wound-up teleporting his body and mind directly into the storage hull of our magnificent, warp-speed spacecraft!'

"Window of Opportunity"

The May Installation Meeting assigning new officers for the Hammonton, New Jersey Lions Club had just adjourned, and afterwords, two recently-appointed minor functionaries were discussing their basic roles with an elderly club member in the upstairs bar of Rocco's Town House on North Third Street. The all-too-garrulous District 16-C Governor had already departed the premises, and Liontamer Mitchell Spencer, Tailtwister Michael Giberson, and feeble Past President Julius Stetson were standing at the tavern's bar, casually engaged in a genial conversation over their after-meeting cocktails.

"It's good to see new blood coming into the club and accepting active roles," eighty-two-year-old Julius Stetson praised the local Lions Club's two new energized recruits. "I was a charter member of the club way back in 1963," Julius informed his respectful listeners before sipping his cold *Southern Comfort* on the rocks. "And we had only a dozen members when John F. Kennedy was the country's President, mostly businessmen owning stores and properties up on Route 30. One guy had a liquor store; another guy was a produce broker; a third had a gas station and auto' repair garage, and a fourth fella' owned a popular diner that stayed open until three in the morning," old Julius Stetson reminisced. "Those fun-loving guys are all dead now, and I'm the only original charter member left. At the time, the town's Kiwanis and Rotary clubs were the top civic organizations in Hammonton, and the fledgling Lions were like the town's orphan upstarts. After the Lillian-on-the-Lake eatery closed for business," Stetson related, "our tiny club had to meet in the small back room of the Hacienda Restaurant, while the hotshot and snobbish Kiwanis guys got priority and enjoyed their meals inside the big dining area."

"Hacienda Restaurant?" Mitchell Spencer politely interrupted Julius. "I've never heard of it!"

"Where have all the years gone? The stucco, Spanish-styled place used to be located at the intersection of *Route 30* and *Route 206* where the Rite-Aid Pharmacy is now situated," Lion Stetson nostalgically revealed. "The Hacienda was demolished back in the late 1970s, just a few years before either of you two whippersnappers were ever born, let alone conceived."

"Were you a conscientious Lion when you joined the club?" Liontamer Mitchell Spencer courteously inquired. "I presume you must've been. I mean, I've never heard of a vegetable vendor selling rotten tomatoes from his fruit and produce wagon! You had to be a true-blue Lion right from the outset in order to have been a dedicated member all these years."

"Like yourself, Mitchell, I started-out as the lowly Liontamer, taking care of the club's banner, gavel, gong, microphone, and table podium," Julius nonchalantly informed his avid audience of two. "Then I was promoted. The next year, I became the Tailtwister, the club sheriff levying fines on members that came late to a meeting, or who had forgotten to wear their club pin on their jacket lapel, or who had neglected to wear their membership badge, or who neglected to have their Lions International Card in their wallet. And if the member checked-out okay with those essential credentials in their possession," Julius bragged and prattled before imbibing a swig of sweet liquor, "I'd then fine them on the spot if the violators couldn't answer a simple question like 'Who founded Lions International in 1917?' or 'Who challenged the Lions to become Knights of the Blind at an early international convention'?"

"Melvin Jones was the founder of Lions International," Liontamer Mitchell Spencer proudly answered with an air of certainty evident in his voice. "And Helen Keller gave an important speech at the early convention you had mentioned and got the first wave of Lions interested in becoming champions for the blind and crusaders for the hearing impaired. She also encouraged the Lions to help the less fortunate in their communities. But unfortunately," Mitch Spencer continued his informal lecture, "presently the government is taking over the function of charity through welfare programs and redistribution of wealth, so I fear that the need for service clubs assisting the needy is rapidly diminishing all throughout the country."

"Okay, Wise Guy," old Julius Stetson amiably stated with a smile. "Who was the first president of Lions International?"

"Melvin Jones?" Mitchell tentatively answered. "Obviously, yes. I'm quite certain that it must've been Melvin Jones if *he* was the founder of Lions International!"

"No, Mitch. it was a man named Dr. W. P. Woods, so that'll be a dollar fine!" knowledgeable club historian Julius Stetson joked and amply laughed. "And as the District Governor had lectured tonight, our international headquarters is in Oak Brook, Illinois, just outside Chicago. But over the years, Lions International has grown to over 30,000 clubs in over 150 countries, and our international membership now totals nearly one-and-a-half-million members,"

Julius confidently reviewed. "In fact, Gentlemen. In many parts of the world like in India and Japan, for example, it's a distinct honor to become a philanthropic Lion."

"You must be pretty bored with all of the redundant routines and monotonous speeches after nearly a half-century of involvement?" high school English teacher Mitchell Spencer asked his sponsor and mentor. "I mean, Julius, how many times do you have to hear the same rhetoric about membership drives, the value of newspaper public relations, and the need for participation in club fundraisers?"

"Well, I gotta' admit," Julius replied and then paused to carefully select his next words. "Over the years, our charity fundraisers have switched around. In the beginning, we had a Turkey Shoot, and we also collected money donations out in front of a grocery store for White Cane Day. Then later on, we had a Bike-A-Thon and sponsored a Tri-Ath-A-Lon, mostly because four ambitious state troopers had joined the club and insisted on us having fundraisers that focused on physical fitness. Now, of course," Julius paused and elaborated, "we have the Gold Raffle Dinner where we give-away seventeen-thousand-dollars in cash and prizes. And as you two members know, we also loyally sell muffins, pies, strudel, and turnovers at the annual Blueberry Festival in late June. Those two events alone earn the club over twenty-thousand-bucks a year, and I predict that someday, both of you two greenhorns will be chairmen of those two highly-profitable fundraisers."

"Well, Lion Julius," Mike Giberson commented before swallowing-down the remainder of his cordial drink. "What in your whole recollection were the craziest things you can remember the local Lions doing back in the good old days?"

"Ha, ha, ha," aged Julius Stetson giggled and then smirked. "In the beginning, when there were only men in the club, we did some nifty things. It was sort of like a fraternity for adult males. Once we hired a stripper to entertain us in the back room of an out-of-town bar to honor the achievements of an outgoing president. Another time, twelve of us journeyed in a van down to Ocean City, Maryland, and we paid a surprise visit to an enterprising club member who owned several thriving summer boardwalk businesses own there," Stetson recalled with a wide grin. "The shocked fella' treated us all to a fantastic crab and spicy shrimp feast at Phillip's Restaurant. But the neatest occurrence that I can recall involved a new member who had transferred into the Hammonton Lions from a club up near Yonkers, New York. Yes, that zany new member precipitated something special."

"Tell me quick, what happened!" Tailtwister Mike Giberson insisted. "I have to soon get on the road and pick-up my son at the elementary school after his Tuesday night basketball practice. I don't want to keep his coach waiting as a babysitter."

"Well, this new member, his name was Henry Thomas, had three of his old friends drive down from Yonkers, New York, and lo and behold, the mischievous culprits stole our club bell. So, eighteen of us Hammonton rascals rented a gigantic RV and drove up to Yonkers to retrieve the bell, according to standard Lions' custom. The idea behind that kind of good-humored theft is designed and endorsed by all Lions' clubs to promote fellowship and subsequent visitations to other clubs in order to advance the cause of sharing a good time."

"Is that all?" Giberson asked in a disappointed tone of voice. "I was expecting something a little more dynamic! Did you guys ever retrieve your club bell?"

"You didn't allow me to finish my terrific story!" old Julius facetiously balked. "On the way up to Yonkers, I was driving the mammoth RV on the *New Jersey Turnpike*. Traffic was bumper-to-bumper early that evening. The other guys were pretty inebriated by that time when we had reached the vicinity of the Newark Airport, and I must confess, including myself. In the midst of the massive automobile congestion," Julius expounded on his tale, "I awkwardly tried changing lanes, and in the process, I partially ripped-off the RV's back bumper when a stubborn tractor-trailer driver wouldn't let me switch lanes. There wasn't any noticeable damage to *his* big rig, but the RV bumper was more than a trifle mangled."

"What happened next?" Tailtwister Giberson curiously asked. "Did you have to pay for the bumper repair? Did you have to buy a new one? Either way, it must've cost you a decent fortune!"

"You're too impetuous, and in my opinion, Mike, your spoiled kid and his impatient coach can wait for you an extra five-minutes at the school gym!" Julius chastised the recently installed club enforcement officer. "It was during the early '70s, yes, during the Carter Administration, and there was gas rationing and long gas station lines everywhere," Lion Stetson recalled and shared. "Anyway Fellas', on the way back from Yonkers, we stopped near the north end of the Garden State Parkway to purchase gas. At the time, a fuel rationing crisis was rampant across the nation, and if your license plate ended in an even number, you could only buy gas on an even number day of the month. Well, it was an even number day, and we had an odd number ending to our RV's license plate, so the attendants refused to sell us fuel."

64

"How did you get home?" Liontamer Mitchell Spencer wanted to know. "This story is now becoming quite intriguing. How did you avoid being stranded a hundred-and-twenty-miles away from Hammonton in a gas-guzzling RV?"

"You're just as immaturely impulsive as Tailtwister Mike Giberson is!" Julius Stetson merrily chided Liontamer Mitch Spencer, before imbibing another tasty gulp of sweet *Southern Comfort*. "The four audacious state troopers in the club, all of them thoroughly groggy from gulping-down hard whiskey, well, they showed the suddenly alarmed attendants their State Police ID badges, and blatantly flashed guns from their shoulder holsters. The State Cops told the petrified gas station employees that *they* would be accused of harmfully obstructing justice since the damaged RV was on a secret drug raid mission, and consequently, the totally intimidated gas station guys immediately filled us up without any further controversy whatsoever."

"Ha, ha, ha! That was rich!" Tailtwister Michael Giberson commended the old-timer. "I wish I had been in the RV to see the frightened expressions on the gas station workers' faces! But how did you ever get the rear bumper fixed!"

"Well, now Boys, that's another fascinating tale that actually happened!" Julius Stetson merrily maintained. "When we eventually got back to Hammonton, the already drunk member who owned the large garage up on Route 30 got into the RV's driver seat, put the immense vehicle into reverse, and then violently slammed into the cinder-blocked side of his service station. Miraculously, the bumper was pressed back into its proper place without any notice of ever being in an accident, or ever being tampered with."

"That's really an incredibly-nifty narrative!" Mike Giberson congratulated old Julius. "Sorry Guys, but I gotta' split! Hope to see you both in two weeks at our next meeting."

After the newly appointed Tailtwister departed the sparsely populated Rocco's Town House bar area, Julius Stetson had a personal question to ask Liontamer Mitchell Spencer.

"Mitch, I'm a fairly good judge of human character, and I think you're a fine young man. I honestly believe that you remind me a lot of myself when I was financially struggling back in the midst of the 1950s recessions," Julius prefaced his odd and unexpected remarks. "I hear that you're thinking about dropping out of the Lions Club for money reasons. I know that you're an excellent high school English teacher, and I'm also aware that you make just an ordinary income."

"Well, quite frankly Mr. Stetson, unfortunately, I've accumulated considerable debts that I find myself drowning in," Mitch confided. "My divorce last year set me back big time; I have a tremendous mortgage on my home out on Second Road and I have to pay for my former wife's new condominium over on the bay in Brigantine. I have to pay her alimony, along with child support for our two kids now in her custody, by the judge's ruling. And finally, I have accumulated over forty-thousand-dollars in high interest credit card debt. My overwhelming total financial obligations are in the neighborhood of..."

"A half-million-dollars," sage Julius Stetson passively declared before finishing his second delicious whiskey. "Like I said, Mitch, I really like you and feel sorry for your unenviable plight. As you might know from town gossip, my wife is dead; I have no children of my own, and I absolutely despise my still-living avaricious niece and greedy nephew on my deceased wife's side. I'm eighty-two years old and have bad cases of colon and prostate cancer. Confidentially, the doctors at Jefferson Hospital over in Philly' say that I have only a month or so left," the old gentleman frankly divulged. "It's too late for me to incorporate you into my will. But should you happen to read my obituary in the local papers, I'm going to give you an extra back door key to my mansion over on Third Road. After my death, you must go to my residence immediately to avoid any complications with my money-hungry niece and nephew." The old man then reached into his pants pocket and exhibited a common key, finally surrendering its possession to the astounded, wide-eyed young Liontamer.

"What will this key lead to?" Mitch marveled and uttered, intensively scrutinizing the ordinary-looking object very closely. "Specifically, what's it really for, other than to gain access to your home? Of what value is it to me?"

"Inside my cluttered master bedroom closet, you'll find a big wall safe concealed directly behind and above my shoe rack," Julius indicated without showing any emotion. "In the safe, I'm going to leave a half-million-dollars in cash for you to pay-off your massive debts, so that you can start your life all over again and avert the grievous mistakes that have brought you to the threshold of bankruptcy. You'll find that *that* same key will open both the back door and the master bedroom closet wall safe."

"I can't believe your unexpected generosity!" Mitchell Spencer exclaimed, getting the attention of several idle tavern patrons seated on the opposite side of the oval bar. "Thank you so very much! You're an absolute Godsend!"

"But please, listen carefully, and fully heed my words," benefactor Julius Stetson whispered to his jubilant, prospective beneficiary. "When I had been a flashy show business performer back in the late 1940s, I had amassed a fine reputation as a class-act magician. Inside my hall cedar closet, I've painstakingly had constructed what I call 'my Window of Opportunity', which will become *your* 'Window of Opportunity'. Open the stained-glass window leading to a hidden room, and I promise that you'll discover additional rare treasures awaiting you!"

All that totally-thrilled Mitchell Spencer could do was stand there at the bar with an astonished-but-grateful expression upon his florid countenance, all the while wildly imagining exactly what the mysterious 'Window of Opportunity' could actually be.

* * * * * * * * * * * * *

Two weeks passed, and the English teacher faithfully carried the 'gift key' in his pocket to Hammonton High School every single workday. 'Julius said that I must go to his home as soon as I learn of his passing and use this back door key immediately so that I can remove the half-million cash from the closet wall safe, and then determine what's behind the mysterious 'Window of Opportunity' inside the cedar closet,' Mitchell kept reminding himself during seventh period while his advanced academic students were taking their *Hamlet* written examination.

That Tuesday evening, Lion Julius Stetson did not attend the bi-weekly club meeting, and it was reported that the aged member was home suffering from a mild spring sinus infection. And at the meeting, it was reported that the old gentleman seemed to be in good spirits when the distinguished elderly 'Past President' had called the club secretary and had informed the club executive of *his* legitimate excuse for being absent.

An additional two weeks passed, and another scheduled Lions Club meeting commenced at Rocco's Town House. After the customary Pledge of Allegiance, the opening prayer, and the traditional Lions' Toast, during *his* introductory remarks, the club president announced that revered Lion Julius Stetson had "suffered a devastating stroke" that afternoon and that the eighty-two-year-old-multimillionaire had been rushed by ambulance to Mainland

Hospital in Pomona, the renowned state-of-the-art medical facility being seventeen-miles east of Hammonton.

'My cousin Helen Reynolds is a night nurse in the emergency room at Mainland Hospital,' Mitchell Spencer astutely and mentally associated. 'I'll quietly text message her during this boring meeting to learn more about Julius's condition. My cousin's very reliable. I'm sure that if Helen is not in surgery right now, she'll be able to give me an update on my benefactor's condition in the form of a prompt reply.'

Forty-five-minutes later, just before the standard meeting ending "fifty-fifty drawing", Mitchell received a return text message from nurse Helen Reynolds stating that Julius Stetson of Hammonton had died at 7:35 p.m. that evening, and that his next of kin were presently being notified, along with a prominent Hammonton undertaker.

'It's happened! God rest *his* soul! The initial suspense is now over!' Mitchell sadly evaluated with perspiration appearing on his forehead, just before he won the sum of thirty-dollars in the fifty-fifty drawing. "I'd like to give the money I've just won back to the club!" Spencer articulated as the seated members unanimously gave him an appreciative round of applause.

Then, an image of the prospective half-million-dollar 'cash bonanza' focused inside Spencer's actively racing mind, and the Liontamer's thoughts greedily contemplated the swift acquisition of his highly anticipated good fortune. 'I'll act calm and collected; pretend that nothing relevant has occurred, and then unobtrusively leave the meeting and evade the subsequent small talk and chitchatting as soon as possible. Next, I'll waste no time being off to Julius's mansion to claim my spectacular windfall before his covetous niece and nephew, or the Hammonton Police can beat me there to check his home.'

Every operational phase at the Third Road mansion smoothly developed and transpired, just as Julius Stetson had accurately described to Mitchell Spencer only weeks prior to the old man's demise. The designated key easily opened the back door. After surreptitiously flicking on a flashlight to locate the master bedroom's closet, the eager interloper anxiously moved the vertical shoe rack, and the ecstatic searcher easily located the wide-spaced wall safe. The key insertion worked perfectly, and just as dependable Julius Stetson had predicted, the half-million-dollars in hundred-dollar-bills had been left inside the safe, stashed in a utilitarian white linen bag.

'Oh my God! My life has been rescued from disaster!' Mitchell Spencer euphorically reckoned. 'I'll never forget *your* compassion and your kindness! Thank you Julius! Thank you from the bottom of my heart! Now to find the Window of Opportunity in the hall cedar closet to retrieve my special bonus!'

* * * * * * * * * * * *

Mitchell Spencer hastily maneuvered his way down the straight, light blue-carpeted hallway, and soon his curiosity found the object of his quest. In the center of the long corridor, the highly-focused, intensely sweating house-explorer quickly located the door to the prized storage room. 'It's locked!' Mitchell instantly recognized and regretted. 'Ah, the magic key also opens this closet door, too! I believe that Julius had mentioned *that* isolated fact to me! I'll close the door behind me, turn on the overhead light, saving the batteries in my flashlight. Then, I'll carefully open that beautiful stained-glass window at the other end of this closet. I see that it features two heavenly angels blowing their celestial golden trumpets. I can't wait to discover my promised bonus reward!'

After cautiously accomplishing those rather facile, elementary tasks, the perspiring searcher was completely thrilled about admiring the singular and resplendent 'Window of Opportunity', and his totally engrossed mind never for one suspicious moment ever comprehended that his physical existence had been permanently locked inside the enormous rectangular cedar closet.

Firmly gripping and holding the linen bag containing the half-million-dollars, the obsessed young man gently lifted the bottom window frame, and much to his utter shock and horror, Mitchell Spencer's body was instantaneously sucked inside the aperture by a powerful, mystical supernatural force.

And before the frightened and petrified victim had a chance to either scream or shriek, the mystical Window of Opportunity quickly descended like a guillotine blade, and the device forcefully slammed shut. Incredibly, the magnificent pair of handsome angels that had splendidly decorated the inimitable, stained-glass portal momentarily transformed into malicious-looking, red-skinned demons. And then, the wicked window that had been so maliciously constructed inside the cedar closet's back wall abruptly disappeared into oblivion.

* * * * * * * * * * * *

A dimly lit dense fog shrouded and enveloped a cold and barren subterranean swampy moor. The vigilant and awesome Black Angel of Death patiently awaited the arrival of the en route, newly acquired transmigrating soul, for to the gargantuan immortal winged creature, time was not ephemeral, and its mundane passage had no boundaries or particular definition. Finally, the rejuvenated spirit and psyche personage of one wily Julius Stetson materialized on the hazy and nebulous moor. The space/time voyager's past personality now parasitically residing inside the physical appearance of its new host, one Mitchell Spencer.

"I must compliment you on a most propitious and effortless spiritual transfer!" the austere-looking Black Angel bluntly stated. "I must confess that your diabolical Window of Opportunity trick has again been skillfully employed. The deceased spirit and soul' of your targeted subject has been symmetrically aligned with and absorbed into your former eighty-two-year-old frail, lifeless body. And simultaneously, your former corrupt spirit, by virtue of *our* contract agreement, is now speeding on its way to Hell. Now Sir, alias Julius Stetson, your unscrupulous heart and mind, by virtue of your devious canard, have been meritoriously transplanted into Mitchell Spencer's vernal form, and you've successfully earned a new extension to your mortal existence. And as you're well-aware, you've coincidentally inherited and obtained a vibrant new, slightly-used soul to complement your new virile body. And just to think," the thwarted and outsmarted Black Angel uttered and summarized, "our friendly relationship all started around three-hundred-and-ninety-years ago in Florence, Italy during the time of..."

"During the time of Galileo and the despicable Inquisitions, when scientific thought was readily condemned by the unrelenting Catholic Church bureaucracy. Technological progress was deemed sheer heresy," the newly exchanged spirit of Julius Stetson answered the sinister Devil's Messenger.

The dead man's resurrected soul was now-residing inside Mitchell Spencer's strong, vernal anatomy. "That's when I felt compelled to sign my binding contract with *you!* But as is outlined in Paragraph One, *you* can only mortgage my soul when I fail to find a vulnerable substitute every six decades or so."

The Black Angel was somewhat perturbed that his subject had again evaded *his* relentless pursuit. "Wily Magician, I promise to apprehend your soul and escort it to Hell the first time you fail at performing your simple-yet-odious deception. Yes, but upon rehashing our odd history together, Sagacious Sir, I recollect that our second devilish encounter had occurred during..."

70

"During the Great Age of the Illuminati in Southern Germany; yes, Black Angel, in medieval Munich, and if I also recollect, a half-century later, our third assignation, like the second one, had similarly transpired in this very same gloomy moor. That specific third development had happened immediately after *my* dupe's death in Marseilles, France during that intellectual genius Voltaire's most-splendid Age of Enlightenment."

"Affirmative, but please don't forget one significant detail Masterful Wizard," the solemn-faced and lugubrious Black Angel articulated, showing a defeated, frowning expression evident on its formidable-looking visage. "You're no longer Julius Stetson, but technically, to the not-too-brilliant human world, you're now Mitchell Spencer, professional educator. Do you plan to continue your mediocre career as a high school English teacher?"

"Hell no, Black Angel! As Mitchell Spencer, I'll wisely use-up my remaining sick days, and then, I'll resign from the school district effective July 1st," the self-centered, four-century-old, re-formatted human being replied. "And of course, I still have in my possession my luxurious mansion, which naturally I had perceptively willed to myself (Mitchell Spencer) along with my five-million-dollars in my Merrill Lynch stock account, and also my five-hundred thousand dollars in cash now concealed inside *my* upstairs cedar closet. The glorious and reliable Window of Opportunity, which as you've already acknowledged, was really an exceptionally clever trap, because it was *my* very necessary Window of Opportunity that was exclusively designed for *me* alone to live another fifty or so years inside this naïve, gullible idiot, Mitchell Spencer's youthful body. Perhaps I shouldn't criticize my new self so severely!"

"That's precisely why my immediate superior and awesome Commander-in-Chief Lucifer positively covets *your* calculated cunning so much. Because Sir, your charming character is insanely disingenuous, and you indeed are a virtual expert at executing marvelously heinous schemes!" the Black Angel commended his illustrious and very lucky mortal acquaintance. "Tell me now, Triumphant One. Will you be attending the dupe's, or should I say *the unfortunate victim's* funeral? After all, as bizarre as it may sound or seem, you will be *your* own fortunate heir."

"Yes, under the circumstances, *that* benign social gesture would be the appropriate and ethical thing to do, since as you've just mentioned Angel Friend, I, Mitchell Spencer, have been delegated as *his* sole and exclusive beneficiary!" the re-generated medieval alchemist and potent accomplished sorcerer cleverly remarked. "And soon thereafter, Black Angel, I'll be moving to another unsuspecting community; that is, after I legally acquire and sell my inherited Hammonton mansion, ha, ha, ha! I think and believe that I'll try living in Italy again!"

"Well now," the contemplative Black Angel very respectfully addressed its human companion, who apparently was reveling in achieving *his* recently earned new lease on life. "You always accomplish your 'transmigration of soul tricking routine' within the required seventy-two-hour parameters. I suppose that our next incidental meeting will be in approximately another fifty-to-sixty Earth years, when *your* then decrepit spirit and debilitated psyche will again require replenishment, reincarnation, and transmigration into a new body," the Black Angel matter-of-factly declared.

"That is absolutely correct!" the rejuvenated, wily Alchemist wholeheartedly verified. "To be sure as reality!"

"Indeed, Dracula and his vampires have nothing noteworthy over you!" the enormous Black Angel stoically admitted. "Good luck in scamming another unwary young male, while you again gamble your already-damned soul. And I congratulate you for adroitly eluding your eternal fate! I feel obligated to inform you, Mitchell Spencer, that my supernatural senses confirm the reality that my Satanic Colleagues now have the former Julius Stetson's body and soul in their custody, while the former Mitchell Spencer's suspended pristine soul is presently on moral probation, comfortably residing inside *your* new, young, human form."

"So long, my four-century-long Satanic Friend!" the most fortunate, resourceful magician replied. "Truthfully, I think I need a change in venue from living in Hammonton, New Jersey. First, I intend to move down to South Padre Island, Texas and begin a new fresh existence. But this time I think I'll join either the Kiwanis or the Rotary Club down there near the Mexican Border. When I tire of Texas, I'll then migrate over to wonderful Italy. I presume we'll again rendezvous in this same ominous swampy moor a half Earth century or so from now!" the mortal soul enthusiastically commented. "Over the centuries, this Window of Opportunity bait idea has worked extremely well for me, and as is my standard practice, I won't deviate one iota from again successfully using it in the future! Fearsome Black Angel," the shrewd Alchemist declared, "my proven strategy might sound like an overused cliché, but the fact of the matter is, 'Nothing really succeeds like success'!"

72

"The Duck Pond"

Salvatore "Duke" Miduri, a diversified business mogul, owned three enormous junkyards in the Hammonton, New Jersey vicinity, and state authorities suspected that each of the trio of fairly profitable operations was a money-laundering front for illicit Philadelphia Mafia drug distribution, prostitution, loan sharking and also gambling racketeering. Frustrated federal and state officials had often investigated notorious and controversial Salvatore Miduri, but the sly Sicilian culprit and his burly bodyguard lieutenants had never been convicted of engaging in criminal activity, even though "the Duke" was constantly under intense police scrutiny.

"The Duke" and his two brash bachelor cohorts lived in a fabulous mansion that had a long winding paved front entrance, and the rustic tree-lined lane leading to the estate was situated at the very end of Oak Road. Salvatore Miduri's seven thousand square foot palace had been built next to a large three-acre duck pond that coincidentally bordered on New Jersey owned Wharton State Forest.

The State Pinelands Preservation Commission theorized that Salvatore Miduri had been polluting the oval-shaped duck pond, but since the reputed villain had owned the hundred and fifty acre property years before the Commission had been appointed in the early 1980s, the regulatory body had no jurisdiction over the land because Miduri's extensive "boundary estate" had already been "grandfathered into the Pinelands' statutes.

Much to the Duke's dissatisfaction, in 1997 the New Jersey State Police had obtained a search warrant to excavate the lawn on three sides of Salvatore's mansion and to dig both to the left and right of Miduri's very massive maintenance building, where the "Palermo and Messina Construction Company" owner kept his heavy-duty equipment including six dump trucks, four bulldozers, two front-end loaders and a still-functional rusty steam shovel. The storage structure's rear wall was located only twenty feet from "the pristine duck pond," and over the years *that* particular "environmental hazard reality" had vastly irritated the concerned bureaucrats sitting on the State Pinelands Commission.

"The State Cops were searching for dead bodies and the incompetent fools were relying on information supplied by a couple of stool pigeons just released out of the Trenton Prison," Salvatore orally reviewed for the ears of his personal henchmen Nick "Blitz" Bartuccio and Patsy "the Bonebreaker" Olivo. "The fuzz had conjectured that the corpses had been buried on my Oak Road property because my home was pretty rural, out here in the South Jersey sticks, and they thought it would be convenient for the Philly' mob to dump off and bury certain uncooperative victims here as a safe haven."

"That's right Boss!" hit man Nick Bartuccio promptly agreed. "You've not only been annoyed and pestered by the nosy Pinelands' jerks but also by the feds, the state goon squads and the lousy local cops too. It's a good thing ya' hired those top notch defense lawyers from Newark to represent you in court."

During the initial verbal exchange shared by the other two underworld confederates, Patsy "the Bonebreaker" Olivo had been mentally engrossed in admiring an exquisite wall fresco rendition of the scenic duck pond. In the background the cherished artwork featured thirteen mallards passively swimming while in the forefront the mural portrayed six splendid ducks flying towards the pond on the left and three pheasants marvelously hovering amongst the cedar trees to the right.

After glancing through the mammoth bay window and then gazing outside at the three dimensional body of water, tough guy Olivo decided to join the casual conversation. "Ya' know Boss, I think the cops waited until 1997 to get their search warrant permittin' them to dig for bones because up until that time, you were friendly with some big Trenton and Atlantic City politicians and also closely associated with some Philly' professional baseball and hockey players that would frequently go wild mallard hunting at the pond in the fall. But after your high level political pals left office," Bonebreaker Olivo contributed and insisted, "that's when the crummy State Cops went to the county judge and…"

"And got their stinkin' permit to start shoveling turf, sand and dirt away to try and discover some clues to indict the three of us and put our butts in the slammer," Nick "Blitz" Bartuccio boisterously finished Patsy "the Bonebreaker" Olivo's background statement. "And when the State Cops failed to uncover any evidence, that's precisely when…"

"When I stepped-up and vigorously sued the State of New Jersey and consequently won a handsome ten million dollar defamation-of-character lawsuit," Salvatore "Duke" Miduri articulated and then indulgently laughed. "The damned State Cops were punished for not doin' their due diligence and for naively listenin'-to unreliable witnesses, and next the taxpayers got really riled-up because their precious hard-earned revenue money had been neglectfully and stupidly squandered on an expensive wild goose chase, ha, ha, ha!"

"And Boss, you were smart enough to get those costly defense attorneys from Newark who make over ten times as much dough as the less-talented federal and state prosecutors do," Blitz Bartuccio haughtily chuckled. "There's a definite reason why the lawyers you had hired make ten times more than the prosecutors do. It's because they're more skilled at the art of evading the law than the district attorneys know about the science of enforcing it," the ruthless aide persuasively argued and then chuckled. "The highly paid defense lawyers that we had workin' for us knew every loophole and technicality to eventually win *our* case."

"But in the Boss's situation Blitz," Bonebreaker Patsy Olivo diplomatically challenged his counterpart's position, "there was no convicting evidence and the jury regarded the inept State Police investigation team as bungling intruders violating our esteemed Mentor's First Amendment civil rights. Then the State had to also pay for all of the bushes and landscaping that the embarrassed State Cops had damaged or ruined during their clumsy frantic-but-futile ground rummaging."

"Boys, we've been together as close pals ever since we attended the Waterford School over in Winslow Township and then barely graduated from Edgewood High," Sal Miduri nostalgically reminisced. "I mean Guys, I hate to sound sentimental but nearly everybody in Waterford is a Miduri, a Midilli, an Iannaco, a Bartuccio, a…"

"Calabria, a Mauriello, a Sarappa, an Illiucci or a Sindoni," Blitz Bartuccio relevantly added. "Truly Boss, Waterford and Hammonton are like one big Cosa Nostra with a lot of Sicilian inbreeding showing in each town!"

"Yeah Boss, most of our Waterford cousins are now either workin' construction for you or seriously manning the three junkyards," Patsy Olivo matter-of-factly pointed out. "If ya' study our family trees, us Waterford Italians are almost as inbred as Cleopatra's ancient Egyptian royal family was before Julius Caesar ever sailed his warship up the Nile! I think that *that's* the only fact I remember from my high school Ancient History seminar."

"Patsy, you remember more than I do from that boring class. But why do you two Imbeciles keep callin' me Boss!" cigar smoking Sal Miduri affectionately ridiculed and then characteristically cackled before casually flicking his ashes inside a convenient tray strategically located upon his expensive mahogany desk. "Who do ya' think I am, Bruce Springstein! Ha, ha, ha!"

* * * * * * * * * * * *

In 1995, the local Hammonton Town Council had declared a building moratorium on all new house construction to abide by recently legislated strict New Jersey forest conservation laws. In the early 1980s the New Jersey lawmakers in Trenton had established the creation of the omnipotent Pinelands Commission, which had the expressed authority to regulate population growth in and around the "environmentally sensitive" Wharton State Forest. Since Salvatore "Duke" Miduri had owned and already occupied his hundred and fifty acre duck pond property prior to the creation of the Pinelands Commission, the flamboyant Mafia figure was essentially exempt from the authority's strict land and water management control.

According to careful definitions enforced by the powerful bureaucratic Commission the "New Jersey Pinelands" extended from Absecon just west of Atlantic City to Atco seven miles west of Hammonton and from Vincentown seventeen miles north of the Hammonton/Waterford agricultural community district all the way to Vineland, seventeen miles south.

The newly defined terminology "Pinelands" had Hammonton and its proud peach and blueberry farmers (along with third-generation large land owners) managing lands located directly in the middle of the "pine barrens core area" where building and population growth was both restricted and limited and where new houses inside the town's jurisdiction (that weren't connected to water and sewer lines) were now required to have the expressed written approval of the "Almighty Pinelands Commission." However, as had been legally established, Salvatore "Duke" Miduri's acreage and his corresponding duck refuge were not affected by the austere Pinelands Commission rules and mandates.

But Hammonton farmers, along with big acreage landowners like Miduri, *were* incidentally deeply affected by the Pinelands and its governing Commission. Since *their* land value was now exclusively restricted to farm use property (that would ordinarily be worth a hundred thousand dollars an acre to an entrepreneurial real estate developer), it was now devalued to a meager five thousand dollars an acre because presently only other farmers or "wealthy environmentalists" would want to purchase the land for agricultural or ecological preservation purposes. Real estate competition had virtually been eliminated for the sake of " green conservation."

Consequently, because of very stringent Pinelands regulations Hammonton fruit and vegetable growers had trouble borrowing money from banks and from farm credit bureaus in order to conduct their businesses since *their* credit lines were determined by using their now devalued land assessments as "basic collateral." It cost most area vegetable growers three hundred thousand dollars of "seed money" to get their operations started each spring because big bucks had to be placed on the table as down payment to purchase the upcoming summer's fertilizers, sprays and special customized packages and cartons (with the farm's brand names printed on them) and in addition, payrolls had to be met before crops were ever picked, packed and shipped along with other myriad miscellaneous accumulative spring expenses.

Duke Miduri had become disgusted and had gotten out of agriculture in 1998, defiantly stating publicly to the *Hammonton Gazette* that "Peach, apple and blueberry growers would in the future be doomed by not being able to secure viable credit from banks and from other regional and national lending institutions."

Farmers doing business in Hammonton's "highly governed and restrictively regulated Pinelands core area" were also limited in deciding exactly *who* could build houses on their property. Their children were allowed to build new homes on three-acre tracts and if immediate family was not involved, desperate farmers had to otherwise have their land parceled into ten-acre zones if they wanted to sell those sub-divisions to non-family strangers (with a lot of money) desiring to erect rural dwellings on such sizeable tracts.

Since the autocratic New Jersey State Pinelands Commission required "core area residents" to hook-up to Hammonton city water lines and to town sewer lines, new population growth was hampered by the State in the name of "natural environment preservation."

And when the old outdated Hammonton sewer plant began operating at full capacity, a restrictive building moratorium was adopted and enforced and the Town Council had to conform to the State's inflexible land-use mandates. "Thanks to the liberals in Trenton, my land's now of little value or use," Sal Miduri had been quoted as complaining in the *Hammonton News*. "The State is driving honest area businessmen out of operation just to save the damned pristine water underneath the Pinelands for the unworthy residents of Philly' and New York!"

The Hammonton area farmers along with peeved real estate developers boldly challenged the Pinelands Commission's authority in State courts, claiming that the new environmental laws were "Unconstitutional" and that the statutes violated the farmers' rights to own and sell land at face value. The disgusted real estate entrepreneurs maintained that their "civil rights" to build and make profits were also being abused. The costly litigations were aggressively pursued but in the end the various challenges to State Authority were to no avail. The Pinelands Commission prevailed and won every legal wrangle intensively argued before sympathetic judges and the resultant court decisions maintained that the "State's general good" was being upheld by the intelligent planned regional conserving and by the prudent preserving of South Jersey forests, lakes and wildlife.

But the wily Hammonton farmers suspected that the real reason for the "stranglehold" Pinelands legislation (and its accompanying land restrictions) was more than mere discrimination against fruit and vegetable growers.

Joseph Wharton of Philadelphia, founder of the prestigious *University of Pennsylvania* Wharton School of Business once owned extensive sections of South Jersey land, which today is known as the Wharton State Forest. Wharton was a venture capitalist at heart whose ownership of the pineland forests (on either side of *Route 206* surrounding Atsion Lake and vicinity) had by coincidence seven trillion gallons of excellent pristine water reserves laying directly under the virgin forestland, and the attendant Pinelands were fed by the close-to-the-surface Cohansey Aquifer.

Capitalist Joseph Wharton's grandiose scheme was to pump clean fresh water from the Wharton Forest Tract to the Philadelphia and New York metropolitan areas and then economically profit from his diligent endeavor, but near the end of his life the nineteenth century investor/entrepreneur changed his mind and heart and benevolently donated the beautiful acreage to the State of New Jersey.

The shrewd Hammonton farmers had suspected all along that the Pinelands building restrictions were not so much about protecting the surface pine trees as the State of New Jersey had adamantly asserted but that the real issue was undeniably about preserving the seven trillion gallons of pristine water lying beneath the forest trees as an emergency reserve water source for Philadelphia and New York during a time of dire regional crisis.

* * * * * * * * * * * *

A Med-Evac helicopter along with a New Jersey State Police surveillance chopper were stationed at (and serviced inside) a maintenance hangar at the Hammonton Municipal Airport. Seated inside the small airport's coffee and snack shop were New Jersey State Police Colonel Ed Siscone and his helicopter pilot for the day Lieutenant Greg Donio. The two were conversing at a square restaurant table, informally exchanging anecdotes and mutually enjoying their respective bacon, eggs and toast breakfasts. The pleasant dialogue was centered upon the pair's scheduled survey/observation flight over the nearby Wharton State Forest and the adjacent Atsion Lake area.

"I understand, Greg," Colonel Ed Siscone mentioned between chews, "there're over seven trillion gallons of fresh water lying directly under the Pinelands Forest. Could you ever imagine that? Over seven trillion I said! Sounds almost as humungus as the upward spiraling national debt!"

"Yes Colonel, and I believe the vast water supply is referred to as the Cohansey Aquifer," Lieutenant Donio politely verified. "I've read where *that* water along with its intended use has been in heated dispute around South Jersey for over a century. But now it finally looks like the environmentalists and the conservationists have gotten the upper hand over the covetous real estate developers and the stubborn area farmers."

"And quite frankly Greg," achievement-oriented Ed Siscone confided, "during our upcoming routine scouting patrol this morning I'd like to fly over that unscrupulous thug Salvatore Miduri's plush mansion at the end of Oak Road. Do you know that vicinity well?"

"Yes, indeed, Colonel!" the recently assigned pilot answered. "I've studied that section of Hammonton on various land and aerial maps. Wasn't Miduri the guy who..."

"Who took *us* to court and with the help of some slippery and unethical mob attorneys, the dastardly crook made the State Troopers look like a bunch of defective rank amateurs. If ever I get the opportunity," Colonel Siscone promised, "I'd like to get even with that no-good corrupt scumbag! Of course Greg, my comments to you are strictly off the record!"

"Yes, Colonel," Lieutenant Donio replied with a broad grin before sipping some hot coffee from his steaming cup. "I too would like to see justice served. That outrageous swindler Miduri and his two Sicilian henchmen deserve to be jailed for life and I can honestly sympathize with your desire to incarcerate the whole pack of

Hammonton affiliated Mafia types, none of whom are any credit to humanity."

"Remind me to recommend you for a promotion right before I retire from the force in six months," Siscone facetiously suggested to his new trooper acquaintance. "What do ya' say Greg!" the Colonel then stated in a more imperative tone of voice. "Let's gulp the remainder of our delicious java down and get today's in-air action show initiated!"

The two state troopers ambled out of the airport coffee shop, briskly paced to the helicopter pad and then entered inside the expensive machine. After Lieutenant Donio confidently manned the chopper's pilot seat and checked the gauges on the control panel, he nonchalantly started the blades rotating and the machine methodically lifted the police whirlybird off of its landing spot. As the craft glided over a desolate-but-dense section of pine-barrens, Colonel Siscone and the amiable pilot rekindled their general repartee.

"It's a gorgeous day to be flying," the chopper operator cordially opined to his superior. "I know from perusing my assignment sheet that we're gonna' do some forest fire prevention observations with the rangers' division and then perform some cursory air surveillance to see if any hunters are illegally prowling the woods with their shotguns. Which way should we be heading first?"

"Parallel Route 206 north up to Atsion Lake and then swing over across Indian Mills and Shamong. That's where Route 541 skims Burlington County and then travel southwest towards Atco. Next we'll conduct a cursory inspection of Winslow and Waterford Townships over in Camden County and after that episode is completed, we'll be returning back to Hammonton to terminate our itinerary. And easy on the throttle!" the Colonel commanded his subordinate. "I honestly get a trifle sea sick with even the slightest irregular motion, even when I'm on a deep sea fishing boat riding out a minor rain shower!"

Nothing extraordinary had been spotted within the perfunctory two-hour survey so the trooper pilot began navigating his craft over that section of the Wharton Forest existing between Winslow and Waterford Townships. Suddenly the alert State Police dispatcher at South Jersey Folsom headquarters voiced an urgent message to the Colonel and the Lieutenant.

"A seismograph in New Brunswick has just recorded a 5.2 earthquake with its epicenter in western Atlantic County and the scientists at Rutgers University indicated that the event had occurred only fifteen minutes ago," the on-the-ball dispatcher transmitting the verbal communiqué related. "This is a rather small vibration as earthquakes go, but whenever we rarely have a jolt here in New Jersey, it's usually in the range of 2.3 or 2.4. Nothing to worry about, but we figured we'd keep you two airborne guys updated about what's happening down here on Earth!"

"Thanks, Seth," Greg Donio radioed back to central command at Folsom. "We'll be landing back at the Hammonton runway in about ten minutes. We appreciate hearing your update! Ten-Four Seth, over and out!"

"Well, if that doesn't beat all!" Colonel Siscone exclaimed as the helicopter zipped a thousand feet high over Flemington Pike; then it soon passed over Walker Road followed by Pine Road. "An earthquake happening and shaking-up civilization right here in the good old Garden State. Say Lieutenant, what's that beehive of activity going on outside Sal Miduri's mansion! There's something weird occurring in the vicinity of the duck pond!"

"Oh my God!" Lieutenant Donio boomed as his pupils widened to their fullest. "The pond's completely empty with only mud showing and now I think I see objects sticking-out of the black wet bottom. Colonel, grab those binoculars wedged between our seats and take a closer gander of what's actually down there."

"This is incredibly bizarre! Absolutely astounding!" the Colonel bellowed as he slowly focused the lenses to allow for a more accurate sighting of the radically altered duck pond. "There're bundles of cash sitting there in the black mud and oh my God, and I can see human skeletal remains sticking-out from all over the drained pond. So *that's* where Miduri was keeping his skeletons, not in a back closet but in his cherished duck pond!"

"Miduri and his two hit men have seen us and they're now scurrying to that black Lincoln parked next to the mansion," the pilot reported and pointed-out to his commander. "We'll follow them overhead until some of our men in their highway cruisers can tail and arrest them."

"I'll bet you dollars to doughnuts Lieutenant that the brazen crooks are fleeing to Miduri's two-engine plane he keeps fueled at the airport," Colonel Siscone hypothesized and stated. "Hand me that microphone! I'll send out an emergency bulletin alerting our patrol cars to intercept the three thugs right there if indeed the municipal airstrip is their intended departure destination."

* * * * * * * * * * * *

Driver Blitz Bartuccio along with passengers Sal Miduri and Patsy Olivo were apprehended and immediately handcuffed at the intersection of Union and Middle Road. Officers in four New Jersey State Police cars and in two Atlantic County Sheriff's Department patrol vehicles had participated in the chase that eventually ended less than a mile from the Hammonton Municipal Airport.

Much to the credit of the speed and efficiency of the pursuing lawmen, not a single bullet had been fired during the entire high-speed "containment operation." A week later a gloating Colonel Ed Siscone met with Captain Ted Hoover and Sergeant Mark Bertram, the dedicated state troopers that had comprehensively conducted the extensive bone-search and cash excavations at Sal Miduri's Oak Road mansion.

"Colonel, back in the 1990s we had made what appeared to be an archeological dig at the suspect's place of interest," Captain Hoover firmly insisted. "The lawn on three sides of the house along with the grounds on either side of the heavy equipment storage and maintenance building had been roped-off into quadrants before we meticulously performed our investigation. But apparently *our* efforts had been outsmarted by savvy cunning criminals."

"And furthermore Colonel," Sergeant Mark Bertram chimed-in, "Ted and I had expert SCUBA divers from the Shore Division Barracks at Bass River scouring the length and breadth of the duck pond delving for evidence. All aspects of our, please pardon the expression Colonel, of our *wild goose chase* came up empty-handed. How could we have missed all of the cash hidden in the water along with all of the skeletal remains that had surfaced? The whole complicated conundrum defies reason!"

"And how did the pond become drained down to its muddy floor so that you and Lieutenant Donio could see the evidence in the mud from inside your whirlybird?" Captain Hoover asked. "Don't the laws of physics define the parameters of reality any more?"

"One meaningful question at a time please," Colonel Siscone suavely requested of his addled underlings. "You two very excellent men are not at fault in any way, shape or form, so kindly get off your guilt trips. Instead Gentlemen, our very best minds were deceived by some very shrewd and deft criminal subterfuge. In fact," the unflappable Colonel calmly vociferated, "if it weren't for the minor 5.2 earthquake that South Jersey experienced just before noon on *that* extremely fortuitous morning, that nefarious thug Sal Miduri and his two sinister cohorts would not now be sitting in separate jail

82

cells awaiting their individual arraignments in the Mays Landing County Courthouse today."

"What do you mean?" Sergeant Mark Bertram incredulously asked. "How could the minor earthquake have made the pond drain? It doesn't seem logical or plausible? Was that coincidence really a cause-effect phenomenon?"

"Ha. Ha, ha!" Colonel Siscone loudly laughed, relishing certain knowledge that his mind possessed to which his two fledglings were totally ignorant. "Here's the scoop Men! Miduri had excavated a fifty-foot-deep tunnel originating from inside the side maintenance building that then rapidly descended down horizontally underneath the center of the duck pond. It appears that the contemptuous racketeer had taken a chapter out of either the Viet Cong or out of the al Qaeda terrorists' playbook!"

"I can now visualize the scenario you're describing!" State Trooper Ted Hoover realized and exclaimed. "The tunnel was so deep that even if *we* had dug down six feet during our search, which we did, and even if the hollow had been directly underneath us, which it probably wasn't most of the time, then *our* digging team would've never discovered it regardless of how conscientious and thorough our on-the-ground excavations had been."

"Well, Ted, the original tunnel entrance inside the maintenance building had been deliberately cemented over so you never considered digging inside where the heavy construction equipment was being stored," Colonel Siscone revealed, "but unbeknownst to all of us, a second entrance has recently been discovered fifty feet in back of the duck pond where your search expedition never considered exploring or digging. Does that specific information illuminate the remainder of the mystery?"

"I now fathom what you're saying!" Captain Ted Hoover recognized, mechanically nodding his head up and down. "The concealed Wharton Forest back tunnel entrance was the only access used once the passageway had been dug-out and later covered-up from inside the metal-framed storage building. And so we could never identify what was really happening from our frequent air reconnaissance because all of the initial tunnel activity had already occurred from inside the enclosed heavy equipment storage structure!"

"Exactly!" the Colonel affirmed and concurred. "And when the larger-than-usual earthquake happened just before noon, the secret tunnel's wooden beam supports, similar to those in old abandoned gold mines out West, well they shook and then consequently, an abundance of loose sand and dirt situated directly beneath the duck pond came pouring into the narrow cave-like passageway below. Soon the assorted bundles of cash along with the eerie-looking skeletal remains became buoyant and surfaced and then the convicting evidence instantly became visible from the air, all cash bundles and bare-bone anatomies strangely lying in the black wet surface mud!"

"That's really a very fantastic set of coincidences to *ponder*! I suppose that the moral to this bizarre story is that it truly matters greatly to have all of your ducks in a row during a rare New Jersey earthquake!" Sergeant Mark Bertram imaginatively quipped.

"I don't think you're quite ready to replace either Jay Leno or David Letterman on late night television!" Colonel Siscone reflexively grinned, mildly admonishing Sergeant Mark Bertram. "But I do believe that one thing's for sure Men. I don't think that Salvatore "Duke" Miduri and his nasty henchmen Nick "Blitz" Bartuccio and Patsy "the Bonebreaker" Olivo will ever again be prominent movers and shakers in the ever-proliferating New Jersey crime syndicate world!"

"Etymologies"

Dr. Bradley Sinclair had been a distinguished English Professor at Glassboro State College in Glassboro, New Jersey and easily survived the smooth transition when the institution of higher education transformed its identity to Rowan University in 1992. The language scholar's parents Keith and Frances Sinclair were currently on vacation in Europe with *his* wife Sharon's folks Peter and Grace Gargone so *that* circumstance left Brad the important responsibility of presiding over the customary Thanksgiving dinner, which that year had been scheduled to take place at the Professor and Sharon's Pitman, New Jersey home.

Attending the traditional annual November family feast were Brad's son Joe Sinclair, a junior at Rutgers University's Cook College Campus in New Brunswick, son John Sinclair, a rambunctious sophomore at Camden Community College and youngest son Stephen, an unsophisticated sophomore at local Pitman High School. Brad's sister Jessica Sinclair was an old maid secretary at Atlantic City Electric Company and was also comfortably seated at the Thanksgiving dining room table (with three wide leafs added to satisfactorily accommodate everyone). To complement the crowded seating arrangement, Sharon's aunt and uncle Mildred and Fred LoBiondo of Bridgeton, New Jersey and Professor Brad's aunt and uncle Katherine and Jerry Caggiano of Cherry Hill were also in attendance to indulge in the tremendous Sinclair family meal.

'The problem with my family and with Sharon's kin as well as with my three kids is that none of them value academics like I do,' Brad thought as he surveyed the other chatty relatives seated at the great oval oak wood table. 'My three kids are so spoiled, vain and self-centered and they generally only want to talk about themselves and their pet interests. I know what I'll do to irritate them. I'll dominate the conversation with knowledge-oriented rhetoric and when my opinionated sons start talking about their nonsensical hobbies and sundry amusements, that's precisely when I'll interrupt their egotism and start prattling and embellishing the conversation utilizing one of my favorite English lexicon topics, word etymologies. I love the history and origin of words that have filtered into our noble Anglo-Saxon derivative lexicon and I'll just perpetually deluge everyone with an abundance of nomenclature until all those drivellers under the age of twenty-three shut their pathetic traps,' Dr. Sinclair decided. 'I'll begin employing my stealthy strategy as soon as I'm finished saying grace. I trust that the other adults seated at the table will eventually fathom my benign purpose and allow me to persistently pester and aggravate my three offspring.'

"Many people think that Rutgers is an Ivy League college but actually it's not," junior Joe Sinclair declared before passing the mashed potatoes to Aunt Katherine Caggiano. "I think the reason for that ridiculous fallacy is because the first college football game was played between Rutgers and Princeton and Princeton is definitely a bona fide Ivy League school. At Princeton, Harvard and Yale," Joe pontificated with perfect clarity, "nearly every building on campus has a thick patch of non-poison ivy crawling up its walls."

"I.V.!" irascible college sophomore John Sinclair jested. "I had an I.V. when I was admitted to the hospital last July for dehydration. Pulled through the procedure in spite of the easily distracted doctors and nurses inside the noisy emergency room."

This juvenile utterance on the part of his second eldest son was Professor Brad Sinclair's golden opportunity to deftly inject his etymology practice into the ongoing dialogue. "You know John," Dr. Brad declared like a true blue authoritative pedagogue. "You had just mentioned the month of July, which obviously came from the name Julius Caesar and in a similar manner, the month of August sprung from the emperor Augustus Caesar's identity. Other months of the year represented on our modern-day Gregorian Calendar attribute their origins to Latin deity names prevalent in Roman mythology. For example," the eminent Professor paused to measure the impact of his boring lecture on his captive audience, "Jupiter's scheming wife was the goddess Juno and that's where June actually began and Mars was the fierce god of war and that's where March had its appellation originate. And don't forget the Roman minor god Janis giving inspiration to good old January."

"Who really cares about such trivial things Dad?" John Sinclair defiantly stated. "Say Joe, what ever happened to that fraternity brother of yours that wanted to join the Army infantry? Say Aunt Jessica, could you please pass the hot Italian bread basket along with the high-calorie butter?"

Before Joe Sinclair could ever answer his sibling John, the head of the zany clan, Professor Brad Sinclair, initiated an informative exposition on how certain words had evolved. "Well John, as you might know the word infantry, like the word 'infant' comes from the Latin reference *infantre*. The Romans would always put their clean-shaven youngest soldiers or their 'infantre' on the front line of battle
86

to provide them with combat experience. And speaking of Roman soldiers, pretty soon Joe you'll be in the American work force and collecting a salary, which is derived from 'sal' and the ancient Latin *salarium*, because salarium happened to be Roman coins paid for the soldiers' salt, which was regarded as legal tender exchangeable for salarium. It was sort of a primitive commodity/cash bank if you will. And naturally," Dr. Sinclair methodically emphasized, "the Roman word 'frater', meaning 'brother,' well, it is the root of the notion of having a fraternity or a cultural brotherhood at a non-Ivy League university such as Rutgers."

Trying to change the subject to a more conventional theme, obstinate Joe Sinclair aptly mentioned, "Are our grandparents touring Germany, France or Italy right now? Which country is it? Does anyone remember in what Mediterranean country the elders are 'traveling' through right now? Say Steve boy," Joe cockily solicited the youngest clan brother, "I'm really starving for some decent grub. Could you please pass the turkey dish and the hot ham platter over this way?"

Before anyone could respond to Joe Sinclair's inquiry concerning his grandparents' European itinerary, Professor Brad Sinclair, aptly seated at the head of the table, felt an intense obligation to elucidate. "I believe Joe that your grandparents are now in Germany touring Hamburg and Frankfurt, which by the way is where our terminologies 'hamburger' and 'frankfurter' originated. And I think they'll next be touring Bologna in Italy, where of course baloney was first processed and also on Sunday they'll be in the Champagne region of France. And don't forget," the sagacious university teacher continued his extended monologue, "they've flown over the Atlantic from America to Europe and that ocean got its name from the Lost Continent of Atlantis, which was reputed to have existed just west of the Pillars of Hercules, which as you know would be Gibraltar in Southern Spain, and correspondingly, the mountain cliff Abyla is on the opposite Northwest Africa side of the mouth of the Mediterranean, which incidentally roughly translated means 'sea between the lands.' And did I mention the word America?" Professor Sinclair rhetorically asked to further annoy his somewhat peeved three offspring. "Yes indeed, *that* wonderful word phenomenon had a very authentic beginning, the term being derived from the name of a famous mapmaker, Amerigo Vespucci, a proud contemporary of Christopher Columbus, whose unique I.D. credit appeared on early maps of the New World used by adventurous Spanish and Italian explorers and other sea-roving navigators. And incidentally,"

Professor Sinclair loquaciously articulated, "when the accomplished navigator Ferdinand Magellan first saw the ocean off the coast of California, he called the mass of water the *Pacific* because it was so passive, peaceful and calm-looking."

The other adults seated at the enormous oval dining room table covered their mouths and giggled as they all finally realized Professor Brad Sinclair's modus operandi, much to the chagrin of *his* three egotistical 'Who cares?' sons.

"And one other thing I had neglected to tell you attentive boys in regard to your grandparents touring Europe and *that* issue is that the term 'travel' had curiously originated from the word 'travail,' which loosely defined means 'hard work,' since in olden days all sorts of land travel was indeed difficult work when the stage coach or covered wagon's wheel unexpectedly fell off while the pioneers' laborious modes of transportation fording a river or stream suddenly ran into a mobility problem that obviously had to be immediately addressed and repaired."

"Pop, my brothers and I aren't complete *dunces* you know, and we believe that you're sounding entirely too repulsive and speaking for Joe and Steve," disgruntled John Sinclair adamantly stated, "we' all wish that we could escape your prolific academic propaganda, and to tell you the plain and simple truth Dad, you aren't boring one of your graduate classes over at Rowan! You're totally boring us!"

But Dr. Brad Sinclair was not through with his mischievous intent of verbally frustrating his three sons and so the erudite scholar persisted in his stellar eloquence. "Well John, your usage of the word 'dunce' is most fascinating because the expression was created in reference to a certain follower of a fellow named John Duns Scotus, whose disciples were alluded to as Dunsmen, or dunderheaded dunces. And furthermore Son, your recent employment of the specific reference 'academic' actually pertains to the ancient Greek school of Plato commonly called the Academy back in ancient Athens during the time of Pericles, Socrates and Aristotle, who hung around the Parthenon up on the Acropolis in Athens. And naturally of course," Professor Sinclair prodigiously expounded, "the prefix 'acro' means 'up in the air' and obviously is related to the terms acrobat and acrophobia, the irrational fear of heights, and the second part of 'Acropolis' is 'polis' meaning city, and our English words police, politician, metropolis and Indianapolis all have their singular beginnings with the root word 'polis'."

The other adults seated at the Thanksgiving dinner table were thoroughly enjoying Dr. Brad Sinclair's unique lesson presentation and so the relatives enthusiastically gave the long-winded orator encouragement by rendering his effort a brief round of applause, which was not-at-all savored by the professor's three sons.

"Pop, I think you're on some kind of an idiotic *mission* and poor Steve, John and I have to sit here at this table like *mesmerized slaves* and listen to your boring *monopoly* of the family's conversation," Joe Sinclair hostilely protested. "Our ears are aching and our brains have become numb! We all wish that we could be tanning ourselves on a beach in Florida right now and effectively *escaping* your disastrous drivel."

"Joe, you just said a mouthful that demands immediate attention and explanation," the determined father replied while pretending to be absolutely serious and solemn. "First of all, if I were on a mission I would now be standing on top of the Alamo in San Antonio, Texas. Secondly, the word 'slave' you had just uttered probably came from the Slavs, people of Slavic origins, remotely related to the Vandals who had sacked, pillaged and destroyed Rome in 455 A.D. Hence, anyone who behaves in a similar marauding manner today is labeled a 'vandal.' And certainly," Dr. Sinclair specifically clarified before clearing his throat, "the term 'mesmerize' honors Franz Anton Mesmer, an 18th century German physician who had industriously studied early hypnosis and analyzed what *he* had described as animal magnetism in *his* volumes of writings. And finally Joe," the father stressed, "you had uttered the word 'monopoly,' which is a combination of two Latin roots, 'mono' meaning 'one' like in 'monorail' and 'monotony,' and 'poly' meaning 'many' as exhibited in 'polygon' and 'polynomial.' And oh yes my fully alert Boys," Brad Sinclair noted and added with a broad smile displayed on his countenance. "The wonderful term 'escaping' has its roots in the desperate act of a Roman criminal lowering his head when being arrested and thus the suspect would attempt to get away by 'escaping,' or exiting his 'cape'."

"Perhaps we could talk about something else more relevant to modern times other than obscure word histories!" Mrs. Sharon Sinclair diplomatically recommended after observing the disgusted expressions on her three sons' florid faces. "Boys, what would you like to receive for Christmas gifts this year? The big holiday is only four weeks away, you know!"

Brad Sinclair was instantly inspired by his wife's practical suggestion and therefore felt it necessary to comment on *her* constructive language deployment. "Honey," the wily professor expressed to his devoted spouse, "you just inadvertently stated several very intriguing etymologies, or what lexicographers contend constitutes the science of word origins, which ostensibly should not be confused with 'entomologies,' or the laborious scientific cataloging and analysis of myriad insect varieties. As you probably know wife Sharon," the college instructor snobbishly declared as his three peeved sons frowned and grimaced in disgust, "Christmas is an important holiday, and all holidays originally were *holy days* like Thanksgiving, Easter and even Halloween, which means 'All Hallows Eve,' or the night before All Saints Day, and Halloween occurs two days prior to November 2nd, All Souls Day on the Christian calendar. And when we think of saints and souls, we naturally think of dead people, ghosts, ghouls, goblins and the like. And considering your mentioning of the term 'Christmas' Sharon," the encyclopedic professor indicated, "the three Wise Men that had brought to Bethlehem gifts of gold, frankincense and myrrh were the *Magi*, and consequently, our modern word 'magician' had emanated from the archaic stem 'Magi'."

"God, I wish I was in Florida playing tennis or golf right now!" Steve Sinclair announced, holding his cerebral headache inside his cranium with both hands. "Joe was right a few minutes ago! Yes, I too definitely wish I was in Florida right this moment!"

"Florida comes from the Spanish word 'flores', meaning flowers," Professor Sinclair instinctively articulated, "and many other states have unique word origins too. For example Steve, Pennsylvania means 'Penn's green woods,' for as you well know and savor, 'sylvan' refers to 'green forests' and 'Penn' connotes with the commonwealth's founding father, famous Quaker William Penn! And Steve," Professor Brad continued his enduring but not endearing narration, "your oldest brother Joe had said the word 'disastrous' around ten minutes ago. 'Aster' is the Greek work for 'star,' and so as a result, 'disastrous' means 'from the stars,' which is the essential idea behind the pseudo-science known as 'astrology,' which places questionable credence in superstitious Zodiac Signs and horoscopes; and Steve, even the seemingly innocuous term 'catastrophe' contains the Greek root 'aster,' suggesting that a calamity on Earth had been caused by obscure powerful forces out there in outer space that had somehow manifested into a 'world catastrophe,' which incidentally is the worst kind of 'trophy' a person could ever receive."

"Brad, I think that your sons are not-at-all enamored with your cavalier parlance along with your aristocratic attitude," Aunt Mildred LoBiondo opined as her hungry husband Fred scooped out several heaps of string beans and carrots and then awkwardly plopped the

90

mixed vegetables onto his empty plate. "Your redundant speech about how various words were formed is causing some degree of alarm to settle in your boys' minds."

"Yes Brad," henpecked Uncle Fred concurred in order to establish harmony with his wife's perspective on the relative value of artfully mastering etymologies. "Although Mildred and I know that your intentions are basically quixotic, your boys on the other hand seem to regard your overall demeanor as being a bit sinister."

"Good ones Fred!" Brad exclaimed just before allergy-suffering Uncle Jerry Caggiano egregiously sneezed into his brand new handkerchief. "Quixotic relates to the pure-but-naïve idealistic character of Don Quixote, who in Spanish literature believed he was a knight several centuries after knights had disappeared from the face of the Earth as being the personal bodyguards of kings. And just prior to your mentioning of 'quixotic,' Mildred had alluded to 'cavalier,' which incidentally and remarkably describes a haughty gallant French knight on horseback, the word having its genesis in the Latin/Italian 'caballus,' or horse. And incidentally my dear Fred," Brad belabored his monotonous verbal exercise, "the word 'sinister' comes from the Latin/French 'sinister' meaning 'left handed,' as opposed to 'dexter,' which is Latin and sprung into our English word 'dexterous' after being adapted and assimilated into the Anglo-Saxon vernacular. And so Fred, during the Middle Ages, men always shook hands using their right arms and palms to show that they weren't carrying any dangerous weapons and that they were openly friendly because 'left-handed' people were regarded as unlucky and 'sinister' and right-handed people were thought to be skillfully 'dexterous' and therefore possessing normal ability."

"Truly remarkable stuff, Brad!" Uncle Jerry praised as Aunt Katherine gave her longtime marital partner a solid dig in the ribs with her left elbow. "The boys shouldn't be *alarmed* in the least by your admirable extensive knowledge!"

"Oh, thanks, Jerry!" Brad Sinclair pleasantly replied. "I had almost forgotten about the verbal past participle 'alarmed.' The term' had originated when European villages were being attacked by invaders and the lookouts would shout, 'All to arms!' And *that* truth reminds me, our word 'siren' refers to beautiful mermaid-like goddesses sitting on rocks that would lure sailors and their ships into perilous dire straits. In fact, in Homer's *Odyssey*, valiant Odysseus and his daring crew were enticed by sirens."

"Your father is being quite sincere?" unmarried straightlaced Aunt Jessica piped-up.

"Thanks for giving me another fantastic word to analyze!" Brad Sinclair impulsively answered Jessica. "Sincere comes from two Latin words, 'sine cera,' meaning 'without wax.' In ancient times sculptors would cover up the flaws in their statues by filling in the various mistakes with wax, so if you are sincere, you're like a marble sculpture that outwardly shows its defects and therefore, you're comparable to being a statue *without wax* because you don't attempt hiding your personality weaknesses."

"Hey Dad, in all due respect, let's talk about al Qaeda, the Taliban or about something else a little more current," under duress Camden Community College student John Sinclair interrupted. "Yeah Pop, let's talk about al Qaeda!" he futilely reiterated.

"Well, John, al Qaeda translated into English means 'the base,' or the cave-like secret camp hideout of that particular clandestine Muslim organization," the Professor coyly answered. "And now you'll be delighted to learn that here's another fantastic Arab/Muslim origin that has furtively wormed its way into our standard English vernacular. And I'm not referring to the word 'Taliban' meaning 'students.' Our pronunciation distinctly known as the word 'assassin' has its basis from the time of King Richard-the-Lionhearted. An assassination is a surprise assault that's designed to kill some unsuspecting enemy VIP. During the medieval Crusades," Dr. Sinclair ardently stated to his trio of restless listeners, "the plotting Arab murder schemers would take a drug 'hashish,' which you youngsters might know as marijuana. After getting drugged-up, the 'hasishans' or 'assassins' would gradually develop the courage to perform their heinous misdeed and raid the camp of their Christian enemy. I mean Fellas', how pernicious can medieval killers get?"

"I guess it involved brawn over brains!" junior Rutgers student Joe Sinclair evaluated and offered. "I suppose way back then that the addicted Arab assassins didn't have too many pharmacies around their war zones to buy their supply of hashish!"

"Well, Joe, actually your timely usage of the word brawn makes me automatically think of the word 'muscle,' and muscle ironically came from the Latin word 'mus,' oddly meaning mouse. So Joe, when you try to impress and charm your lady friends by moving your bicep up and down, it looks like a puny mouse squirming about inside your upper arm!"

"John Boy," Joe said to his equally agitated middle brother, "what do you say we politely excuse ourselves away from the dinner table and go play your new challenging video game where we compete and try to win a barker's Teddy Bear at the *carnival*. Then," Joe

92

Sinclair suggested, "we could come back into the dining room later on for some of Mom's luscious apple pie dessert."

"That reminds me," Dr. Sinclair spoke to Joe as the other elders at the table continued to self-consciously snicker and chuckle. "The word 'carnival' comes from the Latin 'carne' meaning 'meat'. A good example would be the famous Mardi Gras in New Orleans; *that* raucous holiday celebration comes right before Ash Wednesday, or the beginning of Lent. Many people in the past used to sacrifice and do penance by giving up meat after Shrove Tuesday and so they would have great feasts and festivals to commemorate their last opportunity to consume meat or 'carne' before the Lent period commenced," Professor Sinclair pontificated. "So as a result, they would enact a wild carnival festival prior to doing an act of extended penance. And Guys, as far as the usage of the reference 'Teddy Bear' is concerned...."

"We know exactly what you're going to tell us Pop so you can save your breath!" a completely exasperated John Sinclair forcefully declared. "We've all suffered through and heard *this* dull moronic story several times before and if you want to know the honest-to-goodness truth, it sounds like a very disturbing broken record!" the antagonized youth objected. "Teddy Bear comes from Teddy Roosevelt who looked all cuddly and cute with his chubby round cherub face and thick mustache."

"As sure as the word 'czar' was derived from the title Caesar!" Brad Sinclair commended and commented. "Why John! That Teddy Bear recollection of yours was positively amazing! I'm utterly flabbergasted and at a loss for etymologies! You do occasionally pay attention to my pearls of wisdom after all, don't you?"

"Brad, it's a blasted shame but it appears that your three sons view your dynamic rhetoric as being nothing more than very ludicrous prattle!" Uncle Fred LoBiondo guffawed.

"Fred, I'm positively thrilled that you just mentioned the word 'colossal,' which alludes to the once inimitable Colossus of Rhodes, which was revered in mythological times as one of the Seven Wonders of the Ancient World. The gigantic bronze statue stood on two small islands and both Greek trading vessels and warships entered and exited the harbor under and through the huge figure's opened legs. "And one more thing Fred," Professor Sinclair garrulously proceeded, "a popular synonym of 'colossal' is 'mammoth,' which in Paleolithic times was a tremendous-sized woolly elephant having incredible curved tusks."

"I'm gonna' join Joe and John in the den playing the video game Mom!" Pitman High School sophomore Steve Sinclair abruptly announced. "What's thr dessert menu when we get hungry again?"

"Why we're having the usual, apple pie ala mode with vanilla ice cream or you can have homemade pumpkin pie! I've also specially prepared a delicious carrot cake," Mrs. Sharon Sinclair confirmed. "You know Steve that we always have apple pie ala mode and scrumptious pumpkin pie every Thanksgiving!"

"Remember the *ala mode* Steve the next time you're on a mission in San Antonio!" Professor Brad Sinclair energetically bellowed as unimpressed son Stephen eagerly and awkwardly arose from his very neat green and white brocaded dining room chair and then swiftly paced like a determined military soldier in the direction of the Sinclair family den sanctuary.

"Superstitions"

Real estate broker James Brewster was elated, not because he had just completed reading Dale Carnegie's best-selling book *How to Win Friends and Influence People* for the fifth time, but because in March of 2009 the wheeler-dealer had shrewdly purchased a three-year-old beachfront three-story home (with an elevator servicing each suite) on the Boardwalk and 16th Street in Ocean City, New Jersey for the ridiculously-low sum of 1.5 million dollars, acquiring the residence as a vacation home but more importantly, owning and leveraging the dwelling principally as a seasonal investment-return rental property.

'I didn't even need Dale Carnegie's sound advice to negotiate this handsome bargain!' Brewster joyfully reasoned. Being a born-opportunist, the risk-taking entrepreneur wanted to take full advantage of the in-progress economic recession and then in three years, capitalize on the presumed 2.25 million dollar value of the three-year-old beach home should the country's money cash-flow scenario improve back to normal.

'Gosh, how I love these sacrifice home sales, especially when the victimized sellers need cash right away to cover for their divorce allotments or when a family will settlement or estate liquidation occurs. Yeah, Susan and I could make a quick three-quarter million bucks' killing if the weak economy ever manages to cure itself,' Jim thought as he shaved his twenty-four hour whisker growth off while diligently staring into the large master bathroom mirror. 'Or I might just elect to keep the beautiful beach house for entertainment purposes or for the family to use. Even in today's depressed market, fancy Ocean City beachfront rentals go for around seven thousand dollars a week per floor,' Brewster's imagination realized with a brief smile appearing on his face. 'That's a sweet twenty-one grand a week times ten weeks for the June, July and August beach season and now we're talking about an annual income of over two hundred thousand a summer. The entire place could be paid-off in around eight years should I decide not to sell it,' the real estate broker ecstatically considered. 'No matter how I assess the Jersey shore deal, whether I keep it or whether I'll be able to unload it in the future at a handsome profit, it's without a doubt a win-win situation regardless if the national economy rehabs' itself or not! And it's conveniently located and quiet there too, right where the boardwalk narrows at the south end!'

"Jim, who will be manning the Hammonton office today?" Susan yelled up from the downstairs front door foyer. "Is it you or our beloved son?"

"Jeff's gonna' be commanding the 12th Street office and I'll be over in Cedar Brook getting some newly arrived furniture into our new office arrangement," Jim Brewster answered between razor swipes. "Some desks and counters had been delivered yesterday and I gotta' map out where to situate them inside the six re-modeled rooms. That's the last time I'm ever goin' to buy a house and convert it into a commercial building. The township and state bureaucratic red tape was a bit too extreme."

"Yes, the construction costs, zoning fees and licenses were rather tremendous but you've told me on many occasions that that 1950s Cedar Brook home was the only land available along that busy stretch of Route 73!" Susan accurately reminded and yelled up to her forgetful husband. "As you always redundantly state, 'Location, location, location'!"

"What's on your schedule this morning?" the husband hollered down, sticking his head around the bedroom corner so that his wife could see his partially lathered face.

"A woman's work is never done! I'm going to first empty the clothes hamper and then throw the dirty laundry into the washing machine," Susan informed her less energetic spouse. "And Jim, please drive the red Nissan SUV over to Cedar Brook and leave the green Toyota Avalon for me to use. I have some light grocery shopping to do and after returning home from the supermarket, later on this morning I'm going to take a thirty-five-mile trip to Ocean City and inspect every room of our new beach home," the wife revealed. "I want to see if all of the major appliances are working and also see if I have to buy any new bed-sheets, towels or blankets for our highly anticipated eager-to-spend summer rental guests."

"Okay," the husband readily and cheerfully acknowledged. "I'll take the red Murano. It has satellite radio and I can listen to my favorite oldies hits from the '50s, '60s and '70s on the jaunt over to Winslow Township. Do you have any errands you want me to run while I'm gallivanting around this part of South Jersey?"

"Well, yes now that you've mentioned it!" Susan replied. "There's a list of ten items' that I want you to dispose of once and for all down at the Hammonton dump. I've decided that I have too much activity on my plate and I don't have the time to conduct a yard sale to get rid of all of the abundant junk that's accumulated in our garage, in our attic and in our cellar."

"You know Dear that I positively love old relics and that I'm a worthless object collector at heart," Jim laughed, hiding his underlying apprehension. "A lot of the stuff I've kept over the years has a definite sentimental value to me. You know Susan, they're all sorta' like living nostalgia to me! I just have difficulty throwing things out ever since my father disposed of my '50s baseball card collection, and from a strictly emotional point of view, I hate to part with personal things that I'm quite especially fond of!"

"Well, Jim, you'll just have to get over it this time!" the wife imperatively insisted. "You can study the items' list that I've prepared over your morning cup of coffee. I couldn't sleep last night so I got out of bed, marched to the computer and started hammering away at the keys," Susan attested. "Truthfully Jim, I was quite surprised to observe that the printer was working again. You'll find the ten items typed-out on a sheet of paper and placed on the kitchen table. I'm really tired of looking at them scattered all over the residence! As the woman of the house, it's my firm position that those ten useless things have to be thrown out once and for all!"

Jim finished washing-up, put on a pair of jeans and a blue cotton shirt along with his casual black loafers and then descended the stairs and cheerfully sauntered into the kitchen. After concocting his instant coffee and adding his standard two sugars and cream, James Brewster sat down in his usual chair and closely examined the prescribed list of objects.

'Susan can't be serious!' the husband immediately thought. 'These ten things each have a very special meaning to me. Oh no! Here are several bits of nostalgia occupying space in the garage. First is my two-tone brown pair of ice skates from the 1970s, second is my initial set of golf clubs and accompanying bag, the set left over from the late '80s and third, Susan's itemized my twelve cartons of books from when I tried my hand at self-publishing my helpful manual of real estate tips. Too bad that the 1992 literary work only sold three-hundred copies, mostly to family and friends who felt obligated to buy them hot off the presses.'

Five other items stored in the garage and in the attic further disappointed the reader. 'Susan wants to throw-out the fall harvest farmer stand that I put on the front porch steps every October 15th. And then there's the taillight cover to my old yellow Volkswagen convertible, *our* first car after we had gotten married. How could she do this to me? How could she do *this* to *us*?' the husband regretfully concluded. 'And furthermore, Susan indicates that the token spare snow tire hanging on the left garage wall has to go. I love that memorabilia even though snow tires are no longer in vogue. And then there's Aunt Millie's disassembled bed that's stored in the attic. And oh no, the 28 inch by 28 inch old bathroom mirror from the guest bathroom that had been replaced just two years ago. That twenty-five-year old mirror is still along the left wall in the garage and it's leaning against the sheet-rock right below the spare snow tire.'

Finally, Jim's eyes arrived at the two remaining objects placed on the list that still remained stored down in the cellar. The rusty English racer bicycle that Brewster had owned and had proudly ridden in his glorious youth along with a bent screen (once belonging to the front storm door) that incidentally has been collecting cellar dust for over two decades.

"Susan, you can't be serious about me throwing this wonderful stuff out this morning!" Jim Brewster exclaimed to the kitchen table rather than face his tenacious wife, who had just coincidentally entered the room. "You're asking me to eliminate plenty of rich history here! Plenty of *our* rich Brewster family history!"

"Either the ten things go or I go!" the on-the-move wife loudly threatened her false ultimatum from the laundry room just off the den. "And if I go, I get the Ocean City beach home as part of the general divorce settlement and you can keep this two-story colonial and live happily ever after right here in Hammonton!"

"Okay, Honey!" Jim reluctantly conceded. "I promise to dispense with the assigned ten things in about an hour!"

* * * * * * * * * * * *

One of the main principles of Dale Carnegie's informative book *How to Win Friends and Influence People* maintains that the consummate salesman must first cleverly get the prospective customers talking about themselves. Eventually the targeted client feels self-conscious about his or her personality dominating the conversation and then he or she will ultimately request vital facts and money statistics from the congenial sales person. But ironically, Susan's 'austere rubbish edict' had Jim not talking about himself but instead, talking *to himself*. 'I'll pull the red SUV out of the garage, lower the back seats to allow for more room and then sadly fulfill Susan's inflexible command,' the now-melancholy man of the house organized his 'surrender for marital truce strategy.'

After swallowing down a bowlful of wheat cereal and milk, the emotionally disheveled husband obediently gathered the ten
98

specified articles from the garage, attic and cellar and after using his imagination, distressed James Brewster carefully loaded and methodically arranged the assorted objects inside the rear of the red Nissan Murano. Soon the disenchanted object gatherer, with sweat beads trickling down his forehead and cheeks, was seated behind the wheel and making a left turn out of his Valley Avenue driveway and motoring on his way to the town's Eighth Street dump.

Then, feeling vanquished and disappointed, Jim's mind began reviewing the history of each of the ten items that his wife had firmly wished to be discarded. 'This undesirable process will cost me at least a hundred dollars town dumping fee!' the anguished man behind the steering wheel lamented. 'And the municipal garbage attendant at the gate will act like it's a difficult burden and a tremendous chore for him to dispose of the ten random things, each of which means something special to me.'

But then the *down-in-the-dumps* broker's mind realized that he had not only kept the ten dispensable items for their 'sentimental value,' he also had kept them for various worrisome 'superstitious reasons.' Slowly the individual pieces of the man's mental jigsaw puzzle began to re-form into a plausible configuration that now vividly suggested to the SUV driver that a sense of overwhelming bad luck would soon result from the ten items disposal.

'The two-tone brown ice skates were from my youth when my family had lived in Levittown, Pennsylvania. That winter I was with two friends skating on a frozen creek. We were having a friendly competition, racing towards the finish line, a bridge that was under Edgely Avenue. Each of us had to duck down in order to cross the imaginary finish line but then I recklessly lost my balance, foolishly believing that I was winning the contest. I abruptly collided with the bridge's concrete structure going at full speed and wound-up with a concussion. Being only semi-conscious and my mind in a daze, my two fourteen-year-old companions instantly panicked, rushed to a nearby house and had the owner call for an ambulance,' Jim recalled. 'That's the last time that I've ever gone ice skating and it all now seems like a terrible recurring nightmare even though the near-tragedy dramatically happened over thirty years ago!'

Then, Jim's mind concentrated on the rusty golf clubs and the dirty plaid red and black checkered carrying bag. 'I was playing golf with some Rotary Club business friends over at the Pine Crest Country Club on Folsom Road. After the ninth hole, we decided to take a lunch and beer break. I casually called Susan at home only to learn that Aunt Vera and Uncle Leo had just been killed in a violent automobile accident down in tidewater Virginia, not far from Uncle Al's place at Sandy Point on the Potomac. The old golf clubs and bag along with the two-toned ice skates are all negative omens that if trashed, might again unleash a bad event or even a series of bad events to occur and interrupt tranquility in my life.'

As Jim Brewster made his habitual left turn onto Bellevue Avenue, his mind recollected the twelve cartons of unsold books neatly stacked directly behind the driver's seat. An hour after the twelve cartons had been delivered via UPS, an electrical fire had broken-out in the garage when one of the boxes had been pressing against an electrical cord used to operate the car doors. 'It's a good thing I keep a fire extinguisher attached to the garage's back wall or else the minor blaze could've erupted into an inferno and destroyed the entire house!' the real estate broker recollected and concluded. 'To this day I believe that there's a distinct cause and effect relationship between receiving those boxes of books and putting them in the garage and igniting the consequential blaze that resulted,' the failed author believed.

The horizontally packed straw hat fall farmer figure attached at its base to a blue-painted half cinder block was the SUV's item number four. 'Yes, right after the colorful outside fall decoration piece had been purchased at the Berlin Farmers Market back in the '70s, the stock market had simultaneously collapsed because of the oil and gasoline crisis. That's when Susan and I lost over a hundred thousand dollars in our mutual funds' portfolio and *that* sizeable investment was never recovered,' James Brewster disconsolately remembered as his right clenched fist hit against the padded leather steering wheel. 'I don't need a similar financial disaster such as an expensive law suit coming out of nowhere or a crisis involving an unforeseen legal problem with the new Ocean City beach house. But certainly,' the very superstitious driver recognized, 'nostalgia is not the main reason for me desiring to keep the ragged-looking autumn four-foot-tall porch farmer. I absolutely fear the consequences of getting rid of it.'

Upon passing his 12th Street real estate office, and then making a left turn at the next traffic signal onto First Road, Jim's mind thought about the yellow taillight frame that had been hanging from the right wall pegboard in the garage. 'That Volkswagen was my first car and Susan also loved driving the convertible around town on shopping errands and on quick excursions to the pizza parlor and to the custard stand,' Brewster recalled as he drove his red SUV past Greenmount Cemetery. 'But the same day that my wife had a fender-bender while
100

being rear ended at a stop sign at French Street and Packard, I had fallen off of the side porch roof. Our son Jeff had thrown a Frisbee up there and when I went to retrieve it using an aluminum ladder,' Brewster's memory rehashed, 'I slipped and then tumbled down, taking the entire rain gutter with me. Fortunately my only injury was a sprained right ankle, which still aches whenever the barometer's mercury fluid falls. Well, as a result of my tumble, at least I can predict certain approaching rain patterns with the aid of my prognosticating right foot!'

The obsolete snow tire that had been hanging from the left garage wall ever since the early 1980s was the next thing to be mentally assessed by the now-paranoid lugubrious driver. 'That February day I had bought a set of snow tires at Pep Boys over in Berlin,' Jim's memory accurately reminded him. 'That evening Susan and I had gone to Philly' to see the play *Man of La Mancha* at the Walnut Street Theatre. When we eventually returned to the parked car after the performance had ended, the front passenger side window had been smashed and the vehicle's interior vandalized. The right snow tire had been slashed with a knife and the one in the back of the SUV is the only remnant remaining from that snowy winter night's horrible discovery,' the driver remembered. 'Naturally, the Philadelphia cops never were able to apprehend any suspects and my insurance company did pay for the damages after I had submitted a carbon copy of the comprehensive police report.'

Aunt Millie's bed that had been faithfully preserved in the house attic was another cause for the neurotic fellow's concern and distress. 'How could I ever forget the negative significance associated with that bed?' Jim, who had never walked under a leaning ladder, who never stared more than a second at a black cat or who never intentionally stepped on a sidewalk separation crack apprehensively evaluated. 'That brisk late September morning I had to borrow Uncle Bill's truck to drive down to Aunt Millie's stone home in Bridgeton. During that early fall afternoon I managed to successfully re-assemble the bed in the upstairs spare room when I learned from Susan that Grand-Pop Tony had died at his winter home in Miami, Florida. Grand-Mom Anna had an extremely hard time making arrangements to fly his body to Philadelphia and the poor woman had to be a passenger on the same jet plane in which her deceased husband was being flown as human destination cargo from Miami to Pennsylvania.'

Upon alertly turning from First Road onto Eighth Street, Jim thought about his symbolic superstition connected with the large garage mirror that had once occupied a space above the dual basin vanity in the guest bathroom. 'Back in 1994, after the mirror had been removed by carpenters and replaced with a new one, I had taken my mother to Harrah's Casino in Atlantic City to treat Mom upon celebrating her seventy-fifth birthday. Much to my utter shock and anxiety, Mom had suffered a simultaneous heart seizure and low sugar attack and when I turned around, she was lying unconscious on the casino's carpeted floor. Thanks to quick action by on-duty paramedics and nurses, an ambulance was soon summoned. Mom was rushed to the Atlantic City Hospital on Ohio Avenue and her life was fortunately saved. But honestly,' Jim nervously deduced, 'I don't savor the idea of getting rid of that mirror out of fear that something even more terrible and horrendous might be set into motion. I gotta' salvage that ominous thing, one way or another!'

At the intersection of Eighth Street and Second Road, Jim Brewster remembered the last regrettable time he had ridden the rusty English racer bicycle that later had been stored and forgotten in the cellar. 'I was riding ten miles from Hammonton to Batsto in a Kiwanis Club charity fund-raising event. I had raised over a thousand dollars from various friends and relatives who were generous enough to sponsor me in participating in the annual 4th of July event. While not paying particular attention and experiencing some mild exhaustion, my front tire inadvertently hit a stone on Pleasant Mills Road and before I knew it, the bike had careened into a swamp and I had been flung off the seat, landing in a briar patch and thus later requiring seven stitches to patch-up my annoying wounds. But needless to say,' Brewster analyzed, 'I was deeply embarrassed from my cycling misadventure because I was unable to finish the ten-mile-long course and obviously, my delicate pride had been injured much more than my aching body had been!'

Finally, as Jim's shiny sleek red Murano ascended the bridge going over the six lanes of heavy Atlantic City Expressway traffic whizzing by below, the anxious driver contemplated the relevance of the screen from the front storm door that had been leaning against the basement's cinder block wall for the past fifteen years.

'The same April 1995 day that a wicked mini-cyclone micro-burst cut a swath across my property, I noticed that the screen to the front storm door had been bent from the violent swirling winds,' the fidgety SUV navigator remembered. 'After I had removed the screen and then assessed the extensive tree damage on my front and back lawn, I dashed upstairs to change my clothes and get into some more appropriate work jeans, for I intended to use my chain saw to cut-up

102

the downed tree branches into smaller pieces. After changing my attire, I astutely observed a column of termites emerging from a crack in the master bedroom wall and I spent the next three hours vacuuming the swarming bugs as the destructive army of insects exited the wall's floor molding one-by-one in a single file procession. That monotonous vacuum cleaner task I steadfastly performed rather than attending to the many downed tree limbs populating my front and back yards.'

As the red Nissan Murano finally approached the very remotely located Hammonton Town Dump, the saddened driver reviewed and summarized his superstitious instincts. 'Each of the ten articles in the back compartment represents something foreboding or problematic that had occurred in the past,' Jim subjectively hypothesized, 'and I have a good deal of anxiety building-up inside my heart that tells me that something bad is going to happen if I surrender the ten useless items to the town refuge center. I know what I'll do!' Brewster excitedly determined as he halted his vehicle at the main gate entrance. 'I rent and keep a storage unit at the 'Hammonton Self-Serve Lock and Go Depot' over on Egg Harbor Road where the old Hammonton Farmers Market used to be. That's where I store all of my lawn real estate signs and I just happen to have plenty of room inside there to accommodate all of the junk in the SUV's back cargo area. I'll just squirrel-away the ten treasured relics inside my rental unit rather than transfer the items to the Town of Hammonton for a hundred-bucks expense. Call it a weird phobia haunting my mind but I feel that I must protect my family from some lurking imminent danger. I dread that something sinister or malignant is about to occur as a result of me honoring Susan's command to get rid of the ten bad-luck relics!' the real estate man irrationally theorized. 'Then after I safely deposit the ten cherished articles at the Self-Serve Lock and Go Depot, I'll hurry over to the new Cedar Brook office on Route 73 and start figuring-out where the recently delivered walnut desks and counters have to go!'

* * * * * * * * * * * *

"Hey, Mack. You've come to the right place. It looks like ya' got a hundred bucks worth of junk to discard," the Hammonton Dump's garrulous gatekeeper estimated and quoted. "That's what the town charges for either an SUV or a half ton pick-up truck full. And don't worry Pal! I'll give ya' a receipt whether ya' pay me cash or pay me by check or credit card."

"That's okay Sir, but I've just changed my mind and have decided to keep the old heirlooms," Jim apologetically replied. "Perhaps my wife will have a late spring garage or yard sale. We could always use the extra cash."

"Well now, that's the first time I've ever heard *that* story!" the grimy-looking heavy-set gate attendant laughed, then roughly wiping some excess chewing tobacco juice from his lips with his left hand. "Are ya' sure ya' don't want to part with that antiquated English racer bicycle ya' got back there? I restore antiques like that as a hobby. I'll give ya' twenty-five bucks for it right out of my own pocket. With a little elbow grease and a can of spray paint I could make that baby look like it was brand new!"

"No, thanks!" Brewster explicitly answered. "Maybe the bike shop on the Pike near the lake can rehab' it for me a few years from now and I could save it for a future grandson, whenever I finally have one to give it to. In fact Mr., I used to ride this bike when I was in junior high. I think it was sometime during the Richard M. Nixon Administration! Ha, ha, ha!"

The real estate man slowly backed up, turned his handsome SUV around on the dump's gravel entranceway and then headed north on Eighth Street toward downtown Hammonton. 'Susan will never know that I've deliberately relocated the ten items inside my private utility shed. I'll just fib a little bit and tell her that I had religiously followed her exact instructions and that the undesired ten items are no longer in the garage, attic or cellar.'

Five minutes later, James Brewster pulled into the wide asphalt driveway where he could access his individual twelve by twenty-five foot rental space at the seldom busy' Hammonton Lock and Go Storage Depot. No sooner had the superstitious fellow stopped his shiny red vehicle that his cell phone rang and the readout indicated the phone number of his Hammonton residence. After awkwardly fumbling with the electronic device, Brewster's right thumb finally pressed the correct button.

"Dad!" an out-of-breath Jeffrey Brewster yelled. "I just stopped at your house to ask you a few questions. All of the doors were locked so I used my old house key to gain entrance via the side laundry room door. When I got to the front foyer," the son huffed and puffed, "Mom was lying there near the front door, unconscious with the half-full dirty upside-down clothes-basket laying on the tile right next to her, and then I noticed that the empty grocery bags were still on the kitchen table. I quickly dialed 911 and thank goodness the Hammonton Rescue Squad just arrived at the house; the paramedics put her on a stretcher and now she's riding in the ambulance on her way to the best area hospital."

"What do the paramedics think is wrong?" Jim loudly exclaimed. "Did she have a stroke or a heart attack? Does she have a concussion?"

"I don't know!" Jeffrey responded in a stammering tone of voice. "The rescue squad guys said that Mom's vital signs were weak but they believe that they had stabilized her before she was transported in the ambulance. They're now taking her to Virtua Hospital in Berlin! That's' where I've going right now after I finish talking with you!"

"Listen, Jeff! I'll meet you at Virtua in about twenty minutes so that in the meantime you can get an update on your mother's condition! Talk to the doctors in the emergency room suite and see what you can find out after she's admitted! Those doctors at Virtua are among the best in South Jersey. If there's a more serious problem that needs prompt urgent attention, we'll have your mother transferred to Thomas Jefferson Hospital over in Philly'."

"Okay, Dad!" the son comprehended and agreed. "It's a good thing that I dropped by or else Mom would still be lying there on the cold floor completely knocked out! I'll see you at Virtua just off Route 30 in Berlin as soon as you get there." Click.

The superstitious father hastily stepped on the accelerator and sped out of the entrance-way of the modern private storage facility. His prime destination was his white two-story colonial home on Valley Avenue where he would swiftly-but-carefully place the ten items back in their precise former locations in the garage, in the attic and in the cellar. After speedily accomplishing *that* reversal of 'bad luck harbingers' to his personal satisfaction, the now-paranoid real estate broker began driving the twelve miles west to Virtua Hospital.

'I'm glad I honored my sixth sense instincts and decided to keep the ten accursed objects rather than throwing them out at the town dump!' Brewster reckoned as he speedily veered out of his driveway onto Valley Avenue. 'It's my duty and responsibility to reverse my wife's bad luck incident that ironically Susan had convinced me to initiate. And now that I've returned those ten items to their exact former places,' the omen-believing man reflected, 'I'll confidently hightail it over to Berlin and relish the fact that my loyal and loving wife has fully regained consciousness.'

Ten minutes after the ten 'evil articles' had been returned to their definitive positions inside the garage, attic, and cellar, Jim's cell phone again rang and Jeffrey was once more on the other end of the line. The stressed-out motorist immediately pulled over to the busy highway's shoulder to answer the call.

"Hello, Dad! Don't rush getting here! Mom's all right and has snapped out of her precarious state!" the relieved son disclosed in his normal-sounding voice. "The doctors think that she had suffered a mild concussion as a result of her blacking-out and falling!"

"That's absolutely fantastic news!" the jubilant father yelled into his cell phone. "I promise I'll be there Jeff in approximately fifteen minutes. I'll look for you in the visitors' lounge waiting area."

"Okay, Pop! See you there, er, I meant to say 'here'!" the son exclaimed. "There for a minute Dad I had thought that our family had been subjected to some really bad luck!" Click.

'I'm really happy that I trusted my suspicious judgment and decided to keep the ten articles I had placed inside the SUV,' Jim Brewster determined as he cautiously observed the reduced speed limit while passing through Atco. 'If it wasn't for my superstitious nature, then who knows what terrible fate might've been awaiting Susan? I'm never going to get rid of those ten special objects as long as my home remains standing and as long as I'm alive and strong enough to safeguard them!'

"Return from Honolulu"

Ludwik Wisniewski and his wife Olga had originated from Krakow, Poland and then daringly journeyed to the United States by ship, being processed through Ellis Island immigration in 1901. Proud of their Polish heritage, Ludwik and Olga joined other members of the relocated Wisniewski clan then residing outside Posen near Alpena, Michigan, the long grueling train ride from bustling New York City to Alpena being financed by Ludwik's brother Stanislaus, who had already established himself in the "New World" and had successfully founded a logging business, leasing a thousand acres of prime forest ground from the federal government. The ambitious Wisniewski immigrants believed that the eastern Michigan lower peninsula's climate was similar to that of their native Poland and that crucial opportunities for social and economic upward mobility would abound in their "new country."

Almost always during nightly conversations Ludwik and Stanislaus Wisniewski would remind their wives Olga and Agatha about their wealthy aristocratic cousin Teodor Radziwill of Warsaw, Poland, the chieftain of a rich family that had accumulated a colossal fortune in the proliferating steel manufacturing business. But greedy Teodor was too sanctimonious and quite parsimonious about amassing his awesome wealth and the reclusive industrialist never bothered communicating with his struggling Michigan cousins Ludwik and Stanislaus, electing to live a secluded life with his wife Isabel and his pampered son Henryk.

In the summer of 1908, the logging camp owned and operated by Ludwik and Stanislaus Wisniewski had caught fire and Stanislaus and wife Agatha had perished in the wild inferno. Broken hearted and financially ruined, defeated Ludwik and disconsolate Olga (along with their three children) migrated to live with relatives in Baltimore, Maryland, where several years later the bad-luck elders had unfortunately died of pneumonia during the great influenza epidemic that had plagued major American cities just prior to the advent of World War I.

Ten years later, during the Roaring Twenties, the deceased couple's oldest son Josef married an Italian girl named Rita Monzo, whom he had met at an East Baltimore wedding reception, and soon thereafter the newlyweds moved from Dundalk, Maryland to Hammonton, New Jersey, where Josef was employed as a conscientious construction laborer, eventually saving enough money to finally initiate his own business enterprise.

Josef Wisniewski's construction business was on the verge of bankruptcy during the very disappointing 1930s Great Depression, but the World War II years between 1941 and 1947 were rather fortuitous and profitable, and the post war 1950s created an economic boon for industrious hard working entrepreneurs. Josef's "second-life" construction company grew and prospered. But still, the exotic legend of the Teodor and Henryk Radziwill cousins' connection became a popular "Old World tale" often discussed over Josef Wisniewski's dinner table with wife Rita, son Michal and daughter Gretchen. Honoring respect for tradition and ancestral heritage, the family's Polish genealogical history always dominated the children's Sicilian background that had been provided on the mother's side.

"Yes, Kids, your grandfather Ludwik was a great man who with his brother Stanislaus ran into overwhelming misfortune when their logging camp went up in flames just outside Alpena, Michigan," Josef would review at least once a month for the benefit of Michal and Gretchen to hear and appreciate. "And then that widespread influenza plague that ravaged Baltimore was absolutely devastating. So many people along with your grandfather Ludwik and Grandmother Olga had perished during that abominable time period and your grandparents even had to be buried in mass graves since individual funerals were impossible to perform because of the great numbers that had died. Yes," Josef regularly emphasized, "you Kids don't know how difficult things were way back then! Human existence was a far cry from Paradise!"

Josef Wisniewski had died of a massive heart attack in 1980 and his wife Rita from diabetes complications four years later in 1984. Now it was up to Michal to orally carry on and transfer the Wisniewski family legends to his son Frederick, to his daughter Mary Ellen and to his apathetic wife Janet.

"What did our great-grandfather Ludwik and his brother Stanislaus do in Poland before they decided to immigrate to Michigan?" high school sophomore Frederick Wisniewski asked his father Michal. "Were they so poor that they had to travel across the Atlantic on a cattle boat to seek fresh new lives here in America?"

"Well, first of all, Fred," Michal said as his fuzzy mind attempted to organize the family history story, "as I understand it Ludwik and Stanislaus had worked very hard in the famous Wieliczka Salt Mines in Southern Poland and were not once helped by their wealthy
108

Captain of Industry cousin Teodor Radziwill of Warsaw. But just before Hitler and his wicked minions began taking over most of northern Europe in the late 1930s," Michal Wisniewski continued his recollection of significant past events, "Teodor and his son Henryk had advantageously sold their thriving Warsaw steel mill and haven't been heard of since. It's been nearly eighty years following their intelligent financial maneuver and then their subsequent escape to Geneva, and rumor has it that the fabulous Radziwill fortune has been accumulating interest in a Swiss bank account and that Henryk's only heir and bachelor son Leo is living high on the hog and is gradually dwindling down the fantastic estate's value. But as to exactly where the mysterious phantom Leo Radziwill might be living now," Michal summarized and concluded his narrative, "your guess Fred is as good as mine."

"Why do we have to have such a goofy last name like Wisniewski?" seventh grader Mary Ellen asked her seventy-year-old father. "The other kids at school think it sounds funny and too old-fashioned!"

"Actually, Mary Ellen, Wisniewski is a very common surname in Poland, and I believe that it is the third most common last name after Nowak and Kowalski," Michal explained to his somewhat concerned daughter. "And translated into English, 'Wisniewski' roughly means 'from the village of the cherry tree.' That's about all I can tell you about our illustrious family name."

"Oh, Mike, I think that the old story about multi-millionaires Teodor Radziwill and his son Henryk and Henryk's spoiled jet-setting oddball son Leo is just a lot of hot air that's only really designed to generate some much-craved Polish family pride," spouse Janet opined and criticized, much to her husband's general disgust. "And what do you care about foreign cousins you've never seen or known Mike? You've inherited a good business from your father and have been extremely successful on your own without any help from any of those remote and eccentric Radziwills over in Europe."

"Yes, Honey, I guess you're right on that issue!" Michal reluctantly agreed with his totally bored marital mate. "Perhaps the Wisniewskis' of Hammonton, New Jersey are now better off than my distant aristocratic cousin Leo Radziwill is. But you have to understand one vital thing Janet. Family pride is very important to people of Polish descent, and I just have to recognize and value the sacrifices and travails that my ancestors had to endure, especially bravely venturing here to America and boldly seeking their separate fates in a strange new land. I just very much admire their pioneering spirit, that's all!"

"Well, sometimes I wish that I could be given equal time bragging about *my* just-as-relevant Irish heritage," the former Janet Sullivan argued with her left hand on her hip while obediently pouring her demanding husband a second cup of freshly brewed hot coffee. "In the 1890s there was a serious dreadful potato famine back in Ireland you know," Janet maintained from her standing position, "and my valiant ancestors had to overcome obstacles and dilemmas too while trying to make a living subsisting in Boston and New York! I want you to appreciate that your Krakow folks weren't the only ones to pass through Ellis Island while desperately seeking advancement and improvement in their lives!"

"Okay, Janet. I'll concede that excellent point to you," Michal diplomatically compromised. "I suppose that I shouldn't be jealous one iota of that anonymous mogul Leo Radziwell and I must admit that the Irish Sullivans are just as equally as vital to our family's identity and development as are the Polish Wisniewskis of yesteryear. Now Dear Wife," the apologetic husband politely expressed, "Fred and Mary Ellen can swallow-down their hot dogs and relish, but as a token of *our* domestic peace, please pass the kiebasa and the sauerkraut since I'm the only person in this American household that ever eats the delicious stuff!"

* * * * * * * * * * * * * *.

Contracts from highway paving bids and from Atlantic County municipal building improvements had been signed and Michal Wisniewski's M.W. Enterprises, Incorporated was able to purchase three additional dump trucks, bringing the company fleet up to twenty-five. But because of the high cost of heavy equipment, the chief executive had trouble saving cash, always having to reinvest his firm's profits into new machinery and heavy-duty apparatus.

Sitting behind his cluttered office desk on Tuesday morning December 1st, 2009 Michal received a registered letter from Honolulu, Hawaii that the mailman insisted Wisniewski must sign in order to claim. 'I wonder what this must be!' the surprised and curious recipient pondered. 'Oh well, let's see what it is!'

    Adalbert Kaminski, Attorney-at-Law
    Waikiki Beach Hotel
    Honolulu, Oahu Hawaii 96815

November 23rd, 2009

Dear Mr. Michal Wisniewski:

Greetings Sir! It gives me great pleasure to inform you that I have been the principal legal council for Mr. Leonardo "Leo" Radziwill for the past thirty-five years and I have the paramount responsibility of conducting all of Mr. Radziwill's business matters.

As you probably already know from your family's genealogy, Mr. Teodor Radziwill had owned and operated a large steel mill outside Warsaw, Poland just prior to World War II's ravaging most of Northern Europe. Teodor and his son Henryk Radziwill had fortunately sold their flourishing steel plant a year before Adolph Hitler and his Nazi regime had destructively invaded Poland. In a necessary flight to safety, the Radziwills had moved to Geneva, Switzerland where Teodor had died in 1947 and as you might be aware, then Henryk had passed away in 1976.

The letter went on to explain that Michal's distant cousin Leonardo Radziwill had been suffering from cirrhosis of the liver for ten years prior to succumbing to the dreaded disease on October 6th of 2009. The flamboyant international playboy client Mr. Leonardo Radziwill had been a bachelor who had led a very extravagant lifestyle owning fabulous mansions in Geneva, Tuscany and Monaco. But having no children or immediate family members, in his hospital room Mr. Radziwill decided to conduct a simple lottery among his remaining distant cousins to determine whom his next-of-kin heir would actually be. The attorney's letter then congratulated Mr. Michal Wisniewski for *his* good fortune in being selected from thirteen cousins' names that had been placed into an ordinary shoebox. The Honolulu lawyer stated in his missive that Michal was entitled to receive what was left of Mr. Leonardo Radziwill's dwindling-yet-impressive estate.

Mr. Leonardo Radziwill had inherited the equivalent of thirty million Euros (43 million U.S. dollars) from his frugal father Henryk and upon your fine benefactor's death, a sum of fifteen million Euros (approximately 19.6 million dollars) still remains in three separate Swiss bank and stock brokerage accounts.

Now Mr. Wisniewski, in order to facilitate the appropriate transfer of the willed money over to you, and since I will be conducting business for other clients over the course of the next month here in Honolulu, I strongly suggest that you meet me at noon on Wednesday, December 30th in your already booked Suite #428 at the Waikiki Beach Hotel.

As part of the will settlement (and as the will's assigned exclusive legal executor), I have already had my personal secretary send you four United Airlines plane tickets (upon separate cover) with departure from Philadelphia International Airport to Honolulu with a refueling stopover in San Francisco: one for yourself, one for your wife and two for your two children to vacation on Oahu for ten days during the Christmas holidays from Monday December 21st to Friday, January 1st, 2010, of course, with all expenses paid for by benevolent Mr. Leonardo Radizill's Last Will and Testament.

I am looking forward to meeting you and your family at noon on Wednesday, December 30th at your already booked suite at the Waikiki Beach Hotel.

Sincerely,

Adalbert Kaminski, Attorney-at-Law

Feeling a surge of pure ecstasy, Michal's heart surrendered to impulse and Wisniewski anxiously picked up the phone and called Janet at home to relate to his cynical wife the rather incredible postal news. Janet insisted that her emotionally charged husband read the extraordinary letter over the phone so that she could jot down the more pertinent details on a clean sheet of paper. The construction chief's mind was without a doubt majestically floating on Cloud 9 as he faithfully recited the text word by word.

"I'll have Marge call Hawaii to confirm our paid reservations at the Waikiki Beach Hotel in Honolulu," the husband excitedly suggested. "The construction business is pretty inactive between Thanksgiving and March. My secretary has nothing else more important to do than to call Hawaii about this hotel reservation item. The matter ought to occupy some of Marge's time on such a lazy December 1st morning."

"Better yet, Mike," distrustful wife Janet voluntarily answered. "I'll call Hawaii myself and verify the reservations for the prescribed dates that have been pre-scheduled for later on this month. I just want to make sure that we're not being victimized by a fantastic mean hoax of some sort."

"Okay, Honey," Michal eagerly agreed while the consummate dreamer was secretly contemplating the magnitude of his great inheritance. "If it is some sort of quirky trick, it's a most expensive one at that for the unscrupulous person perpetrating it!"

A half-hour later Janet contacted Michal and enthusiastically confirmed that everything appeared to be on the up and up, both at the Waikiki Beach Hotel main desk and with the United Airlines ticket counter. Both marriage partners were satisfied that the exceptional provisions depicted in Leonardo Radziwill's will (as described in Adalbert Kaminski's letter) were authentic and that the dispensing of the multimillionaire's huge estate was indeed perfectly legitimate and on the level.

"And Mike, our four placements are in the first class section of the plane, which automatically entitles us to more comfortable seats than the passengers riding in coach along with more terrific food choices on our meals' menu."

"Janet, I've told you countless times that there was a definite close connection between the Radziwill and the Wisniewski families back in Poland during the late 1800s," Mike bragged and gloated. "And truthfully, I've never had anything negative to say about anyone in the Radziwill clan except the notion that Teodor, Henryk and Leo were all a trifle on the odd side, although I must qualify that poignant statement right now because at this moment, despite *his* cad-like eccentric reputation, I fully appreciate Cousin Leo's abundant generosity."

The United Airlines flight from Philadelphia to San Francisco was quite smooth and the exciting transcontinental trip was only surpassed by the wonderful Pacific flight from the City on the Bay to Oahu. The accommodations at the luxurious Waikiki Beach Hotel were quite luxurious and the view of the shoreline and the incomparable sight of Diamond Head from Suite #428 were as magnificent as magnificent gets. Even normally sarcastic Frederick and typically contrary Mary Ellen appeared to be mesmerized by the resplendence of the Pacific tropical paradise.

"I can't say enough superlatives to describe this exotic place," Janet marveled and offered upon assessing the panorama from the suite's balcony. "It's a dream come true and perhaps the finest experience of my life!"

"And don't neglect to mention my unbelievable nineteen-million-six-hundred-thousand-dollar miracle bonanza!" Michal laughed as he observed some honeymooners frolicking in the surf. "Who ever said that blood wasn't thicker than water? Make sure that tonight at dinner I offer a heartfelt toast to the memory of the great and noble Leonardo Radziwill! May his immortal soul dwell forever in Heaven!"

The next seven days passed by rapidly, with junkets and jaunts to popular Honolulu tourist destinations such as Pearl Harbor and the revered Battleship Arizona Memorial, the Hanauma Bay Marine Preserve, the Diamond Head State Monument and Volcanic Crater Park, the Iolani Palace, the Honolulu Zoo and the nearby Waikiki Aquarium where colorful fish (indigenous to the island's bays and currents) were on exhibit. And besides those inimitable wonders, the flight over Oahu provided by Island Seaplane Services was both spectacular and sensational.

Finally, noon on Wednesday December 30th arrived on the end-of-year calendar, but much to Michal Wisniewski's instant frustration, Adalbert Kaminski, distinguished Attorney-at-Law, failed to show-up at Suite #428. By suppertime Michal had realistically suspected that he had been the victim of an elaborate and outlandish canard or complicated ruse.

"I'm telling you Janet, there's something more putrid and rancid in Honolulu than that normal *other something* being rotten in Denmark!" the totally distressed husband ranted. "I've never felt as used and as exploited as I do right now! But all of this scheming and planning being done for what reason? I simply don't get it!"

"Yes, Mike. The picnic's officially over! I just called the airport and we have to fly coach all the way back to Philly'," Janet disclosed and reported. "No more filet mignon or lobster tails!"

"When we get back to Hammonton, I'm going to get to the bottom of this weird puzzle if I have to sell three dump trucks to pay for a thorough background investigation," the angry husband vowed with a look of consternation dominating his facial features. "I've

114

never been so befuddled in my entire life and I don't relish the empty bewildered feeling one bit either!"

* * * * * * * * * * * *

On Monday morning, February 1st 2010 experienced private investigator Frank Meyers paid a vital visit to Michal Wisniewski's comfortable Hammonton residence on upper middle-class Golf Drive. Frederick and Mary Ellen were attending their respective public schools so the construction contractor and the veteran private eye were able to conduct a forthright and confidential conversation.

"Well Frank, nearly five weeks ago I had hired you and you've been paid a nice five-thousand-dollar retainer," Michal nervously prefaced his remarks. "Tell me now, what has your research discovered, or should I say 'uncovered'?"

"I'll be perfectly candid with you right from the outset Mike," the baldheaded and rotund P. I. began his comprehensive narrative. "I had twenty-five years in a patrol car on the Atlantic City Police Force and Mr. Wisniewski, I've been a private investigator for thirteen more yearly campaigns. Quite honestly Mr. Wisniewski," the extremely competent investigator qualified. "I've never before been involved in a case like this one, a multi-faceted riddle that required plenty of ingenuity and hard delving and probing to eventually solve. It's extremely unique and complex in many ways and after a great degree of adversity," Frank Meyers swore solemnly, raising his right hand above his shoulder, "I've amazingly managed to piece it all together."

"Well then, Mr. Meyers. First of all," the flustered and deceived Hammonton businessmen verbalized, "what happened to my wife and where is my missing nine hundred thousand dollars? How's that for a double whammy loss?"

After loudly clearing his larynx, Frank Meyers first explained that both the local and the state police departments had been advised of what peculiar circumstances had surfaced and materialized and that the 'All Points Bulletin' that had been sent out to apprehend the two suspected felons had been canceled in order to protect and insulate the 'reputable victim' Michal Wisniewski from IRS scrutiny and prosecution.

"I'm a little confused," Michal honestly stated. "Could you be a little more specific?"

"Mike, the Devil is always in the details," the shrewd reputable detective declared. "Now kindly tell me Sir, did you ever have a devious fellow named Vladimir Kozlowski work for you?" Meyers asked in a slow enunciation.

"Why yes! Kozlowski was a road tar foreman for my firm for about seven years until we had an explosive argument over a paving and slurry seal job we were doing down in Stone Harbor," Michal recollected and stated. "Vladimir was generally a good industrious worker but he had a chronic problem with alcohol that induced his nasty temper to surface from time to time, especially when he wasn't completely rested or sober. Why are you asking me about this indignant fellow Kozlowski?"

"Well Mike, after your wife Janet had found out that you were having an affair with your vivacious secretary Marge Dixon, who incidentally has been married three times as you probably know," Frank Meyers added and vociferated, "she began seeing your fired guy, this love-competitor nemesis Vladimir Kozlowski when you weren't around. And of course, their every rendezvous was stealthily done out of your wife Janet's spite and jealousy!"

"And so," Michal replied after taking a much-needed deep breath, "my wife wasn't molested or kidnapped like I had originally thought. She had run away with that two-bit loser Kozlowski. What an unfaithful Jezebel Janet turned out to be!"

"Precisely," the private investigator concurred with his paying client's opinion, nodding his head in full agreement. "And your wife knew all about the nine hundred thousand dollars that you had skimmed from the business over the course of the last decade. She fully knew that you had kept the dough stashed in your cellar inside the slat vent to your air conditioning duct. So while you were away merrily vacationing with the family in Honolulu," Meyers continued his rather fascinating exposition, "Janet's lover/accomplice Vladimir Kozlowski, alias Swiss Barrister Adalbert Kaminski, Attorney-at-Law, decided to pull a clever scam on you as vindictive punishment for your infidelity to your wife and for your incidental firing of your amorous on-the-prowl former road foreman."

"This is all very bizarre and incredibly sophisticated!" Michal acknowledged, exhibiting a stern grim expression on his now-florid face. "I fully understand that since the nine hundred thousand had never been reported to the IRS on my past tax returns, I would then have to pay hundreds of thousands of dollars in back taxes that I don't really have at hand. What a tight Gordian knot I had tied for myself!" the thoroughly duped man verbally realized. "When the skimmed money was finally noticed stolen from the cellar air conditioning duct, I couldn't report it to the local authorities because then eventually, an IRS investigation would have me losing my business. But tell me Frank," Michal Wisniewski questioned with an astonished look showing on his face, "what was this roundabout Hawaii adventure and inheritance marathon all about?"

"That's all simple elementary school logic," Frank Meyers answered and indulgently laughed, and then the hired researcher begged for forgiveness after admitting to his gross indiscretion that had been inadvertently directed toward his shocked and beleaguered client. "I figured that your cheating scorned wife and this Kozlowski gigolo knew all about your historic infatuation with the Radziwill steel moguls from Warsaw. Consequently," the savvy detective concluded his extraordinary exposition, "after you had coincidentally fired Mr. Kozlowski, he couldn't be hanging around your house and deliberately be breaking into your air conditioning duct by removing the latticed vent cover. And so, the audacious pair concocted this magnificently creative scheme where...."

"Where I temporarily forgot all about my nine hundred thousand dollars concealed in the cellar air conditioning duct and foolishly focused my concentration on the nineteen and a half million dollar non-existent reward, the evasive illusion at the end of my fantasy rainbow," Michal gasped and uttered in complete animosity. "The two creative rogues capitalized on my desire to become twenty times as wealthy as I presently am, or was, and they next coyly sweetened the pot and enticed me with an all-expense-covered Hawaiian vacation for me and my family. That was the maraschino cherry on top of the all-too-tantalizing hot fudge sundae," Wisniewski regretfully determined. "And while I had been unsuspectingly touring the splendid sights of Oahu, Vladimir Kozlowski, alias Lawyer Adalbert Kaminski, sneakily entered my house with a door key provided by my wife and then..."

"And then unimpeded, the deplorable scoundrel without any interruption easily pilfered your stashed nine hundred thousand clams that had been concealed inside your cellar air conditioning vent!" Frank Meyers attested. "The entire Hawaii ruse was just a neat scam to skillfully shnooker you and get you away from Hammonton for a week or so in order for the common thief to casually purloin your hidden basement treasure."

"But the whole deceitful plot must've cost Kozlowski at least thirty thousand dollars when you consider the round trip plane tickets for four, the lavish hotel accommodations and the cash allotted for the trip's food expense account!" the still astounded Michal Wisniewski vigorously complained. "And the worst aspect of the entire fiasco is that I had been betrayed by my formerly trusted two-timing wife!"

"Indeed!" P.I. Frank Meyers exclaimed. "In effect, this Vladimir Kozlowski character and your deceitful wife ingeniously collaborated to achieve something mighty imaginative. They offered you an artificial twenty-million-dollar whale in exchange for a real nine-hundred-and-sixty-thousand-dollar rare tuna and you swallowed their absurd outrageous proposal, hook, line and sinker! And when you and your family arrived in Hawaii, that was Mr. Kozlowski's confirmation signal to fly back to New Jersey from Honolulu to enact his sly cellar duct heist, which naturally you will never report to the local authorities out of fear of punitive IRS retribution."

"I suppose I deserve this uncouth outcome as atonement for me being so covetous," Michal deducted and confessed. "I guess I've been pummeled both in love and in money because I had been a naïve foolish greedy dreamer believing that the high-flying aristocratic and super-sophisticated Radziwill family of Warsaw, Poland cared one tiny scintilla about the lowly Wisniewskis of Krakow."

"Soldier of Misfortune"

Dr. Angelo DeMarco had recently retired as the head psychiatrist at New Jersey's Ancora State Hospital in order to devote his full time to expanding his private practice, which was located inside a second-floor office suite at the southeast corner of 2nd Street and Bellevue Avenue, Hammonton, New Jersey. The psych' physician was perusing a letter received from Noreen Pearson, the wife of a twenty-five-year-old Army Corporal, and the distraught enlisted soldier had been complaining to his spouse of severe migraine headaches, of terrible repetitious nightmares, and also the afflicted young serviceman was often heard uttering "indiscernible gibberish" during his erratic nightly sleeps.

Dr. DeMarco considered the prospective case study of his latest accepted patient, Jack Pearson, to be quite novel and intriguing, because in her curious letter of introduction and referral request, Mrs. Noreen Pearson had thoroughly described her husband's insistence that he had been suffering from symptoms of a baffling multiple personality disorder caused by regenerative experiences of 'organized, chronological, military service reincarnation.'

The psychiatrist's receptionist/secretary politely escorted Mr. Jack Pearson into Dr. DeMarco's spacious office, where initial casual conversation gradually led to the standard doctor/patient interview. The mental health expert explicitly explained to Jack that all human beings were similar in that humans respond to general fundamental needs and drives, but each person's relationship to his or her behavior is expressed in an individual, unique, and specific way.

"Frankly Jack, there are basically two types of needs," Dr. DeMarco pontificated to Pearson. "Physical needs such as the need for food, shelter, and clothing to protect the body from the elements, and then there're also human psychological needs, such as the need for approval, acceptance, attention, self-esteem and last buy not least, the need for love and security. And then, of course Jack," the eminent psychiatrist sternly continued his monologue, "there are those strong basic drives that often motivate and compel people to act, such as the characteristic hunger, greed, and sex drives. Your unusual mental condition might very well be a combination of any two or more of the traditional needs and drives that comprise the 'typical human profile'. Now Jack, your very concerned wife Doreen stated in her letter that you believe that you're over two-hundred-and-fifty years old! Is her remarkable assertion true?"

"That's correct Dr.," the somewhat addled patient quite matter-of-factly answered. "But the stressful dreams that I've been having stay in my subconscious mind, and I'm frustrated because I can never fully recall any specific details of my involvement, anywhere from the beginning of my restless slumber to the end. All I can remember about my dreams, or should I say 'my nightmares', is that I'm predictably engaged in some kind of major war battle. But in each instance, the battles are with all kinds of different enemies of various nationalities. Now please tell me, does that odd portrayal make any sort of sense to you?"

"I believe that I see what you're attempting to explain!" Dr. Angelo DeMarco stated, pensively rubbing his clean-shaven chin. "Since my ten o'clock appointment has canceled because *that* patient has developed flu symptoms, I'll have up to two-hours to objectively observe your deportment under hypnosis. I'll be recording and evaluating your verbal responses to my oral prompts. Now Mr. Pearson, I find the notion that you honestly think that you're around two-and-a-half-centuries old very fascinating indeed! I think that your abnormal nightmare events represent a distinct challenge to my general knowledge of human behavior and development. Let me ask if you are now emotionally ready for me to delve into your psyche, your id, and your ego?"

"Yes, Dr. I've seen enough of this sort of stuff in the movies. I presume that I should first lie down on your leather couch over there," Jack indicated, pointing at the comfortable-looking piece of furniture with his index finger. "Honestly now, for my sake and for my wife's peace of mind, I hope that this experimental session turns out to be successful."

"If possible, Jack, when you respond to a particular question, please inform me of the exact setting of your mental manifestation; that is," the psychiatrist stipulated and then paused to perfectly enunciate his additional words, "provide me with the exact year of the incident you're describing. And also, if you could, tell me the geographic location where the battle that you're directly involved in is taking place. I trust, Mr. Pearson, that you'll be able to do that simple task without experiencing any harmful duress or emotional stress."

Jack then voluntarily assumed his horizontal position upon the soft black leather sofa, and in a matter of several suspenseful minutes, Dr. DeMarco had effectively hypnotized Pearson, using a watch dangling and oscillating from a gold fob chain. When the soldier/patient appeared to be fully relaxed, the all-too-confident mind doctor commenced with his formal interrogation, which a remote camera was capturing on film.

"Please remember Mr. Pearson, you still possess your free will and should only verbally respond to my well-intentioned suggestions and comments if you so desire. Now then, as a brave and loyal soldier of history, where are you located now, Jack, and what time period is it?"

"I'm somewhere in Massachusetts in June of 1775," Jack began his bizarre recollection. "Yes, I'm helping in the effort to fortify the Charlestown Peninsula. The British barges are currently ferrying opposing troops across the river, and my commander, Colonel William Prescott, has ordered me and the other soldiers to make a stand and defend Breed's Hill. We had held our ground twice, but now we've run out of gunpowder," the hypnotized subject expressed. "The redcoats are shooting at us, volley after volley. Boston and vicinity must not fall to the enemy! Oh my God!" Jack exclaimed. "I'm wounded; shot in the back while I was turned around and reloading my musket! My legs are paralyzed. The pain from my shoulders to my hips is excruciating! I'll never be able to escape the peninsula alive! I'm passing out! Everything's hazy all around me! I'm sure I'm dying! Goodbye cruel world!"

"All right Jack, you're safe and sound now, and you've miraculously fled the enemy. Your pathetic injuries have completely healed!" Dr. DeMarco declared as his eyes noticed that his patient's changed breathing was gradually becoming more normal and regular. "You've been safely evacuated out of the Battle of Bunker Hill, and you've triumphantly endured *that* important-but-pivotal conflict of the American Revolutionary War!" the mind doctor loquaciously communicated. "I now recommend that you take ten deep breaths, and then again tell me where you are and what activities are occurring in your immediate vicinity."

Jack had effectively calmed-down from his initial ordeal, and the stabilized patient very deliberately articulated that the new date was January 8th, 1815, and that Pearson, along with other assigned riflemen, were occupying an entrenchment while observing highly-trained units of British soldiers marching in neat rows directly into the pre-set American trap. General Andrew Jackson soon gave the command to "Fire!", and the ambushing American marksmen easily defeated the advancing, hostile-but-surprised foreign enemy. But during the termination of the rather fierce engagement, a blast from a

121

distant cannon sent Jack Pearson hurtling through the air, his fragile body being violently crushed upon impacting a sturdy tree trunk.

"I am an avid student of history and evidently, you had just participated in the Battle of New Orleans during the War of 1812," Dr. DeMarco immediately recognized and related. "But don't worry one iota, Jack; you've apparently endured and survived your ordeal with flying colors! If my memory of history serves me correctly, the battle was unnecessary because a peace treaty had already been signed at Ghent, Belgium, several weeks before the violent conflict had happened. But because of the lack of speedy communications across the Atlantic Ocean," the highly-skilled consultant elucidated, "neither the British commander, General Edward Parkenham, nor your own dauntless General Andrew Jackson were ever aware of the cease fire being in effect! You're doing quite excellent, Jack!" Dr. DeMarco praised. "Where are you now?"

"It's February 23, 1836, although in truth, I haven't looked at a calendar or an almanac for several months," the amazing military patient prefaced. "There's this popular belief of 'Manifest Destiny' going all around America, and presently, Texas Territory is under Mexican dominion. I'm standing on a rampart, so to speak, defending a Spanish mission, the Alamo, so I suppose that Davy Crockett, Jim Bowie, and me are all 'on-a-mission' to fight to the death using our muskets as clubs. That is, after our ammunition supplies have been used up. Oh, how agonizing!" Jack Pearson anguished with conviction from his trance-like state. "A Mexican bayonet has just entered my chest and I'm bleeding to death while lying helplessly on the ground. My spirit is about to exit my body. Oh Lord, please save me! Forgive me for my numerous sins and grant me life everlasting! Lord have mercy on me!"

'My patient's entire narrative is positively incredible!' Dr. DeMarco marveled and contemplated. 'This very special man, at least according to this subject's extraordinary testimony, is an actual true-blue American patriot! And he's candidly and persuasively presented his recollection of virtually almost dying three consecutive times in precise chronological order, originating with the Revolutionary War, followed by the War of 1812, and now Jack's vividly describing his heroic actions during the quest for Texas independence at the Alamo in 1836. If I recall from my knowledge of U.S. history, the battle was a major episode in the prelude to the Mexican-American War where General Sam Houston eventually vanquished Santa Anna at San Jacinto,' Dr. DeMarco's keen mind imagined. 'But how could Jack Pearson possibly be inventing such phenomenal fiction while being totally submissive and obediently compliant under professional hypnosis?'

Dr. Angelo DeMarco then hypothesized that according to the patient's exceptional 'already-established time line', Jack would naturally next declare his personal association with the Civil War. The man's unique narrative was unlike any commentaries that the psychiatrist had ever before heard in *his* noteworthy thirty-five-year professional career. To the astounded interviewer, Jack Pearson was like an addiction, and Dr. Angelo DeMarco wanted more of his subject's strange attestations.

"What's your next war adventure?" the captivated questioner courteously and suavely interrogated. "Verify for me, Jack. Are you fighting for the North or for the South?"

"Definitely for the Union Blue!" Jack emphatically confirmed. "It's September, 1862, I believe, somewhere in Maryland at a creek called Antietam near the town of Sharpsburg. My commander, General McClellan, has vigilantly pursued the Grays there, but then backup Confederates have unexpectedly showed-up coming from the direction of Harpers Ferry, West Virginia. During the wild and bloody confrontation, I've just been mortally wounded and am rapidly losing consciousness. I've got enemy shrapnel in my arms, stomach, and legs!"

"Well, Jack, I have good news to relate. You've magically managed to survive the bitter Antietam altercation unscathed," consoled and comforted the veteran interviewer. "And you're fortunate to have come out of that formidable war zone still alive and able to speak! Your escape to safety is borderline miraculous. Over twelve-thousand brave Union soldiers had perished in the wild siege," Dr. DeMarco, amateur historian, expounded in a soothing tone of voice. "All because General Robert E. Lee wanted to record his first victory on land that had been controlled by the North. But in the final analysis," the mind-doctor indicated to his new patient, "Lee had to admit being out-manned, and subsequently, the Confederate General reluctantly retreated his exhausted army from Maryland back into Virginia."

The professional examiner was not especially skeptical of his new client's veracity, but the mental health expert suspected that Corporal Jack Pearson might just have been suffering from delusional imaginings, with certain ideas being spontaneously generated from *his* most creative subconscious mind. Dr. DeMarco accurately anticipated that his subject's next graphic depiction would entail *his* supporting role in the Spanish-American War that had begun in 1898 with the sinking of the battleship Maine in Havana Harbor, occurring during Republican President William McKinley's Administration. The excited psychiatrist then expertly transitioned Jack into *his* new dangerous scenario.

"I had fought with Colonel Teddy Roosevelt's Rough Riders at the Battle of San Juan Hill, but fortunately for us, only mostly enemy Spanish soldiers were killed during the brief encounter," Jack uttered and disclosed in a more relaxed oral delivery. "But because of poor sanitary conditions and camping-out in a mosquito-infested tropical environment, I did almost die in Cuba, but not from any destructive cannon blast or gunfire. I had somehow contracted a repugnant case of Yellow Fever, and then somehow avoided passing-away on August 1st, 1898, exactly one month after Colonel Roosevelt and his rambunctious Rough Riders had basically run rough-shod over their intimidated Spanish adversaries."

"And if I may suggest your next wartime engagement, I suppose that twenty or so years later, you were part of General John J. Pershing's advancing American Expeditionary Force in France," the knowledgeable history buff/psychiatrist asked his immobile, mesmerized patient. "I've avidly read in various encyclopedias where over two-million American soldiers had valiantly fought in France during the famous 'Lafayette We Are Here!' campaign. Did you ever sing the famous song *Over There?"*

"Yes, I did sing that inspiring George M. Cohan marching song in the rural sectors of France in 1918," Jack rather lethargically confirmed. "I had gotten separated from my platoon after the left side of our trench had been demolished by a direct mortar hit. Bloodthirsty and aggressive German soldiers surrounded me near the Siegfried Line, and I was immediately captured and tortured somewhere inside a dense forest without ever having a chance to raise my hands and formally surrender."

"Well, in the 1930s there was the Great Depression scourge, along with Prohibition in America, and then there was the infamous rise of Adolph Hitler and his Nazi regime in Germany in the mid and late '30s," Dr. DeMarco recalled and commented. "And after the Japanese squadron planes attacked Pearl Harbor, the United States responded to the belligerent assault by joining the Allies to fight the Germans, who were aligned with the Italians under Mussolini and also with the Japanese imperialists' fearsome military juggernaut. And don't forget, Jack, the Jewish Holocaust, too, where over six million innocent people perished for no apparent reason at all, except for probably being Hitler's personal scapegoat!"

124

"World War II was an abomination, an absolutely atrocious ugly conflict waged against brutal and ruthless German fascists," Jack Pearson uttered in a monotone voice from his trance-like state. "My Army unit was advancing north inside Italy, and we were about to fight for control of Rome and then move on towards Florence in Tuscany. We were hunkered-down, occupying a building in the town of Cassino, situated about midway between Naples and Rome," the perplexed man lying prone on the black leather sofa orally reviewed. "The Allies' planes then bombed the monastery at the top of Monte Cassino, thinking that it had been housing German and Italian troops. But then, an errant shell landed squarely on top of the building I was in, and I instantly was injured in my face and hands from what might be today described as 'friendly fire'!"

"Well, Jack, after World War II, the U.S. troops returned home. And there was a tremendous industrial renaissance throughout the entire land with suburban communities and shopping centers popping-up outside and around every major urban metropolitan area," Dr. DeMarco lectured to his now quietly-resting patient. "The short-lived peace was interrupted, however, with the initiation of the Korean War between the North Korea Communists and the United States. Was that particular war in your experiential repertoire?"

"No, Sir. I don't recall any Korean War," the placid patient maintained. "Instead, I remember the year being 1968. I was savagely wounded by a Viet Cong surprise sneak attack outside a coastal city called Hue. Apparently, my platoon had wandered too close to an underground enemy tunnel hatch entrance, and before I knew it," Pearson stammered and then regained his subconscious confidence, "three of my companions and I were viciously attacked, and two of my buddies died, being cruelly maimed by several tossed hand grenades that landed near their American targets."

"And by virtue of deductive logic, because of a time sequence war pattern you've experienced over the last two-and-a-half centuries, I reckon that you had to also be a participant if not a casualty in the 2003 Iraq War?" Dr. DeMarco speculated and conveyed. "Were you also a victim in that modern-era conflict?"

"Yes, Sir. I did eventually die after receiving a bullet to my throat. I had passed-away inside a temporary Kuwait military tent hospital, after the sudden firefight I had been describing flared-up near the Iraqi border," pallid-faced Corporal Pearson divulged. "All together, I have accomplished dying, or nearly dying, nine times in nine separate American Wars. But each time, I had other last names than Pearson; names like Adams, Jensen, Douglas, Johnson, Burns and McFarland, but in each instance, my first name was always 'Jack'. I trust that my stated observations have managed to clarify certain important psychological concepts for you!"

Having to learn and ascertain another salient relevant fact, inquisitive Dr. DeMarco momentarily hesitated, his keen mind grappling with another question while his eyes gazed upon and studied inimitable Corporal Pearson. The patient was dressed in civilian attire, still lying flat upon the black leather couch.

"Jack, in my professional opinion, I find your unconventional multiple war lives' account to be both most absorbing and most incomprehensible. Now please tell me, were you married during your nine former soldier existences, and if so, was your wife's name Doreen in each instance?"

"Yes!" the subject affirmatively replied. "Yes, I had been wed!" Pearson confidently reiterated.

"Was your wife the same Doreen to whom you're presently married?" the now-enamored psychiatrist asked. "Think carefully, for *this* matter is of utmost significance!"

"No! Each time it was a different Doreen with red, black, brown, or blonde hair!" the patient explicitly insisted. "But if I may add, each of my nine former wives was in her own way an intelligent, beautiful woman, that fact I am sure."

"Well, Jack, I've performed a bit of elementary math' in my head and have arrived at the statistic that, assuming that you were at least twenty-years old when you had been wounded at the battle of Bunker Hill, you've lived approximately two-hundred-and-fifty- years as you've already convincingly asserted. And according to my calculation estimates," Dr. Angelo DeMarco conjectured and maintained, "most of the time intervals between the various wars that you've chronologically cited were on the average in the range of twenty-five years apart. I've achieved arriving at *that* temporal mean average length by simply subtracting twenty-years from two-hundred-and-fifty, and then dividing the number two-hundred-and-thirty by nine!" the authoritative mind and emotion evaluator declared. "The basic arithmetic tends to support and justify your claim that you're born again every twenty-five years; mature to adulthood like any normal adolescent would, and then coincidentally, are injured or die in warfare, just about every standard generation. This uncanny recurrent sequence means that..."

"Means that I'm on a schedule to soon be wounded or die for the tenth consecutive time," Corporal Pearson completed his perceptive mentor's statement. "Oh my God! I think my brain's entering into a

126

panic attack! I'm being overwhelmed by a weird-feeling, a definite death anxiety!"

"Listen carefully to my strict directions, Jack!" Dr. DeMarco imperatively instructed. "I'm going to count backwards from ten. When I reach the number 'one', I'll snap my fingers, and you'll slowly come out of your deep sleep, and then be as good as new. Ten, nine, eight, seven, six…."

* * * * * * * * * * * * *

"Five, four, three, two, one…."

When Dr. DeMarco snapped his fingers, the office setting instantly became a thick dark fog, and the next thing that the psychiatrist knew, the mind expert was occupying a bunker surrounded by a wall of sandbags and that he and Jack Pearson were in Army uniforms nervously preparing for imminent combat. Plumes of dense smoke were billowing skyward in the background. Assessing the illogical situational anomaly, the alarmed and panic-stricken psychiatrist felt compelled to ask, "Jack, where the hell are we? What's going on?"

"It's now April of 2017, and we're on a plain somewhere in northern Israel, getting ready for the Battle of Armageddon! It's all very feasible and rational. The truths of Biblical prophecy must be fulfilled, you know!"

"What do you mean when you say that Biblical prophecy must be fulfilled? Are you totally insane or drastically inebriated?" the obviously incensed and apprehensive transported psychiatrist demanded a plausible explanation from his new-found companion. "Stop being so damned vague and evasive! Be more specific when answering me, Corporal Pearson!"

"It's all a matter of exact Cosmic Divine Inspiration that is actually quite ubiquitous throughout the entire Universe!" Jack endeavored explaining to the thoroughly-puzzled and perturbed mind doctor. "Believing is so much more vital to a human being than is the practice of abstract scientific thinking! Any avowed cynic or skeptic could engage in the simple act of doubting!"

"Your wife was right about your nonsensical verbalizations! Stop speaking this incessant, ludicrous gibberish of yours! Explain yourself before I lose my temper and get violent!" the now-terrified mind doctor loudly yelled like an asylum maniac.

"I really don't fear dying at this particular moment like you do!" Jack cryptically and enigmatically answered. "The laws of the

Universe prescribe that a person must die ten-times to reach his or her ultimate destiny. After the final ninth reincarnation," the Corporal methodically articulated, "the individual's Karma has been finally attained upon rendezvousing a tenth time with the immortal Eternal Force. There's one thing I've neglected to tell you, Dr. DeMarco. I want you to know that I've actually died nine times and *not once* as you currently believe, you frivolous Fool!" Jack Pearson solemnly informed his fit-to-be-tied listener.

"Jack, I don't want t die!" Dr. Demarco shrieked.

"So, when we're both exploded into the hereafter, Dr. DeMarco, I'll be emotionally content traveling to my ultimate destiny, commonly referred to as Nirvana, because Dr., *my* final spiritual examination will have ended, and I will have then successfully passed the obligatory Karma test. Don't you comprehend what I'm expressing? My ten assigned life-and-death Earth cycles will have been finally satisfied. My restless soul will have finally achieved harmony with the Great Universe! When *you* die, you'll have to die nine more times!"

"But what about me?" the psychiatrist bellowed into the Corporal's serene-looking face. "What is to be *my* personal fate?"

"I've finally found you, Dr. Angelo DeMarco, as my gullible soul replacement, and you're now my foolish victimized substitute; you're futilely trapped in a three-century series of future life/death reenactments," the Army Corporal apprised his greatly dumbfounded Army Private counterpart.

"But Jack, that's *your* eternal status! Tell me more about what's going to happen to *me?*"

"As I've stated, you must die nine additional times, thereafter, that is, following your about-to-happen first expiration in order to fulfill your Eternal Karma. And then, after you eventually die nine additional times, as I certainly will have soon accomplished, you'll progressively become spiritually purified. Then, your troubled soul can finally exist in total tranquility with the Endless Universe," Jack Pearson candidly conveyed to his still-astonished and totally alienated, neurotic, army bunker mate. "Then and only then, Dr. DeMarco, you and your pseudo-science psychiatry, along with your immortal soul, will at last be accepted by the omnipotent Powers-That-Be. And after ten deaths, your total being will finally be integrated as One' with the wisdom of the Supreme Cosmos! Oh God!" Jack joyfully exclaimed. "I just can't wait to die for the tenth and final time, and majestically reach my Ultimate Karma!"

128

"Trestles, Overpasses & Blue Skies"

Inspector Ned Carson sat at his office desk on the third floor of Philadelphia's Race Street "Round House," casually watching vehicular traffic flowing in both directions across the Ben Franklin Bridge connecting Pennsylvania with New Jersey, the span being a mile-long distance across the historic Delaware River. Carson's reverie was instantly broken when his office partner Detective Timothy Ransom entered the room carrying two fresh cups of coffee, and then respectfully handed one of the steaming Styrofoam containers to his appreciative thirty-year-veteran colleague.

"Tim, every March right before spring arrives on the calendar, I get the strong urge to get out of the congested city and use a week of my treasured vacation time to go either hunting or fishing with you," Inspector Ned Carson mused and said. "But I gotta' confess that our good wives have been quite understanding in allowing us to participate in some valued male bonding at suburban bars, and Jenny trusts me when I'm away from town at a distant convention with you for a week or so."

"Joanne feels the same way when I'm far away from the dregs of downtown Philly' hanging out in Maine or North Dakota with none other than you," Detective Tim Ransom amiably agreed before taking a sip of just-brewed java from his hot cup. "Ned, do you remember last year when we were on our last adventurous escapade up in Maine hunting big-buck deer? We bagged us two terrific trophies that our taxidermist Gordie had stuffed and mounted for us. My twelve-point buck head and accompanying antlers is now proudly displayed hanging over my brick fireplace as a souvenir of that terrific expedition into the wilderness."

"How could I ever forget *that* madcap excursion we had up North?" the Inspector replied with a smile. "Our hilarious hunting guide claimed that *his* grandfather had a left leg that was wooden between the knee and the ankle while the thigh section along with the foot were genuine normal flesh, blood and bone!" Ned Carson gleefully exclaimed. "And after listening to that old-timer's exaggerated travesty, I reckoned that *we* were all much more than a little smashed from drinking six rounds of boilermakers and so I was the first to call it quits and march off to my cabin to seriously prepare for the next morning's hunt. Quite frankly Tim, I enjoy hunting dangerous criminals as much as I do wild animals!"

"And after you were snoring and sounding like a wild unconscious boar in your bunk sack," jovial Detective Timothy Ransom reminisced, "our illustrious guide was giving me a tin ear about how he had proudly voted for James Buchanan when he had turned twenty-one and finally became eligible to cast a ballot. I told the old animal scout that it was impossible for him to do what he had maintained and swore he had performed because James Buchanan was the fifteenth President of the United States just before Abraham Lincoln, and *his* lackluster administration was even before the Civil War ever started at Fort Sumter," Ransom embellished his story. "But the demented and totally soused guy was adamant and then poured himself another full glass of whiskey."

"Well, how did you counter the intoxicated fool's outrageous and preposterous statement?" Inspector Carson wondered and asked. "Did you put the cuffs on him before he became violent? I must've slept through the whole weird fiasco over in the other cabin. There's only so much stupidity I can endure, ya' know!"

"Well, Inspector," the amiable Detective chuckled and then proceeded with his recollection, "I felt obligated to tell our eighty-year-old drunken bearded guide that our English word "okay" had originated from another nineteenth century American President named Martin Van Buren, who incidentally was often called 'Old Kinderhook' because he had originated from Kinderhook, New York. Anyway," Tim Ransom continued with his extremely boring anecdote, "when Van Buren's aides would agree with *Old Kinderhook*, the subordinates would often say 'O. K.,' and that's precisely how the birth of our simple word 'okay' came to be."

"Did *our* inebriated guide buy the factual tale you were selling him?" Inspector Carson deliberately asked to keep the ludicrous dialogue going. "Certainly, he must've been impressed with your great storehouse of accurate-but-trivial knowledge. You were once a history major in college I believe."

"Well, Ned, all the old geezer did was indulge himself and flagrantly gulp down the remaining six ounces of cold rye liquor in his glass, put the glass on the table and say 'Okay' to me. Then the old fossil-face lowered his chin and entered into the deepest sleep I've ever witnessed," Detective Ransom humorously elaborated. "Quite candidly Ned, I've never been so entertained in all my life! Say, Inspector. What do ya' say that after work we have a temporary change in venue from our ordinary humdrum existence. We'll call our wives and tell them we're workin' a couple of hours late on next year's tight budget and then get out of town and drive across the
130

bridge over to Jersey. There's a new hot stripper from Arkansas performin' her act over at the Aquarius Club just south of Camden, in fact, not too far from the Walt Whitman Bridge. I think the broad's stage name is Daisy Maisy and that her fantastic erotic dance routine is Daisy Maisy Gone Crazy!"

"Great suggestion, Tim, but my bowling team's havin' an important championship match tonight over in Penndel and I gotta' be there since I'm both the captain and official cheerleader. Ha, ha, ha!" Carson loudly guffawed. "I'm the captain tonight at the bowling alleys but at the moment I'm merely a rank inspector sittin' behind my desk here at humdrum police headquarters. But confidentially, I like your tempting Jersey stripper club idea so ya' gotta' give me a rain check for one sunny day next week."

The two amused center city working chums next momentarily discussed their upcoming planned July deep-sea white marlin fishing trip to Ocean City, Maryland that was slated to commence out of Captain Bill Bunting's Bayside Marina and they also reviewed the prospect of going down to semi-tropical Miami the following summer to try their luck at the more formidable Atlantic Ocean blue marlin fish variety.

"Great idea, Tim!" the Inspector appreciatively complimented. "The blue marlin off the coast of Florida can be twice the size and weight of the white marlin we get off the coast of Maryland. We can arrange a week-long trip and take along the chatty wives and pesky kids. There're plenty of activities to keep our two tribes busy while we're out in the ocean meetin' the challenge of reelin' in the big blue game fish. I'll bring-up the subject with Jenny and the kids over the supper table," the thirsty-for-thrills Ned Carson promised his loyal friend. "All we have to do is get our boat captain and his mates a little smashed like we did with the hunting guide up in Maine and then have ourselves a real misadventure getting lost out there somewhere in the middle of the Bermuda Triangle."

* * * * * * * * * * * *

Attractive office secretary Karen Stone brought in the morning's mail and city edition newspapers for the Inspector and the Detective to read. The *Philadelphia Inquirer* headlines were quite depressing with murders, robberies, assaults and rapes running rampant throughout the more dangerous police precincts in the metropolis. But one particular mail item was specifically addressed both to the Inspector and to the Detective, the peculiar postal delivery being a small square package having no return address, and the strange object caught the Inspector's immediate attention. Using his handy penknife, Carson casually slit open the plain brown wrapper and the co-recipient was surprised to examine what appeared to be a computer-made recording disc, which he then placed onto the D Drive tray of his desktop Hewlett Packard tower.

"This is pretty unusual!" Inspector Carson mentioned to his crime-fighting colleague. "Some gutless incognito person has sent us an anonymous disc. I'm not *that* computer literate, Tim, but I don't think it's a video DVD. Let's see exactly what it is and what kind of message it might contain. Perhaps it's just a blank hoax of some sort or some misinformation specifically designed to steer us in the wrong direction! I'm pretty sure that it's home-made and not professionally or commercially produced in a recording studio, at least that's my initial opinion at the moment!"

"My normally latent curiosity has suddenly been stimulated!" Detective Ransom exclaimed as he casually reached for his Styrofoam coffee cup on the Inspector's gray metal desk. "This must be some sort of wacky practical joke being played, that's my first perception. Who in their right mind would take the time and trouble to send that mediocre-looking disc to you, er, I mean to *us*!"

After inserting the circular item into the appropriate computer tray, several seconds later the familiar popular music tune of the Monkees 'Take the Last Train to Clarksville' blasted through the device's speakers. The two befuddled law enforcers looked incredulously at each other and then burst out in merriment at trying to decipher the minor mystery that had unexpectedly interrupted their congenial conversation. Carson and Ransom's brief period of entertainment was soon negatively affected by a disturbing news flash coming over the police bulletin wire.

"Is this a lousy coincidence or what Inspector?" Detective Ransom dubiously asked his department superior. "A murder victim's body has been found dangling from a railroad trestle on Flemming Pike, Winslow Township, New Jersey and the person had been smashed by an unsuspecting farmer driving a truck along the rural road at fifty-miles an hour and going beneath the isolated overpass. How gruesome and heinous!"

"Especially if the victim was still alive when the wicked impact occurred," Inspector Carson evaluated and suggested. "Could you imagine the intense terror that the dangling human must have experienced?"

"I hope it wasn't that gorgeous Arkansas stripper that's doin' her dancing-routine thing over at the Jersey Aquarius Club!" Tim Ransom awkwardly replied to try and break the room's moment of gloomy depression with an element of levity. "But Ned, I presume that the deceased *person* is a male. Do you suppose that the culprits were the South Philly' Mafia? They have plenty of ties with unscrupulous Jersey junkyard dealers, especially in the Hammonton and Winslow Township areas. And also Inspector, this kind of callous premeditated killing tactic does seem to fit *that* Mafia syndicate profile perfectly! And the poor innocent farmer driving the truck under the train trestle feels really guilty for accidentally crushing the dead guy's anatomy and simultaneously sending *his* tortured soul to the afterlife!"

"Yes, Tim, I lean more towards the South Philly' Mafia being the perpetrators rather than let's say area street gangs like the Crypts and the Bloods or let's say even further, a cell of organized Islamic jihadists too!" Ned Carson concluded.

"But Arab terrorists are now concentrating more on smaller targets because the larger ones are so well protected," Detective Ransom speculated and declared. "That's their radical change in strategy on how they're conducting their clandestine heinous terror acts. Their new philosophy is to create public panic by ruthlessly and brutally killing individual citizens in bizarre ways rather than by sensationally blowing up national monuments, tall skyscrapers and the like."

Karen Stone re-entered the office with another square brown-wrapped package in her hands. "Inspector, I had forgotten to deliver this piece during my last rotation around the offices. It's addressed to both you and Detective Ransom."

The attractive secretary then handed the second sealed music disc to the somewhat startled Police Inspector, who anxiously unraveled the external covering and then hurriedly placed the new homemade object into the D Drive computer tray.

After Karen Stone had departed the office, the men's ears readily discerned the lyrics and accompanying rhythm to the catchy 1940s Glenn Miller Orchestra song 'Chattanooga Choo-Choo.' And to add to their overall astonishment, a female news reporter instantly appeared on the right wall's flat screen television and the young lady began describing an incident that had recently happened a mile south of the Tullytown/Levittown train station platform near Edgely, Bucks County, Pennsylvania. A man's body that had been suspended-by-ropes had been obliterated beyond recognition by a speeding New York to Philadelphia AmTrak train. Additional relevant details concerning the commission of the dastardly and egregious crime were currently unavailable, but it was next announced that the Bucks County Sheriff's Department was feverishly working on the case.

"There's a definite pattern being established here and I think that someone's trying to implicate *us* into this bizarre series of nefarious events!" Inspector Carson theorized and conveyed to his devoted associate. "Tim, I think I'm developing a distinct aversion to popular train songs! I'm never going to take the Jersey Transit train from Philly' to Atlantic City again! Nor for that matter, the always dependable SEPTA High Speed Line transit across the Ben Franklin into Jersey!"

"I know the exact same feeling you're presently experiencing Ned!" the seated grim-faced Detective concurred. "Could *we* be prospective earmarked sitting duck targets on the hit list? I'll run a quick background scan of all possible Mafia figures that either you or I have put behind bars during our distinguished law-enforcement careers," Ransom instinctively indicated. "I dislike mentioning this glaring detail Boss but we're no longer third party investigators searching for or examining evidence and attempting to convict nefarious suspects. Really Ned, I believe that we're now marked men on the targeted victims' list and I think that we're being deliberately harassed and stalked by professional hit men! Here's what's bothering me in a nutshell. The whole thing is like *they're* the dominant cats maliciously toying with and taunting *us* vulnerable mice before arbitrarily deciding to eliminate our puny butts from mortal existence."

* * * * * * * * * * * *

The next several weeks, Ned Carson and Tim Ransom had received five additional homemade CDs from the mysterious anonymous source: 'Midnight Train to Georgia' by Gladys Knight and the Pips, 'Mystery Train' by Elvis Presley, 'Peace Train' by Cat Stevens, 'Love Train' by the O' Jays and 'Freedom Train' by Lenny Kravis, all of which materialized into five corresponding victims dying after being dangled by ropes from respective train trestles and overpasses in Pleasantville, Camden and Burlington County, New Jersey and in Croydon and also near Norristown, Pennsylvania. Inspector Carson and Detective Ransom became even more baffled

134

and apprehensive as each successive horrible incident was being vigorously investigated.

"This sequence of major felony incidents is too sophisticated to be a wave of easy-to-solve atrocities caused by local Crypts and Bloods' gang-related feuding," Inspector Carson insisted. "Most of the train sacrifice victims have been upper middle class suburban whites that apparently seem to have no significant city or regional gang affiliations."

"And the bodies were in far worse shape than being merely dismembered or wickedly decapitated as you've already alluded," Detective Ransom rendered an appendix to his partner's murder-motive theory. "I hate to sound too visceral but the corpses were severely mutilated, no, they were more-than-likely gruesomely pulverized with blood and tissue disgustingly smeared and splashed all over the concrete trestles and overpass column supports. Whoever is behind this heinous skein of sadistic killings must have an evil black heart," the detective ascertained. "What about Arab or Muslim terrorists? Do you see any valid connection there?"

"No, I don't think so at this point," sleuth Ned Carson answered. "It's not their type of M.O. The jihadists want to create terror by dynamiting historic monuments or famous places like Times Square or Yankee Stadium where tens of thousand of innocent people congregate or would spontaneously die. The hateful al Qaeda mindset is bent on causing widespread devastation and each primitive act of terror must always be bigger and grander than the barbaric preceding ones! Remember too Tim," Carson paused and emphasized. "You and I are now intimately connected to this hideous crime surge so it's pretty hard for us to be completely objective about cracking the insidious train trestle and overpass pattern. Either the victim is killed by a truck or bus zipping by under a train bridge, or the still-alive person is suddenly pulverized, as a locomotive zooms under a signal support structure. Could you imagine the psychological damage that the diabolical incidents must have on the unwary train engineers after the poor fellows commit involuntary manslaughter at some cowardly thug's volition?"

"Then, obviously, you certainly don't think that these abominable events are random crimes being committed," Tim Ransom surmised and expressed. "Well Inspector, what about the ruthless Philly' Mafia?" the worried detective rhetorically asked. "I've got the names of ten villains that either you or I or both of us have had incarcerated in the last fifteen years. We have Marco "the Brute" Benedetti, Sal "Knuckles" Panachelli, Oliviero "Monks" Bruno, Giovanni

"Undertaker" Perna, Pasquale "the Equalizer" DePalma, Antonio "Digger" Campanella, Angelo...."

"I know who all the treacherous South Philly' Sicilian punks are!" Inspector Carson angrily yelled as he thrice pounded his right fist upon his metal desk. "The ruthless scumbags even play Robin Hood and secretly sponsor several string bands in the annual Mummers Parade! But Tim, I gotta' confess that we have no concrete clues to adequately pursue. Every music disc that we've received has no fingerprints except for those belonging to postal employees handling the mail," Carson reminded Ransom. "And as far as the post office of origin is concerned, all the CDs were separately mailed with the necessary correct postage stamps from different public mailboxes in seven different locations in three states that comprise the entire Delaware Valley region."

"This whole problem is a dilemma of major magnitude!" Detective Ransom exclaimed as contempt mingled with fear occupied his soul. "What does the top brass say about it, you know, the Chief and the other moronic bureaucrats occupying key positions at the upper echelon?"

"They think that you and I are incompetent imbeciles because we're apparently clueless about where to begin," the flustered and thwarted investigator related. "Square One can't be found! And if you want to know my inner feelings," Ned Carson boomed, "I don't personally savor the notion of being suspended by ropes from a train trestle and then being mangled beyond recognition a mere six months before earning my lucrative retirement pension and corresponding social security benefits that I've worked all my adult working life to amass."

On the following Thursday morning, pert and proper Karen Stone nonchalantly entered the third-floor Round House police office and handed Inspector Carson a half dozen square packages sent from six different New Jersey, Pennsylvania and Delaware suburban post offices. The nervous duo very meticulously began opening the newly arrived suspicious items, being very careful not to contaminate potential evidence with their own fingerprints.

The first two CDs opened and played by Inspector Carson had undeniable tractor-trailer themes with C.W. McCall singing 'Convoy' and the second associated tune featured Dave Dudley's rendition of 'Truck Driving Man.'

An apologetic and embarrassed Karen Stone then re-entered the men's office and guiltily claimed that her memory and sorting skills were becoming diminished. "Here's one more piece of mail that I
136

had somehow overlooked," the prim-looking normally reliable department clerk said to Carson as she handed him another plain-wrapped CD, which after being unraveled turned out to be the Eagles singing 'Take It Easy,' a lively song which also personified the truck driving big-rig theme.

The remaining already-delivered packages that had been later cautiously identified by Detective Ransom had (when played via the desktop computer) an observable change in subject venue switching from eighteen-wheeler semi' rigs to familiar bus themed songs. The first rendition was the classic tune 'Bus Stop' by the Hollies, followed by 'Magic Bus' by the Who, 'Barney's Adventure Bus' kids' song vocalized by a variety of unknown chorus singers and finally, 'Ramblin' Man' vocalized by the Allman Brothers, which much to Carson and Ransom's consternation and chagrin featured the famous lyrics: "I was born in the back seat of a Greyhound Bus, rollin' down Highway 41."

"What do you make of these new CDs?" the Inspector asked his dumbfounded assistant. "You don't suppose that...."

"That the method of death has instantaneously transformed from train, trestle and overpass murders to deaths caused by tractor-trailers and buses!" Detective Ransom sagaciously assumed and concluded. "This would be an extremely fascinating case if you and I weren't directly involved as intended victims! We're dealing with an unscrupulous surreptitious antagonist, that's for sure!"

"As the Eagles often sang in 'Take It Easy': 'Don't let the sound of your own wheels drive you crazy," the about-to-retire crime fighter advised his very upset partner. "Tim, what's that new info' appearing over there on the wall TV screen?"

"Two local tractor-trailers have just exploded killing the drivers in separate accidents fifty miles apart," the now-neurotic detective stammered as he slowly read from his own computer screen atop his own cheap metal frame desk. "The first one was going north in Philly' around the Academy Street Exit on I-95 and the second one was demolished on Route 322, the Black Horse Pike in Mays Landing, New Jersey."

"Two distinct-but-simultaneous incidents about fifty-miles apart from each other!" Carson repeated to his shocked and exasperated underling, desperately attempting to connect a few dots. "True, the South Philly' mob syndicate is involved with the freight drivers' union and perhaps we're looking at a couple of stool pigeon whistle-blowing drivers that possibly knew too much info' about internal union affairs. I think that this coincidence might be a blessing in disguise, the two new tragedies finally leading us in the right direction," the Inspector stated with a glimmer of wishful resolution prevalent in his raspy tone of voice. "I hope that we can soon locate and arrest the dirty skunks responsible for these horrific crimes before you and I become deceased entities listed in alphabetical order on the morning papers' obituary page."

"Hey, Boss, an Eyewitness News team over at Exit 5 on the New Jersey Turnpike is now reporting on the flat screen TV that a bus with forty-three passengers aboard has just exploded and has burst into flames outside Burlington. Initial reports say that there are few if any survivors. It didn't take too long for the media focus to go from tractor-trailers to buses!"

"This is really serious business Tim!" Inspector Carson yelled to his already beleaguered subordinate. "Let's get off our rumpy carcasses and get in touch with the Jersey authorities about the recent bus turnpike calamity and then we'll head on over to Academy Street and I-95 and glean some essential data about the horrendous tractor-trailer inferno. I'll tell you one thing Tim. I refuse to be eliminated from this precious Earth before I'm fully retired and safely living in self-exile somewhere on a remote South Pacific island."

* * * * * * * * * * * *

Early the following Monday morning, Inspector Carson and Detective Ransom were drinking their standard cups of morning coffee and reviewing their slate of responsibilities for the upcoming day's agenda. Carson was peering out the window and nonchalantly viewing a Septa High Speed Line Train rumbling across the Ben Franklin Bridge towards Camden, New Jersey.

Meanwhile, garrulous Tim Ransom was commenting about a suspect line-up scheduled downstairs at ten-thirty and a press conference for "annoying media print and TV reporters" slated for after lunch. But introspective Inspector Ned Carson's mind was in a sullen depressed mood since his department's investigation into the series of trestle, train, tractor-trailer and commercial bus-related homicides had (over the span of the last month) become a veritable exercise in futility.

"Ya' know, Tim," the frustrated Inspector began his brief monologue while still staring out the office window at the Ben Franklin Bridge, "some investigators look for a needle in a haystack while other gumshoes search for a haystack in the eye of a needle. But is this perplexing sequence of despicable events really a series of
138

planned murders?" Carson muttered, showing a degree of repulsion in his tone of voice. "Despite all of my time and effort, I can't even find an ordinary-sized haystack or a single needle with which to base a lousy flimsy hypothesis upon."

"I happen to share your disappointment," Detective Tim Ransom sympathetically remarked. "None of the regular punks that *we'* frequently rely on for ratting aren't opening their mouths. They're all afraid of being knocked-off themselves in this crazy and totally savage murder spree caper. They're all like craven scared-to-death pigs with intimidated mass laryngitis; they just aren't squealing!"

"Have we gotten any sort of DNA evidence back from the local coroner's autopsies?" Ned wanted to know. "Perhaps some new-found scientific data could lead to a breakthrough, a dramatic moment of enlightenment."

"The only DNA traces that had been recovered at the area crime scenes have been samples of the victims' tissues and blood and much to my bafflement, nothing tangible pointing towards any particular suspect has been uncovered," Tim Ransom sadly conveyed. "Say Ned, Hudson over in central homicide canceled-out on the Police Convention in Denver on Thursday because of a nasty bout with bronchitis. And guess what? I've been assigned to take his place so I'll be rooming with you for a few nights in Rocky Mountain country. How's that for an inspirational surprise?"

"Unfortunately, Tim, I won't be able to fly out to Colorado until Thursday morning," Carson indicated, disdainfully twisting his head back and forth to demonstrate his overall disenchantment. "I have plenty to attend to right here at my desk in terms of backlogged paperwork so Good Buddy, I hereby predict that I'll see you at *our* already-booked Denver hotel late Thursday evening."

"Sounds pretty copacetic to me!" the seldom-pessimistic, crime-combating assistant rather pleasantly stated. "Maybe a change in environment will get our minds synchronized and thinking on the same wavelength in regard to this rash of insane homicides happening to innocent dangling train trestle victims, to the lives of random tractor-trailer drivers and to the horror of unsuspecting bus passengers. Karen has made all of the arrangements and I'm flying west at 6:15 a.m. tomorrow morning. But I have to be at the airport at 4:10 in order to be processed through the security cattle line. You'd think Ned that I'd get some sort of privileged airport priority since I'm an honorable veteran police department professional."

"Okay, Tim!" Carson robotically answered while ignoring his partner's general dissatisfaction with airport security measures. "It's all settled. Thanks to reservations obtained by Karen, I'll be checking into our Denver hotel late Thursday night. Be sure to set your watch back two hours. I'll buy you a couple of drinks at the lobby bar, that is, after I unpack, and then we'll rack up delectable late suppers on our individual expense accounts."

* * * * * * * * * * * *

On Thursday morning, Ned Carson was seated at his desk reviewing the *Inquirer's* front-page headlines about the inability of the metropolitan police to put together the myriad pieces of the "reprehensible trestle bridge, tractor-trailer and commercial bus conundrum." The Inspector was sipping his steaming cup of coffee when Karen Stone entered his office and efficiently delivered the morning mail, and much to the recipient's displeasure, six separately wrapped and shipped CD music discs were very evident and distinguishable, all present in the morning post pile.

After energetically ripping off the external brown wrapping paper to the half dozen discs, the thoroughly aggravated police investigator was soon immensely horrified upon listening to the opening bars of the newly obtained six haunting song lyrics.

'Oh, my gracious word!' Carson anxiously thought. 'Tim's in immediate jeopardy, but I can't call the airport because they'll think that I'm crazy inventing a plane crash prediction based on several homemade musical CDs I've just received. The Chief and the bureaucratic brass will want me to undergo a psychiatric examination and I don't wish to endanger any of my pension benefits if some quack shrink declares me being mentally incompetent if no plane disaster had ever transpired over Denver! Hopefully there wasn't any major headwind resistance and Tim's plane has already safely landed!'

Carson seriously pondered his psychological dilemma for a moment and then jotted down the theme-oriented song titles and performing artists connected with the six mentally haunting musical discs. 'Let's see now, there's five that had been addressed to both Tim and me and those five are 'Snoopy and the Red Baron' by the Yuletide Singers, 'Come Fly with Me' by Frank Sinatra, 'Jet Airliner' by the Steve Miller Band, 'Leaving on a Jet Plane' by Peter, Paul and Mary and the last one was 'Volare' by Bobby Rydell.

Finally, the fazed and crazed Inspector jotted-down the title to the one song disc that had specifically been sent to *him*: the 1940s' hit 'Blue Skies' by Bing Crosby.

140

The morning talk show gossip on the side-wall flat screen TV was instantly interrupted with a reporter having a very melancholy expression upon his face, announcing that five fatal jet airplane crashes had occurred simultaneously in various parts of the United States. "The first one being reported happened thirty minutes ago over the Air Force Academy in Colorado Springs. The flight had originated from Philadelphia International Airport and had been scheduled to land in Denver. The second jet crash ironically occurred just north of Boston's Logan International Airport and first responder rescue crews are now on the scene and we'll provide you with additional details as they soon become available. The third mysterious and amazingly coincidental crash has happened in the bay near New York's LaGuardia…"

Being very disturbed and emotionally rattled, Inspector Ned Carson grabbed his remote control and fearfully turned-off the wall flat screen television. Perspiration beads rolled down his forehead, cheeks and back. The affected aged man was on the right side of the law but yet malignant-minded devious underworld adversaries were arbitrarily sentencing him to death. Immediately Carson summoned brunette Ms. Karen Stone to his office to do him a special favor.

"Karen, I'm not feeling too well at the moment!" the appalled police veteran declared. "I think I must be having some serious flu symptoms coming on. Please call the airport and cancel my round-trip plane tickets to and from Denver. And while you're at it," the ashen-faced Inspector paused and stammered, "cancel my Denver hotel reservation too! And tell the Chief I believe I need immediate medical treatment and am driving myself over to Thomas Jefferson University Hospital right now."

"The Evil Force"

I, Colonel Cliff Dawson, am accurately recording this incredible account into my personal electronic journal and not into the official ship's log for reasons that will obviously be self-explanatory later on in this narrative. Captain Jeremy Parker and I have been on a courageous ten-year space mission exploring outer space and methodically charting our landmark discoveries for the International World Coalition. Our well-publicized mission was described in the world's media as "an awesome enterprise" and quite basically, I've always been attracted to the prospect of being one of the first 'daring humans' to find intelligent human-like life thriving elsewhere in the nearby Milky Way Galaxy.

Our lengthy expedition started out from Earth in the year 2534 A.D., and it is now, according to our ship's reliable instrument panel, May 5th of 2542. The Newton III is now ready to lift off and leave the planet that Captain Parker and I have labeled EL-741, which is an *E*arth-*L*ike sphere rotating around a Sun-Like star that my cohort and I have named Mater Seven.

But plenty of exceptionally weird and eerie phenomena have happened since our momentous landing on EL-741 approximately forty-eight hours ago, and thus, my guilty conscience would not allow the Newton III to take off until all of the pertinent details have been precisely documented into my personal diary and not into the ship's authentic log.

Captain Parker and I have been close friends ever since our dual graduations from the American Space Force Academy in Cape Canaveral, Florida in June of 2520. Jeremy happened to be a veritable wizard at understanding and repairing complex matter and anti-matter equipment and my 'space partner' was very adept at proficiently fixing warp drives whereas I am highly regarded back on Earth as being an academic expert at comprehending the intricacies of astrophysics and biochemistry.

Throughout our glorious odyssey trek across this sector of the Milky Way our general relationship on the Einstein III had been both cordial and compatible and my comrade and I satisfactorily shared navigation responsibilities and Captain Jeremy Parker and I had cooperatively alternated slumbering inside the spaceship's one and only Deep Sleep Hibernation Compartment, which over the course of our decade-long expedition efficiently slowed down our mutual biological aging process by five years, thus effectively halfing our breathing and our heartbeats.

Captain Parker and I had quite different motivations in volunteering for this very vital space mission. Jeremy had experienced marital difficulties and was divorced without any children and my co-pilot possessed a zealous spirit for adventure and challenge and also, my ambitious comrade always wanted to become historically famous. Jeremy's core aspirations were always goal-oriented and it would be an understatement for me to suggest that throughout his career Captain Parker possessed both the dream and the drive to achieve his valued objective.

As for myself, I am happily married to the former Carol Anderson and we have two wonderful kids, Tom, now age seventeen and Denise, now age thirteen. I had applied to participate in this historic journey because first and foremost, I consider myself an American Union patriot and quite truthfully, I despise all of the mundane conflict existing back on Earth like war, famine, pestilence, political wrangling, drought, disease and human envy, jealousy, greed and abundant spite too, which I assess to be the fundamental roots of all human evil.

Tending to have an introverted nature, I have always preferred to be a loner and as I now recollect, my personality was never very gregarious and convivial at military social events and at gala receptions. And besides, I had reckoned that *our* significant space voyage would be only five years in duration and not ten because of our body-preservation time spent in suspended animation inside the very essential Bio-Chemical Deceleration Chambers. Indeed, I have greatly missed my family during this extensive space voyage.

Although Jeremy and I have visited, explored and thoroughly documented fifty-three unique planets during our current expedition, more importantly, we have successfully located and ambitiously cataloged three special planets very similar to Earth on our interstellar maps, but the only evidence of life prior to our recent comprehensive investigation into EL-741 had merely been primitive microorganisms, new strains of bacteria and various types of peculiar protozoa. Generally speaking, everything seemed rather normal on our galactic 'Interstellar Study' until we had eventually entered the most remote solar system of the Constellation Pegasus.

Upon approaching Mater Seven and eventually orbiting EL-741, Captain Parker was uncharacteristically excited to report that the Earth-like sphere had an atmosphere very similar to that of our native planet, seventy-five percent nitrogen, twenty-two percent oxygen and
144

three percent hydrogen, along with minute quantities of other rare gases. My eminent co-pilot had always been quite eloquent in expressing himself.

"And Colonel Dawson, there's an excellent ozone screen filtering out traces of ultra-violet and infra-red rays so *that* important condition means that the possibility of plant and animal life existing on EL-741 is dramatically heightened," Captain Parker observed and communicated. "This is pretty thrilling Cliff both in scope and in sequence! A good chance exists that over the eons life has migrated from the planet's rivers and lakes onto land just like it had done back on Earth hundreds of millions of years ago," Captain Parker euphorically articulated to me. "Just imagine what kind of fantastic evolution might have occurred over the ages here on EL-741! Just the contemplation of such an evolutionary miracle is absolutely mind-boggling!" my friend indicated. "This extraordinary planetary encounter might be the first genuine human contact with alien life forms in outer space," Jeremy enthusiastically gushed and giggled. "Neil Armstrong should've been so lucky as *we* are right now! That ancient astronaut's biggest accomplishment as an audacious space pioneer was to set foot on the lifeless crater-pocked Moon. We have a terrific opportunity to become internationally renowned back home on good old Mother Earth!"

"Yes, Jeremy," I passively answered, trying my utmost to contain my emotions from running rampant, "but I recommend that you now carefully study the topography of EL-741's surface. There aren't any oceans or seas as far as I can determine; just evidence of various irregular coastlines forming one enormous circular-shaped continent, if you like."

"But look, Colonel!" Captain Parker ecstatically yelled to justify his total fascination. "There's an abundance of beautiful rivers and lakes on that one vast global continent that you've just so aptly described. And there're bountiful forests and trees and vegetation and deserts and mountains too, all fairly similar to those features existing on Earth!" my close friend anxiously vociferated. "The entire planet reminds me of depictions I've read of the American west before the invasion of the Conestoga wagons that traversed through Colorado, Utah and sunny California."

"Well, Jeremy, it's always better to be safe than being either sorry or dead!" I objectively and rationally replied. "I'm not setting foot upon the surface down there until we perform a complete and comprehensive atmospheric analysis and finish a general land elements' probe. But Captain, I must admit that the present daylight

145

surface temperature of seventy-five degrees and polar readings of twenty below zero are indeed favorable and possibly conducive to supporting advanced life forms."

"Okay, Dr. Caution!" Parker promptly jested. "Let's look before we leap. *That* expression ought to be our new motto!"

"It would be nice if we could investigate without having to don our cumbersome space suits," I casually noted, trying to impress my colleague with my calm self-discipline. "But after landing, let's be patient and wait a few hours before we initiate our examination of the physical elements of EL-741. Who knows? We might be able to add a few more chemical items to the standard Periodic Table and become scientifically famous in addition to historically famous!"

Most of the minerals that we had identified on EL-741 were similar to those prevalent on Earth and on other foreign planets that we had recently explored and surveyed: iron, phosphorus, potassium, sulfur, sodium, aluminum, potash, quartz, silicon and gold were in good supply. More remarkably though, certain chemical compounds were commonly detectable in the form of carbon dioxide, sodium chloride along with measurable sugar molecules.

The evidence of carbon dioxide strongly suggested to us that plant life could exist and thrive, and *that* fortuitous factor could consequently support natural food growth through photosynthesis, specifically provided by radiant orange-glowing Mater Seven, which incidentally happened to be a very favorable hundred and twenty million miles away. That intriguing coincidence of satisfactory conditions promoting the possibility of EL-741 surface life represented a distinct and encouraging prospect, and both Captain Parker and I were highly motivated to commence our essential quest, searching for indigenous plant and animal life.

Twenty-four hours after landing on EL-741 (which incidentally rotated on its axis every twenty-six Earth hours), and after determining that the planet's atmosphere was indeed conducive to breathing and walking without the use of space suits and the need for any artificial aid apparatus, Captain Parker and I next intrepidly exited the Newton III's air lock chamber and then bravely stepped down the access ramp, eventually audaciously setting foot onto what later was defined as the "Planet of Evil Force."

* * * * * * * * * * * *

I am not a particularly religious man but I have always viewed my conscience's value system as being one founded on strong moral
146

convictions and upon discreet ethical principles. Throughout my adult life I've generally assessed organized formal religion as being something analogous to superstitious and primitive prehistoric thinking, that is, until I had made certain incidental interactions with the mysterious "Evil Force" that I soon learned dominates EL-741. Now as the Almighty is my witness, I am convinced that some diabolical omnipotent power pervades and controls this God-forsaken planet that Captain Parker and myself had randomly-but-intentionally encroached upon.

Please allow me to articulate the astute recounting of my experiences, all of which I maintain will adequately justify and defend my seemingly implausible and fictitious testimony, for I now believe that any goodness that exists in the Infinite Universe is conversely counterbalanced with a diametrically opposed Evil Equivalent, a contemptible Evil Equivalent that has wretchedly pushed my mind to the threshold of insanity. I shall now be more specific in my elaboration.

After intensively analyzing the remarkable planet's atmosphere and thereby determining that the air was consistently safe enough to breathe, Captain Parker and I boldly exited the Newton III and steadfastly ambled out into what appeared to be a pristine New England environment abounding with late springtime forest deciduous and pine trees, the overall physical landscape exhibiting assorted strange-looking green leaves, branches, pinecones and accompanying needles.

About a half-mile distant from the Newton III we soon encountered a swift-running brook and the two of us followed its rocky meandering path until we eventually arrived at a gorgeous grove comprised of what appeared to be wild peach and apple trees interspersed with random bushes laden with red berries that seemed to be a combination of a raspberry and a blackberry, that is, in their physical three-dimensional appearance.

"This is what I truly love about EL-741," Captain Parker opined and declared. "It's pristine and astronomically remote and now there's definite evidence of delicious-looking luscious fruit growing here. Perhaps there're some human-like inhabitants residing nearby in this desolate vicinity too! Colonel Dawson, I don't want to sound too optimistic but right this minute *this* observation could be the all-too-elusive cosmic missing link that we've been desperately searching for, the crucial connection that decisively proves once and for all that Homo sapiens are not the only cerebral creatures populating our enormous galaxy."

"Jeremy, I want to do a complete property molecular inspection of this alluring fruit before we ever attempt devouring it," I suspiciously answered my best friend. "Ah yes!" I exclaimed as I gazed at the gauge reading being registered on my advanced bio-chemical spectrometer compound-measuring mechanism. "Elements of fructose, glucose, chlorophyll and carbon-related compounds are quite prevalent inside the odd-shaped lavender peach and also inside the purple apple and inside the distorted-looking red and black berries too. I confidently deduct that they're all devoid of harmful toxins or poisons and I'm convinced that the fruit is edible and nutritious as well as being digestive tract friendly."

"This is truly wonderful because I'm sick of all the monotonous processed food meals, artificially flavored juices and all of the tasteless energy tablets we've been swallowing-down for breakfast, lunch and supper," my dependable space associate eagerly stated. "I just can't resist the temptation any longer. With your permission, I desire sampling the berries and the apple facsimile right away. But honestly, I've never liked the taste of peaches ever since I was a youngster, thinking the fuzzy produce to be too sweet for my sophisticated palate. I think I'll pass on eating the peach."

"Okay, Jeremy," I amenably acknowledged. "I'm going to try the lavender peach and the purple apple while your fussy taste buds can enjoy the apple and the red berries. According to the spectrometer's readings," I observed and plainly stated to my companion, "the three kinds of fruit growing here in this valley almost seem to be of chain store quality."

The edible fresh fruit we consumed was positively mouth-watering and I made a mental note of the grove's location and considered it 'a must responsibility' that I should visit the wonderful wild fruit orchard again simply to satisfy my voracious appetite. After simultaneously synchronizing *our* solar-powered watches, Jeremy and I decided to separate and explore north and south respectively and we agreed that we would rendezvous at the aforementioned orchard in an Earth hour. Hence I wandered south while my conscientious partner conducted his separate exploration north along the brook.

After trekking for twenty minutes, my wandering arrived me at a double ridge that was divided by a deep valley. Realizing that my forward progress was impossible, I stubbornly trudged my way back to the vicinity of the exotic peach and apple tree grove.

'I know what I'll do,' I deviously imagined. 'I'll proceed north and meet-up with Jeremy' as he's returning south along the fast-flowing stream. My adventurous co-pilot will be surprised to see me prematurely trespassing on *his* turf!'

As I exited a nondescript patch of pine trees, I noticed my friend stooping down and collecting what appeared to be some sparkling gold nuggets from the brook's bank. 'I'll see if Jeremy is honest enough to tell me about his treasure trove find,' I wisely thought. 'It'll be like a little character test! Surely the gold bonanza will have no special value to either of us until we return back to Earth. Precious metals and paper money are absolutely meaningless commodities up here on EL-741.'

After filling his deep white collection sack with the precious mineral, Jeremy oddly headed west along a dirt trail and then paced through a small-woods and much to my astonishment and bewilderment, he entered a house that was an exact facsimile to mine back in Vero Beach, Florida, inadvertently or deliberately leaving the stucco rancher's front door open.

My palpitating heart became filled with anxiety and curiosity. I surreptitiously ascended the three brick steps and next distrustfully ducked-down on the front porch. Not detecting Jeremy's presence inside, I stealthily entered the foyer, turned right past the living room and then nervously hesitated before entering the master bedroom. Furtively sticking my head through the portal, my disbelieving eyes caught a glimpse of Captain Parker making love to my formerly faithful wife Carol.

'How could this possibly be reality?' I skeptically speculated. 'It must be some perverted illusion or inexplicable hallucination, or perhaps some ugly mental manifestation! Anger is raging inside me! Could the same repulsive scenario have happened in the past on Earth without my knowledge?'

My mind was incensed. I furiously left the area of the familiar-looking house and headed directly for the peach and apple orchard. An innocent-looking Captain Parker showed-up fifteen minutes later than the designated grove rendezvous time, and Jeremy had the unmitigated audacity to offer the lame excuse that his attention had been diverted when he had perceived a giant human-sized frog catching a huge flying insect with its sticky tongue.

I pretended to accept his exaggerated tale as being truthful, but on our long hike back to the Newton III, not once did my avaricious and baneful colleague mention to me either the white linen collection sack full of gold nuggets or his sinful adulterous love affair with Carol.

'Ever since our academic days ay the Space Academy, my rival
Jeremy's always been exceedingly jealous and especially envious of
my numerous accomplishments and awards,' I selfishly conjectured
in defense of my faltering ego. 'He's without a doubt greedy,
arrogant and spiteful and will do anything malicious to pilfer my
pride and ruin my good public reputation! My moral standards have
been impugned by that conscience-less maniac!' I lividly concluded.
'Captain Parker is going to pay dearly for violating my wife's
fidelity to me and he'll suffer dire consequences for not
demonstrating military honesty and integrity in regard to his recent
gold discovery! I swear I'll get my just revenge on that unscrupulous
traitor and marriage-wrecker! I've never loathed anyone as much as I
now wholly abhor detestable Captain Jeremy Walter Parker right this
very minute!'

* * * * * * * * * * * *

My disheveled mind had difficulty fathoming how my
transplanted Vero Beach home and how my cheating wife happened
to realistically appear on Planet EL-741, which logically was over
ten light years away from Earth in the constellation Pegasus and
furthermore, where were the remainder of the homes in my Florida
neighborhood?

On our arduous amble back to the Newton III, Captain Parker
and I exchanged few words but midway during our three-mile
ramble, I did remove from my jacket's pocket and then munch on a
lavender peach that I had previously pulled from the strange-looking
orchard tree. The entire way back to our spacecraft I felt both
resentment and hatred toward my betraying co-pilot.

That evening, after exiting the ship's shower compartment and
then drying my body off with a soft towel, I dressed into clean
clothes and silently stepped into *our* sleeping quarters. Intense
acrimony filled my spirit when my alert eyes detected Captain Parker
assiduously searching through my wallet and at that point in time, I
instinctively suspected that the sneaky thief was brazenly attempting
to pilfer my identity.

Never before had I ever felt such antagonism towards another
human being. Feeling grievously violated and deceived, I quietly
retreated to the galley's pantry to sit at the table and drink down a
cup of ice-cold water, but all the while my offended mind was
strategically contemplating my next move.

150

'Why is Parker rummaging through my personal belongings?' I asked my confused self. 'I know! He's jealous of me, desires to steal my wife and probably also covets my expensive vacation hacienda in Andalusia, Spain! But money and gold have no particular value out here on this desolate end of the celestial zodiac! Property and wealth are irrelevant here on EL-741 too! According to the astronaut's manual,' I continued thinking and evaluating, 'with the exception of military rank during an emergency, all basic relationships between Parker and me away from Earth are supposed to be egalitarian in nature! Now everything's changed for the worse!'

My poisoned mind actually believed that I possessed the uncanny capacity to fully perceive every aspect of Parker's sinister intent. 'The greedy scoundrel envies my rank, despises my ability, resents my integrity, loathes my fame and curses my success,' I irrationally concluded. 'He's now my one and only adversary who is wickedly planning to either harm or kill me! That's why I must plot to destroy the demonic wretch first!'

My ears heard Captain Parker's shoes casually shuffling into the ship's library and then five minutes later they discerned 'my nemesis' striding into our sleeping quarters' chamber. 'Parker must be eliminated because I fear he's secretly preparing to execute me in cold blood! I'll wait here in the craft's library for a half hour pretending to be chewing on a snack and then when he's later slumbering in his bunk,' I cunningly contemplated, 'I'll swiftly perform my wicked deed!' I deviously schemed and determined.

An hour later, I rose from my soft chair and very quietly walked to our small bedroom. 'Forget about implementing the paralyzing stun mode!' I shrewdly decided. 'My avowed enemy must be instantaneously eradicated from mortal existence! Parker's soul is defective and the villain must be eliminated!'

I slowly and meticulously removed my trusty ray gun from my waist holster and while Captain Parker was soundly sleeping under the blanket inside his lower bunk, I mercilessly pulled the trigger and zapped him with the weapon's potent laser beam.

The following dawn, I dragged Parker's limp lifeless body into the heavy equipment room and next awkwardly lifted his heavy corpse into the 'All Purpose Digger's' passenger seat. After pressing a button on the sidewall control panel, thus opening the ship's exit portal, I started the machine's engine and then fanatically drove the versatile vehicle down the Newton III's back ramp.

Not far from the now familiar peach and apple grove, I used the machine to dig a six-foot-deep hole, deposited my vanquished foe's remains into the hollow and then skillfully manipulating the device's levers, I competently covered the makeshift grave with ample dirt. Before departing the vicinity, and exhibiting no sign of remorse, I hopped off the All-Purpose-Digger and forcefully plucked a ripe lavender peach from the nearest fruit tree. Appeasing my sudden hunger, I ravenously ate the juicy fruit.

On my short excursion back to the Newton III, I was confronted with several inexplicable threatening situations. First a ferocious lion-like creature crossed my path but I managed to adroitly maneuver my All-Purpose Digger and scare the awesome fierce beast away with several laser volleys from my handy ray gun.

I next encountered a giant hungry anaconda-like snake and honoring my need for self-preservation, I deftly escaped its imminent danger by adroitly speeding away in my swift reliable contraption. But then a seven-foot-tall squirrel accompanied by a ten-foot-high rat accosted me, and in a flash, I shot at and chased away both apparent existential threats during the height of the emergency.

Soon, a bizarre idea registered inside my addled brain. 'Parker said that he had witnessed a huge frog eating a very large insect,' I neurotically recalled. 'Perhaps he wasn't lying or hallucinating after all! Or maybe he was simply fabricating a tall tale to conceal his guilt for having an adulterous affair with Carol? There must be some lucid logical explanation to account for all of these abnormal crazy things that are occurring on this hellish planet! What is causing these very disturbing evil aberrations to happen?'

When I eventually returned the vehicle to the Newton III, I raised the segmented entrance ramp and next systematically closed and locked all exit portals. I was happy to note that the ship was still there at the landing site and that it had not somehow been stolen or damaged, but when I curiously looked inside Captain Parker's white linen collection sack, it was totally empty and much to my amazement, no glittering gold nuggets were hidden inside.

* * * * * * * * * * * *

As I impatiently sit here in the Commander's Chair ready to take off from EL-741 inside always reliable Newton III, I am pensively reflecting on what exactly had provoked me to act like a savage felon and callously and maliciously murder Captain Jeremy Parker.

My co-pilot had eaten the apple and the red berries and I had consumed the apple and three peaches and had avoided sampling the berries. These relevant factors should be germane for me to better comprehend the true moral dimension of the Evil Force that capriciously governs the myriad strange events transpiring here on EL-741.'Possibly the purple apples eaten by Jeremy and me had caused *us* to independently hallucinate or imagine certain surreal fantasies,' I conjectured.

'Either the purple apple or the lavender peaches caused me to see certain illusions and delusions,' I keenly realized and hypothesized. 'The peaches were more of a hallucinogenic drug than were the purple apples and the red berries. And Parker had tasted the purple apple and the red berries while I had eaten one apple and three peaches. Therefore,' I pondered, 'I had imagined that the incidents I had witnessed involving Jeremy and the gold nuggets at the stream, his affair with Carol along with his scrutiny of my wallet in our ship's bed chamber all were illusions generated as a result of the effect of the combination peaches and apples I had digested. Parker only ate the single apple and a few berries, so *that* action caused him to envision *one* mammoth frog feasting on an oversized bug.'

I next theorized that a chemical synthesis of the ingredients that constituted the peaches and the apple had influenced me to behave like an evil person temporarily possessing a criminal mindset. Somehow the accidental chemical compound mixture in my body had a similar effect to that of the Lotus Plants in Odysseus's extraordinary adventure in the Land of the Lotus Eaters where *his* recalcitrant crew ate of the potent flowers and soon refused to obey their king's incessant commands to leave the idyllic paradise. Because of *this* noteworthy analogy between my zany adventure on this evil planet and the weird Lotus Flower episode described in Homer's *Odyssey*, I have decided to rename EL-741 'Lotus 1.'

'Those golden nuggets, along with the deceitful love affair and also the oversized lion, the immense squirrel and the huge snake were all distracting illusions that my fertile mind had projected into my physical surroundings,' I considered. 'This postulation of mine must be true because the Evil Force on this planet does not know that a lion is many times the size of a squirrel and that a frog is not the same size as a human being. That formerly perverted scenario that I had imagined all makes perfect sense now,' I finally comprehended. 'But the stark reality is that I have murdered Jeremy and now my conscience deeply regrets my grotesque and misguided misdeed. His death was no mental manifestation! It was truly real! I am now a bona fide wanton criminal all because I could not readily distinguish Lotus I fantasy from Lotus I reality.'

After I had started the atomic thrust engines and lifted off the remarkable planet's surface, according to my ship's compass and gyroscope, my course was heading due west. My sensitive pupils then observed a squadron of UFOs flying and then hovering over a gleaming city having enormous skyscrapers and spectacular obelisks along with stunning round and pyramid-shaped majestic edifices. Also quite conspicuous were a plethora of lustrous mass transportation tubes connecting the various outstanding vertical glistening structures.

'My scanners have determined and verified that those distant objects do not in reality exist!' I perceptively realized. 'The vivid visions are only products of my active subconscious imagination being diabolically projected into that distant fantasy environment, all somehow caused (I believe) by the tempting fruit, or fruit combinations that I had eaten on Captain Parker's EL-741. Naturally I'll have to mimic what most dishonest businessmen do when they keep two sets of books: one for the government agents' scrutiny and the other documentation exclusively for themselves. There's no way that this visual rendition that I'm presently observing is going to be entered into the ship's official log. In my own defense, the aberrant and outlandish story of the Evil Force that exists on 'Planet Lotus I' will forever remain a closely guarded secret solely preserved in my personal journal.

As the mythical Satan is my witness, according to *this* Devil's Advocate, Captain Jeremy Parker had died from a lethal unknown virus on Planet Lotus I and out of traditional human sympathy and my' sense of duty, I had respectfully buried his remains somewhere on the alien planet.

"Rapid Crystals"

Harry DeLareto sat erect upon his black leather swivel chair behind his desk in his walnut-paneled Elwood, New Jersey insurance office. The broker was preoccupied making a ten percent depreciation adjustment to the 'inflated claim' submitted by the Nesco Volunteer Fire Department that had recently and ironically burned to the ground in a raging inferno.

On Harry's desk were random additional claims from Mrs. Rhonda Leonetti of Atsion, who had just been involved in an automobile accident, Arthur Noto of Hamilton Township, who had recently collided his motorboat with a Mullica River marina dock and another one from Jennifer Friel, a Sweetwater resident who had experienced severe flooding into her house when the normally tranquil Mullica River had overflowed its banks during a torrential three-day downpour. As DeLareto was fumbling through the assorted bureaucratic paperwork that was frustrating his mental health, the gentleman's very capable secretary Nancy Davenport suddenly buzzed his desk from the adjoining room.

"Harry, Mr. And Mrs. David DeLaurentis had to cancel this afternoon's appointment because their son Alfred has crashed his motorbike into a barn on a blueberry farmer's property over in Hammonton, and they're now at AtlantiCare Hospital in Pomona. The boy's all right but that'll definitely be another injury insurance claim appearing on your desk within the next few weeks," Mrs. Davenport advised her employer. "If you have no objections, I've already conveniently rescheduled them for next Friday at 2 p.m. The afternoon time slot happened to be available on your calendar's weekly planner."

"That's fine with me Nancy as long as there aren't any time conflicts," Harry replied into his desk speaker. "But right now I'm overwhelmed with a deluge of claims we're having so I've decided to take the rest of the afternoon off since as you've just mentioned, the DeLaurentis appointment has been postponed. My wife misses her old police and rescue scanner that she had kept for years on *her* kitchen counter, and she has discovered it laying in our cellar storage area during her annual spring housecleaning."

"Yes, Sylvia's a fanatic when it comes to certain things. Does the device still work?" the friendly secretary curiously asked. "My husband and I listen to ours all the time. We get to know what's happening all over Mullica Township and vicinity and it keeps us informed about burglaries and house fires."

"Yes, but if I recollect, only two of the eight crystals in our set are still functional," Mrs. Davenport's encumbered boss related. "In fact, I have the scanner in the trunk of my car so I think I'll take a drive over to the Berlin Farmers Market. There's an electronics' store just inside the main entrance that might just have updated replacement crystals for the eight channels on the scanner. It's worth a shot in the dark, anyway!"

"Okay, Harry. It sure beats hanging-out at that raucous Pic-A-Lilli Inn over in the pine-barrens on Route 206! I'll lock-up the office at five for you," the faithful and trustworthy secretary assured her appreciative employer. "Good luck on making your important crystal acquisitions. The new digital scanners cost around two-hundred-bucks; at least that's what mine did!"

Harry drove the twenty-miles west from his rustic Elwood insurance office to the bustling Berlin Farmers Market in less than a half-hour. Ten-minutes later, the man-on-a-mission was engaged in a congenial conversation with Mr. Phil Curreri, the affable proprietor of Modern Digital Communications.

"What have you got here?" the storeowner wanted to know as Curreri carefully examined the ancient electronic scanner handed to him by Harry. "This relic looks like it belongs in either the Smithsonian Institute or inside the Ford Museum. Pardon my amusement, but I haven't seen one of these rare babies since the 1970s. It's an Allied Patrolman Pro-7 VHF Scanner Receiver that you've brought here. Ya' know," the chatty merchant prattled, "these types of volume and squelch dials have been obsolete for a couple of decades. Everything today from cell phones, to Blackberry handheld computer devices, to standard police scanners happens to be digital! Was this machine given to you by the stars on *Bonanza?*"

"Well, Sir, I hope I'm not wasting your valuable time," Harry politely answered after clearing his voice-box out of sheer embarrassment. "Six of the crystals don't work at all, and I'd like to replace all eight of them. Do you have any suitable crystals in stock you can sell me?"

"Where do you live?" Phil Curreri questioned his prospective customer. "I might be able to assist you."

"In Elwood, over in Atlantic County between Hammonton and Egg Harbor City," DeLareto informed the very accommodating store proprietor. "If possible, I'd like to get the essential fire department and rescue squad transmissions that are geared to my residential
156

zone. My wife's very fond of this particular relic, and confidentially, she would like to see it working again. I always try to keep the Mrs. happy, ya' know."

"I'll see what I can do for you," the businessman assured his potential patron. "Just browse around the shop while I perform some basic inventory research."

Harry casually sauntered around the fairly attractive store, nonchalantly looking at various cell phones, cameras, and obsolete electronics' merchandise exhibited inside old glass display showcases. Five minutes later, Mr. Phil Curreri exited his cluttered stockroom with eight shiny crystals held in his right palm, which the merchant testified would definitely work in the antiquated scanner that Harry had brought into *his* unique electronics' establishment.

"Let's see now; we have one for the Hammonton Fire Department and Rescue Squad; one for Egg Harbor City; one for Mays Landing, and one for the Folsom State Police Barracks," Mr. Curreri positively articulated. "And here's one for the Hammonton Police; one for Mullica Township Police, and one for the Egg Harbor Police Department. Now, to fill out the entire eight slot channels, here's one crystal that's not been labeled. It might be for the Atlantic City Police, or maybe perhaps it's tuned-in to the Camden cops. I really can't clearly identify the item, but not to sound too cynical or sarcastic," the store owner awkwardly continued his explanation, "it'll give you another workable channel to listen to when things get too drab and monotonous in your rather dull existence living life over there in Metropolitan Downtown Elwood!"

The impressed and optimistic customer insisted that the eight already described crystals be inserted into the unit to ascertain that the archaic scanner was indeed operational. Upon hearing the Hammonton and Egg Harbor City dispatchers' voices and their associated instructions being conveyed to fire personnel and municipal police patrols, Harry was elated and satisfied with the very evident successful results. In fact, it was fairly difficult for the fellow to control his gushing euphoria.

"How much for the eight crystals?" the customer anxiously inquired. "Please give me a good decent price so that I don't have to negotiate, haggle, or dicker."

"What about fifty-dollars for all eight, which would also include my three-minute crystal installation fee?" the proprietor offered. "That modest price would include the state sales tax, of course!"

"It's a deal!" the insurance broker readily and enthusiastically agreed, extending his right arm for a firm handshake. "You've saved

157

me a ton-load of grief this dreary Friday afternoon! If my wife Sylvia's happy, then naturally, *that* pleasant scenario makes me perfectly contented, too!"

On the Route 30 drive from Berlin east to Elwood, Harry cheerfully listened to the song 'Da Doo Ron Ron' by the Crystals on a popular Philadelphia FM oldies radio station. The tune's stimulating upbeat rhythm put the driver into a most favorable mood, and Harry DeLareto imaginatively interpreted the cute coincidence of the female recording group's name and of his recent Modern Digital Communications purchase to be a very good and propitious omen.

* * * * * * * * * * * * *

Sylvia was thrilled that Harry had gotten the eight replacement crystals for the police scanner, and her husband excitedly plugged in the device, which worked like new that Friday evening. Saturday the couple spent the late morning visiting their son Jake, a scholarly freshman at *Rutgers University,* New Brunswick, and the close-knit family enjoyed the afternoon and a late dinner at a crowded Charlie Brown Restaurant

The DeLaretos didn't arrive back home to Elwood until eleven that night, so Harry and Sylvia, suffering from mild exhaustion, didn't turn on their refurbished scanning device, electing to retire to bed and spending a half-hour watching the eleven o'clock news before shutting-off the tabletop television and going to sleep.

The couple spent Sunday morning attending church services in Hammonton, and then having breakfast at Mary's Restaurant, which was situated directly across the highway from *their* parish, St. Anthony of Padua Catholic Church on Route 206. The afternoon hours had Harry and Sylvia strolling the newly renovated Hamilton Mall, where on impulse, the wife purchased a dress and an umbrella; and then later Sunday evening, the pair partook of some adult entertainment by gambling at the blackjack tables and playing the nickel slot machines at Harrah's Casino in Atlantic City, where the frugal DeLaretos had booked a complimentary room the week before, and then stayed at the popular gaming resort overnight.

When Harry returned home from his insurance office late Monday afternoon, Sylvia had a strange look of consternation upon her face. Showing genuine concern, the sensitive husband first consoled his wife with an embrace and then was very diplomatic in his verbal approach and subsequent inquiry.

158

"What's wrong, Honey?" DeLareto sympathetically asked. "Are you upset that we lost a couple hundred bucks at the casino last night? Please don't worry about that trifle! It wasn't any tremendous loss to be concerned about!"

"No, Harry," Sylvia nervously returned. "It's the police scanner that's gotten me all upset. The first seven channels work really well, and I heard all about a minor traffic accident on Route 30 in Hammonton; several ambulance emergency calls, and four police patrol transmissions in Hamilton Township, along with a false fire alarm that had been reported over on Philadelphia Avenue in Egg Harbor."

"Well, I imagine that the voice jargon is still basically the same as in the past," the husband supportively comforted in a bland-sounding voice. "Stuff like where's your twenty means 'give me your location', and 'ten-four' probably still means something akin to 'okay, over.' What's so darn unique and special about Crystal Number Eight? That mysterious one happens to be an extra bonus that the guy at the electronics store had added in to close the deal."

"Harry, I was listening to the scanner around noon and on Channel Number Eight two men were wildly arguing," the very concerned wife related. "The first speaker was loudly accusing the second guy about making amorous advances towards *his* wife, and he threatened to injure the second fellow if he ever tried flirting with her again. It was like a melodramatic afternoon TV soap opera scene, and I felt as if I had been guiltily eavesdropping on a private conversation."

"Let's see if something similar happens tonight on Channel Eight," Harry constructively suggested. "I'm pretty intrigued myself now, too. Your story has really piqued my curiosity. If your description is correct, my theory is that Channel Eight somehow picks up random cell phone conversations, and then makes them public and accessible to our refitted police scanner. We'll wait and see what happens with the refurbished scanner tonight."

Around seven that evening, enigmatic Channel Eight transmitted a rather vociferous cell phone exchange between a boisterous man and an infuriated woman. The incensed female accused the self-indulgent man of philandering and not paying his numerous debts, and the livid husband acknowledged that he was in the process of filing for bankruptcy, while the wife was intermittently screaming that she would soon be filing for permanent divorce. It was a very tempestuous and heated conversation that eventually made Harry raise his eyebrows and compelled Sylvia to cover her offended ears.

"Do you see what I mean about that oddball scanner?" the concerned wife emotionally stated. "That weird Eighth Crystal must be removed and destroyed. It's sort of like an unauthorized wiretap that's randomly intercepting personal conversations that are not intended for public audience."

"Sylvia, I recognized the man's voice in that nasty dialogue we just heard," the husband almost apologetically revealed. "It belonged to Mr. Peterson, a struggling merchant who owns a hardware store over in Mays Landing. I had just purchased several gallons of exterior house paint from his place of business last week. Apparently, his marital life is on the skids," Harry surmised and stated to his still-shocked wife. "I know from local barber shop gossip that Peterson spends a lot of time gambling at boardwalk casinos and at Monmouth Race Track, and that both he and his wife are chronic alcoholics. One glaring truth in this matter cannot be denied," the husband continued his gossip revelation. "Things are not always quite as cheerful as they appear on the surface when it comes to certain marriage relationships."

"I still don't like Crystal Number Eight, and I recommend that you remove it right away," the wife adamantly insisted. "Call it woman's intuition if you'd like, but I have a serious aversion about *that* unethical receptor. It's a definite intruder into other people's lives. It's almost evil!"

"I promise that I'll take the Eighth Crystal out of the police scanner tomorrow morning," Harry pledged, raising his right hand as if taking a solemn oath in a courtroom. "Now, just remain calm and patient. Let's see if any other interesting discussions will occur. You gotta' admit, Honey. Channel Eight is comparable to being a local gossip page gazette!"

Twenty-minutes later, Channel Eight picked-up a frantic cell phone dialogue, whereby a distraught high school girl informed her stunned boyfriend that she had become pregnant and that she wanted him to immediately pay for an abortion. Wanting to keep the new-found knowledge confidential, the suddenly distressed boyfriend agreed to the crying girl's impetuous proposal and stated that he would pay for half of the clinical procedure, as long as their parents never learned about their mutually unsavory situation.

"That scanner device is positively abominable!" Sylvia yelled at her now-fascinated spouse. "We should not be privy to such disturbing private matters, even if the upset girl had been consoled. Who knows what that wicked scanner is going to divulge to us next? A murder plot?"

160

"I recognized that girl's voice we had just heard. It belongs to Gene and Phyllis Riley's daughter over in Devonshire," Harry reluctantly declared. "The girl's name is Carolyn, and she was involved in a small fender-bender over on the White Horse Pike in Hammonton just last month. Her parents had her sitting in my office last week to review the settlement of the insurance claim on her mother's compact car."

"But having an abortion without their parents' knowledge or consent is far different than having a trivial Route 30 auto' mishap," the shaken wife countered. "Harry, that Channel Eight frequency is borderline Satanic! I demand that you dispose of it right this second! It can only bring more harm than good!"

"First thing tomorrow morning," the husband conceded and responded, shrugging his broad shoulders. "Here's my opinion on the matter, Sylvia. If I listen to the scanner all night, I believe I'll have accumulated enough juicy material to be able to author a decent best-selling novel."

A half-hour later, the re-activated police scanner conveyed a very private verbal exchange involving a local man and woman planning a secret extra-marital love rendezvous at the Hammonton Motor Lodge. Sylvia instantly recognized that one of the voices belonged to her close friend Dorothy Bronson of Vine Street in downtown Hammonton, and from evaluating the extremely intimate dialogue, it was easily determined that the male voice belonged to a prominent minister who was the pastor of a familiar church with a large congregation on Bellevue Avenue, in the same community.

"Yes, you're absolutely right, Sylvia," Harry confirmed. "Your friend Dottie has a splendid alto singing voice, and she's the soloist in *that* church choir. And that obnoxious, sanctimonious preacher is a totally hypocritical fraud! What ever happened to moral authority where the devout minister piously leads his flock by setting a fine example?" DeLareto rhetorically asked. "You must admit that this disgusting reverend's immoral behavior is horribly irreverent! He's guilty of being a devious creep! And your friend, Dottie," Harry concluded and alleged, "well, she's nothing more than a modern-day Jezebel; a cheap harlot!"

"Harry, I insist that you either unplug the police scanner and put it back in the cellar, or remove the Channel Eight Crystal and toss it into the garbage container underneath the kitchen sink," the mentally disheveled wife hollered, almost sobbing. "Don't you understand? We're immorally hearing personal, confidential, private information from people that we happen to know, and it's not intended for our ears."

The next Channel Eight transmission captured two female teachers that were employed at a nearby public high school. Unaware of any eavesdropping, the pair was discussing their steamy bisexual love relationship separate and apart from their husbands' knowledge. The voices belonged to Shirley Burgess and Darla Swift, former senior year classroom teachers of Jake DeLareto.

"This entire complicated mess is wholly deplorable!" normally serene and passive Sylvia bellowed as the wife slowly wept. "Harry, this baneful scanner is an instrument of the Devil. It can only bring malicious disgrace for others, and also, detrimental problems into *our* lives now that we're learning all of these terrible personal secrets. I strongly urge you now; take the scanner into the garage and crush it with your sledgehammer!"

"Who would ever suspect that those two reputable high school instructors were practicing bisexuals having a sultry lesbian extra-marital love affair?" Harry replied with his left hand vigorously scratching his head in disbelief. "I mean, Dear. In my mind, a person is either a homosexual or they're straight! There's none of this lousy in between stuff going on!"

"And I always thought that Mrs. Burgess and Mrs. Swift were excellent classroom teachers, each possessing outstanding character!" the wife added before wiping her eyes with a handkerchief. "They've both gotten Teacher of the Year awards. I've seen their photos' last June in the Press of Atlantic City, and also in the two local newspapers."

"And Mrs. Burgess is married to a no-nonsense police chief rumored to have a terrible jealous and spiteful disposition!" DeLareto commented to his already-appalled and rattled wife. "Yes, Honey. If the Chief ever found-out about his wife's odd and morally unacceptable infidelity, knowing his personality, he'd do something drastic about the scandal! That guy has a notorious volatile temper when his brain goes off the deep end!"

"Please, Harry! I beg you! Throw out that despicable Crystal Number Eight before it causes serious trouble! I think it's more dangerous than the proverbial Tree of Knowledge that's described in the Book of Genesis. I don't like making innuendoes or hurtful accusations! But I don't want us having any outside conflict, by either you or me accidentally slandering anyone's name!"

"Sylvia, I just want to hear and savor one more cell phone transmission!" Harry implored his mate. "Then, I pledge that I'll remove the diabolical Eighth Crystal, and get rid of its tempting functionality once and for all. But just to be on the safe side of truth," the husband stipulated, "I'm going to tape record the final cell phone transmission, and immediately erase it if it's simply a mediocre, frivolous, personal conversation!"

At nine-fifteen, the police scanner's Crystal Eight intercepted an extraordinary cell phone dialogue, which Harry instantly recorded on tape. The unique oral language exchange was between two chatty Arab high school students.

"Abdul, have you finished the part about blowing-up the school gym," the first Muslim teenager inquired. "Don't forget the bombs in the auditorium, and also in the library, too!"

"Yes, Saddam," the second juvenile answered. "And are you working or the cafeteria horror devastation enactment? Hand grenades and AK-47s, along with rocket-propelled grenades would have the best graphic impact. Kids and faculty members that luckily survive the lethal blasts will be gunned-down by terrorists with machine guns, all waiting in the high school's exit corridors."

"Great idea, Abdul!" Saddam complimented and acknowledged. "This fantastic massacre will make Columbine High School look like a mere grade school picnic! Soon, the clever jihad will be completed. See you tomorrow morning before homeroom, and we'll discuss any additional details that need to be included."

"Okay, Saddam," Abdul verified. "I'll see your ugly face tomorrow morning in the main corridor!"

Harry and Sylvia sat in their den with their' mouths agape. Then, the introspective insurance broker remembered that their son Jake had often mentioned the two new Arab kids that were now juniors at the local high school, so the father gave his pride and joy a 'surprise phone call' to the *Rutgers* freshman's dorm room.

"Jake, do you remember the full names of the two Arab boys that enrolled in the high school last year? I think they'd be juniors now, and ready to graduate next year. Your mother and I couldn't remember their names."

"They are Abdul al Jameel and Saddam Kareem Habash," Jake lethargically answered. "Pop, I thought you were calling to tell me that you're gonna' buy me a car for my sophomore year. I'll be able to live off-campus, and could use a decent set of wheels to impress the Douglass chicks up here."

"Okay, Jake, I'll discuss the issue with your mother, and we'll see what we can work out for you over the summer months!" the father diplomatically responded. "Good luck on your two new courses! Take care now, Son!" Click.

"Harry, what are you going to do with that tape recording you've just made?" Sylvia asked in a very alarmed tone of voice. "Are you planning to take the tape over to the Atlantic County Sheriff's Office?"

"No, Sylvia. This is a definite terrorist conspiracy in progress, and one of those Arab boys lives only a block away from my brother Ted on Cypress Lane. Yes, I'm first taking the tape over to the local police chief and get his professional opinion about its content," the husband nervously answered, his forehead breaking out in a sweat, despite the den's effective air-conditioning. "And don't worry, Sylvia! I'm not going to mention a syllable about the police chief's wife having a licentious lesbian love affair outside the sacred institution of Holy Matrimony!"

* * * * * * * * * * * *

A week later, Chief George Burgess summoned Mr. And Mrs. Harry DeLareto into his police headquarters' office to review certain aspects of the department's investigation into a possible terror plot, involving two suspected radicalized Arab students at the local high school. The Chief's attitude and general demeanor seemed to be austere and businesslike.

"Well, Folks, you seem to have stirred-up a bees' nest controversy of sorts at the high school," Chief Burgess began his dissertation. "Even the school board has gotten involved. First of all, did you follow my instructions and bring along that' police radio scanner's Eighth Crystal that has apparently generated all of the current hullabaloo?"

"Yes, here it is!" Harry softly replied, handing the shiny object to the police authority. "But the conversation and all of the plotting between the two Arab boys that my wife and I had heard was captured on the tape recorder. You have the smoking-gun evidence in your possession."

"That it was, or at least seemed to be!" the Chief agreed and qualified. "But I wish you'd leave the gumshoe detective work to the police department, and not go free-lancing and pretending to be Dick Tracy or Sherlock Holmes on your own. Are you sure that you hadn't heard any other cell phone transmissions besides the one between young Abdul and this Saddam kid?"

"Well, Chief, Sylvia here had heard one other chat before I had arrived home," Harry awkwardly fibbed. "So then, I figured I'd try an experiment and see if I could tape a cell phone conversation just for verification purposes. But in the final analysis, it seems that I had obtained much more than I had bargained for!"

"Well, Mr. DeLareto," the Chief firmly said, "when a private citizen tapes another private citizen's cell phone conversation without the second party's approval or permission, then that deed could technically be construed as a violation of federal law. But don't panic, because I'm not going to get the county district attorney's office or a federal prosecutor on your case to pursue any felony charges against either you or your wife. I'd prefer to have a peaceful solution if it's at all possible!"

"Why thank you, Chief Burgess!" Harry commented, then taking a very deep breath. "Now, please explain what the Arab kids were doing by talking about a terror act that the pair were scheming to commit."

Chief Burgess calmly explained that Abdul al Jameel and Saddam Kareem Habash were writing a fictional contemporary play for their English teacher Mrs. Darla Swift, over at the regional high school. The 'terror play' was to be entitled "American Home-Grown Jihad," and the school principal had been caught between a rock and a hard place over the First Amendment rights of the Arab students and the high school's 'zero tolerance policy' in regard to students' allusions and references to acts of terror, especially those exhibited as graffiti on school corridor walls, or visible as incendiary emblems and insignias or students' tee-shirts, jackets and coats.

"Mrs. Swift teaches on the same faculty as my wife Shirley does," Chief Burgess stated. "And as you can now plainly see," the high-ranking law-enforcement official solemnly revealed, "Abdul and Saddam were only collaborating on a school assignment project, but even ultra-liberal Mrs. Swift felt uncomfortable about their academic jihad play proposal. She did eventually get the support of the school administration and superintendent, and as a result the short two-actor play will be performed fourth period in her senior English classroom next week. Even the school board had relucatantly approved of the rather peculiar project."

"Sometimes, things don't turn-out to be as they appear on the surface," Harry remorsefully confessed in a phlegmatic and lugubrious tone of voice. "Chief Burgess, I'm sorry that I've caused you so much duress, and I feel really bad about making the false allegations against the two Arab-American boys."

"Well now, their sensitive old-tradition parents were extremely upset about these bizarre circumstances, and have threatened to press charges against you for bearing false witness against their sons, but I think I've adequately smoothed things over if it's all right with you, Mr. DeLareto."

"And what do I have to do to make amends without having to hire a defense attorney, and then appear in court and suffer a burdensome load of ugly newspaper and television news publicity!" Harry wondered and asked, worried about his local reputation. "Honestly, I can't imagine what a dreadful prospective nightmare *that* humiliation would be!"

"First, Mr. DeLareto, write two letters of apology, addressing one each to Abdul and Saddam. Then next, simply go to Joe Italiano's Maplewood Italian Restaurant on the White Horse Pike in Hammonton and purchase two one-hundred-dollar meal certificates, one for each of the boys' families," Chief Burgess confidentially directed. "The two kids and their parents absolutely love Italian cuisine, especially spaghetti and meatballs! Finally, Mr. DeLareto, deliver the two letters and the pair of hundred- dollar Maplewood food certificates to my office no later than next Tuesday! Then, leave the rest to me!"

"Wow, Chief! Thanks for getting me out of a vat of hot boiling water!" Harry gratefully exclaimed. "I really feel relieved. My wife and I are very indebted to you for your fantastic assistance and cooperation."

"And one final thing, Mr. DeLareto!" Chief Burgess remarked with a feigned dour expression evident upon his countenance. "It's a good thing you never recorded any of my family's cell phone conversations while using your police scanner's magical Eighth Crystal!"

"Dream-On"

Session 1

Hammonton, New Jersey resident Samuel Charles Dexter was both depressed and despondent. His recent divorce from his ultra-dominant wife Sharon left the man's mind in an emotional state of shambles. Sam's friends at the Vineland, New Jersey plastics manufacturing company where Dexter was employed as an accountant suggested that the numbers guru should seek professional therapy counseling. One of his fellow co-workers had highly recommended Dr. Adam Neville, a reputable psychiatrist whose practice was at the corner of Landis Avenue and Third Street in downtown Vineland. Samuel Charles Dexter honored his June 7th, 2010 "get acquainted appointment" and was cheerfully escorted into Dr. Neville's office by Miss Emily Jensen, the psychiatrist's secretary and bookkeeper.

"Mr. Dexter, you say in your letter of introduction you've been having peculiar dreams lately that seem to be compounding your mercurial emotional instability," Dr. Adam Neville diplomatically commenced his narrative. "And your well-documented medical records that have been forwarded to me indicate that you tend to be an introvert, that you don't mingle and socialize with others too well, that you have a noteworthy gift for organizing and manipulating numbers, that you have an aggressive Alpha-type personality when threatened or challenged, that you love popular music and that you tend to be a melancholy loner who frequently feels isolated from mainstream society. I suppose that you attribute your overall alienation to your recent divorce."

"That's correct," Sam candidly told Dr. Neville. "Oftentimes I feel jittery and nervous. I've even suffered several anxiety attacks, but fortunately, the terrible onslaughts were at home in Hammonton and not at my workplace in Vineland."

"I see!" Dr. Neville perceptively answered as he quickly jotted down some relevant notes about his initial interview with his new patient. "I believe I can help you Mr. Dexter but your meticulous psychological treatment will require at least one full year to complete. My very competent secretary Miss Jensen has already checked with your insurance company and I'm pleased to inform you that your visits will be totally covered. I'll convincingly report to your employers that you're undergoing light hypnosis to help you deal more satisfactorily with middle age adjustment along with the gradual therapy promoting your general relaxation. Don't fret one iota Mr. Dexter!" Dr. Neville routinely explained. "I'm not going to divulge to your company's management team the exact specifics of our confidential relationship or the precise nature of your mental health *problems,* or for that matter, your 'personal *issues'* as we now like to call them. Is that clear?"

"I appreciate your skilled handling of my rather bothersome condition," Sam replied with a weak smile. "You appear to be very adequately experienced at dealing with corporations and with insurance companies' red tape."

"That particular expertise comes with the territory. Now then, we'll begin your comprehensive treatment sessions starting next Monday at 7 p.m. and we'll continue our remediation program every Monday thereafter for a full year," Dr. Neville related to his new patient. "And Mr. Dexter, I want to again emphasize that our relationship is strictly professional and confidential. Please don't discuss any details of our dialogues with anyone else! I believe strongly in the 'doctor-patient privilege'."

"Don't worry, Dr. Neville!" Sam sincerely declared. "I'm an introvert, remember? I seldom talk with anyone either at home or at work. Even my mother still thinks I'm shy!"

"That's quite fine and perfectly acceptable!" Dr. Adam Neville replied with a forced smile. "Your records from your regular physician show that you have a tendency to feel lethargic. Often-times emotional stress can sap a person's energy and enthusiasm, making *that* individual virtually phlegmatic. Now Mr. Dexter, I'm going to briefly put you under hypnosis for just one hour to measure and study some of your vital subconscious responses. This initial step is very important for me to better understand your underlying subconscious motivations."

"Okay, Dr. Neville," Sam Dexter readily agreed. "Let's get started on guiding me back onto the road to recovery."

Session 2

On Monday, June 14th, 2010 Sam Dexter honored his scheduled appointment with Dr. Adam Neville and at 7:10 the troubled accountant was lying prone on the psychiatrist's black leather couch and the patient's mind was already in a hypnotic state.

"Now Sam, just relax and tell me about your latest dream," the veteran examiner instructed. "Has it been a vivid one?"

168

"Why, yes!" Dexter answered from his subconscious trance. "Every night this past week I've had the same redundant dream, or perhaps it could be better described as a nasty redundant nightmare. I dreamed that I had been trapped all alone in this truly gigantic department store that had three floors connected by escalators and elevators, and each floor never ended. Each department store level was infinite! I roamed, searched and wandered around from department area to department area but there were no exits to any outside or external mall area, no overhead skylights showing a blue sky or even night stars, and also there were no doors or windows to escape my overall entrapment. I felt totally powerless and needless to say, very apprehensive even though the enormous store was illuminated by translucent ceiling light panels. The entire experience was surreal to say the least."

"Did the store in which you were lost have any brand name like Macy's, Penney's or Nordstrom?" Dr. Neville curiously asked.

"No, Dr. It was just a colossal-sized endless department store having tremendously stocked areas!"

"Was there any voice over the intercom directing shoppers to various locations or sections where bargain sales or discounts were going on?" Dr. Neville asked.

"No, in fact there weren't any other shoppers walking around inside the gargantuan department store nor were there any other customers randomly browsing about the various inventories besides myself'," Sam described his imagined-but-troubling emotional dilemma. "And no announcer's voice was ever heard discussing sales or giving directions to non-existent store personnel. But there definitely was background sound. Yes, now I remember. Music was being played over the sound system; yes, the same song repeated over and over again, 'Dream-On' by Aerosmith."

Sam Dexter then went on a lengthy Homeric-type catalogue of all of the departments that he frantically rushed through trying to find an avenue of escape from his illusionary mammoth store's captivity. His frenetic pursuit of freedom had the delirious hostage rushing around like a maniac on all three endless floors, his circuitous odyssey taking him through Men's Clothing, Women's Apparel, Children's Attire, Handbags and Accessories, Jewelry and Watches, Sporting Goods, Shoes Department, Lingerie and Nightgowns, Perfumes and Cologne, Furniture and Beds, Kitchen Appliances, Dishes and China, Bed and Bath, Wallets, Belts and Men's Gifts, Towels and Washcloths, Electronics and TVs, Cameras and

Photography, Toys and Games, Linens, Cosmetics and Lipstick, Luggage and then into Stationery Goods."

"Sam, calm down for a moment," Dr. Neville soothingly instructed. "You're working yourself up into a sweat. But I do find your general depiction to be most fascinating. Take ten deep breaths and then resume your most interesting story."

After honoring Dr. Neville's direction, the patient continued with his recollection. "Well, the monotonous and annoying Aerosmith song 'Dream-On' was constantly playing in the background as I desperately dashed from department to department in a wild frenzy," Dexter revealed to the very intrigued mind doctor. "It was an absolutely horrendous recurrent marathon nightmare as I visited each department on all three floors at least three consecutive times! Then I finally arrived at the thrice visited Hardware area, picked-up a large tool and immediately started smashing the cinderblock walls with the heavy sledgehammer I had discovered."

"Did you manage to shatter the wall?" Dr. Neville wanted to learn. "Did your great effort yield any tangible results?"

"No, the wall was impenetrable, and the repetitious Aerosmith song was making me both mentally crazy and physically exhausted as I futilely hammered away in total frustration. And when I eventually collapsed from fatigue onto the fantasy store's tiled floor," Sam proceeded to communicate, "in reality, I had actually fallen out of my bed and then groggily woke-up upon impacting the bedroom floor."

With the patient then being gently guided out of his subconscious state, the knowledgeable psychiatrist next rendered to bewildered Sam Dexter his initial evaluation about the man's emotional condition and postulated *his* theories about its root causes.

"Mr. Dexter, my interpretation of your fantastic department store dream is that you were lost and helpless among all of the myriad merchandise in your imagined environment simply because you probably felt a degree guilty about being a loner and also you probably feel somewhat guilty about being too materialistic," Dr. Neville hypothesized and related. "Sigmund Freud has proven that subconscious human guilt is often responsible for overt external behavior. As you might know, man's mind is like an iceberg, one sixth above the surface, which represents the conscious mind, and the other five-sixths below the surface, which obviously signifies the subconscious mind," the Ph.D. psychiatrist lectured. "This of course is only a preliminary conclusion and it might in actuality be too premature for me to state it definitively, but I conjecture that you're

170

possibly feeling a burden of self-shame because you've deceived yourself into thinking that you're fundamentally selfish and possessive; hence, you've defensively isolated yourself from mainstream American civilization. I believe that your very graphic department store dream is a creative manifestation of your accumulated subconscious guilt."

"What do you recommend I do Dr.?" Sam asked. "Is there any hope? Is my condition treatable?"

"Like I said, it's really too early for me to give you any thorough or comprehensive professional advice," Dr. Neville evasively stipulated, "but you might want to search for and acquire a spiritual identity; not necessarily a religious orientation Mr. Dexter, but I'm referring to a spiritual identity that affords you an element of joy and satisfaction nonetheless! Better self-esteem will eventually lead to a higher self-confidence level."

"Thanks-a-million, Dr. Neville," the impressed patient gratefully acknowledged. "I like your style and your disposition. I'll see you next Monday evening at 7 sharp."

Session 3

After Sam Dexter arrived at Dr. Adam Neville's modern-looking Landis Avenue office on June 21st, the cooperative patient was again promptly hypnotized by the psychiatrist, who had effectively used a large watch dangling and swinging from a gold fob chain. Dr. Neville was enthused to learn that Samuel Dexter had been having a rather different nightly dream that did not relate in any way, shape or form to any immense and super-capacious department store setting.

"Sam, tell me about your marvelous dreams this past week," the curious interrogator suavely asked. "I know you have plenty to share. Were your dreams exotic? Were they drab? Were they the same repeated dream each and every night?"

"I have dreamed the same thing or theme every single night," Dexter muttered and disclosed. "This might sound ridiculous or absurd but I dreamed that I was the only male on a hot desert island beach and I had been wildly chased through the surf by a thousand or so beautiful native women. But ironically," the subject clarified, "some of the alluring dolls on that anonymous tropical isle were brunettes, some were blondes and some were redheads. But none of the girls were naked. All of the gorgeous ladies were wearing similar red bikinis."

"Did they pursue you through any giant department store on that remote desert island?" Dr. Neville asked his restive subject lying horizontally on the black leather couch. "Forgive my direct questioning Sam, but for verification purposes I'm just trying to connect a few dots and I need some additional information."

"No, there wasn't any department store on that remote island; just some sex-starved really aggressive beautiful girls, all of whom had definitely gone through puberty."

"Did you hear any music in the background when you were being intensely chased?"

"Yes, come to mention it, the Aerosmith rock and roll song 'Dream-On' was perpetually being played over and over, which of course tended to make me very anxious!"

"This is all very fine and understandable, so there's no need to be especially alarmed by a simple fantasy phobia," Dr. Neville communicated to his mildly agitated but still hypnotized patient. "You have a good separation of spatial fantasy because you were on a remote island and not lost inside a colossal-sized department store surrounding. And you seem inspired to be running away from any lengthy relationship with a woman, but as I see and interpret your complex emotional needs, despite your major adversity known as bashfulness, in the end you still desire being pursued and found to be attractive and interesting to the opposite sex."

An hour later, Sam had been skillfully shifted out of his trance-like state and brought back to full consciousness. The doctor and the patient then engaged in several minutes of meaningful conversation.

"Sam, I believe that your subconscious mind has constructed a parallel fantasy to correspond with the fears and anxieties of your conscious brain, a sort of below-the-surface reality-coping mechanism, so to speak," Dr. Neville ascertained and shared. "And this past week you were dreaming where you're being hunted by a thousand lovely women; well now, that suggests that you desire to have a trustworthy love-mate but you feel isolated and hurt by your recent divorce misadventure. And the fact that the women chasing you in your fantasy dream were not nude reveals to me that your mind still possesses a degree of Protestant morality prudishness," the psychiatrist logically deducted and concluded. "But both your department store dream from last week's conference and your remarkable island dream of this week have the Aerosmith song 'Dream-On' being played from some unknown source in the distance. This strange combination of ideas is all rather puzzling,

172

rather perplexing too, since you've already maintained that you like music, especially '70s rock and roll."

"Are *we* making any significant progress, Dr.?"

"I've already told you that any vast improvement won't be noticeable until after a full year of continuous therapy," the psychiatrist evasively answered. "No doubt you've often heard of the familiar expression 'No Man Is an Island?' Well Sam, *that* island comparison I've just articulated and brought to your attention shows me that you don't want to be completely detached from other human beings, especially gorgeous women. I believe that deep down inside your psyche," Dr. Neville hypothesized, "you really crave being connected to a sympathetic female and I suspect, despite your apparent reclusive nature, that you're now in the process of actively searching for the right lady friend, unless *she* finds you first. That's where the bizarre department store scenario is creatively invented and applied by your fertile imagination. You're desperately trying to find someone reliable to assist you in escaping your loneliness, a lady friend," the psychiatrist theorized and verbalized. "And the fact that a thousand stunning voluptuous women are infatuated with you on that desert island only confirms to me that you're in quest of a supportive female companion, but it has to be the right lady out of a pack of a thousand eligible ones. And Sam, don't let the tropical island environment represented in your dream throw your reasoning off course. It's quite evident to me that you're not being too selective either because you don't seem to prefer whether your next mate would be a brunette, a blonde or a redhead."

"Then, I'm not going insane or anything drastic like that?" the somewhat relieved patient asked his newfound mentor. "That's what I truly fear the most!"

"Quite frankly, Sam, I think that you have difficulty dealing with women in everyday reality so the situational island dream theme is how your ever-active mind's fabrications have accommodated *that* ostensible inhibition that's quite prevalent in your fantasy subconscious realm," Dr. Neville elaborated. "Idealistically speaking, Sam, your sensitive ego has been egregiously damaged by your recent devastating divorce, but in your starving soul, I believe that you still desire contact and affection from a lady friend. That's my theory at present, but *that* speculation of mine may change as our weekly sessions continue."

The examiner next asked his easily influenced subject if he had any other dreams in the past month that the paranoid accountant could recall besides the extraordinary department store entrapment and the incredible recurrent island paradise nightmare.

"Yes, Dr.," the trusting patient all-too-honestly replied. "I'm the only passenger sitting on a huge jet airplane without any stewardesses or male flight attendants aboard. But now that you drew *this* particular remembrance to my attention, the familiar song 'Dream-On' was repetitiously being played over the plane's intercom system."

"Well Sam, your unusual tale makes excellent sense and as a matter of fact it's quite self-explanatory," Dr. Neville comforted and consoled. "The prefix 'Aero" in Aerosmith means 'airborne' or 'in flight, or it could also mean 'gasses in the air,' so *that* notion supports the idea that you're riding on a jet plane. And the word 'smith' refers to a working trade like a blacksmith, goldsmith or a silversmith, so *that* particular word connection accounts for you attempting to solve your emotional crisis in your subconscious mind by cleverly inventing disguised symbolic references and graphic terminology."

"Gosh Dr., I'm sure glad that I've decided to consult your skilled services," Sam praised his erudite dream interpreter. "I can't wait for our next session to commence next Monday. These formerly puzzling dreams are beginning to make plausible sense."

Session 4

Sam Dexter was not tardy for his slated Monday, June 28th consultation. Dr. Adam Neville did not deviate from past practice and employed the same administrative therapy pattern as had been applied in the first three sessions, and soon the receptive patient's mind had entered into a deep-but-comfortable hypnotic state. Much to the sagacious doctor's satisfaction, the easy-to-manage subject had recalled several very exceptional dreams conjured-up during the bygone week and then the passive subject accurately related them in full detail to his alert physician.

"I was participating in a crucial archeological expedition-dig on a western state's Indian Reservation and I accidentally discovered some ancient remains that presumably had once belonged to the nomadic tribe's shaman," Sam disclosed from his relaxed prone position on the black leather couch. "And all throughout the entire excavation, the very entrancing Aerosmith song 'Dream-On' was being played somewhere in the prairie background. I believe I'm really starting to hate that catchy song."

174

"You could be uniquely combining and relating words like 'Aero' with 'arrow' and 'smith' with a colonial-type person or possibly with a pioneer-era craftsman," the psychiatrist pondered and summarized. "Your amazingly analytic mind does demonstrate *that* sort of co-relative propensity!"

"Yes, and on last Tuesday night I dreamed that I had been driving, well actually speeding eastbound on the Atlantic City Expressway and heading toward my destination, the Wild, Wild West Casino on the boardwalk," Samuel Dexter recollected and then conveyed. "Well anyway, all along the thirty-mile distance from Hammonton to the shore the enchanting song 'Dream-On' by Aerosmith was featured over my car's radio, no matter what station on the AM or FM bands I was listening to."

"You seem to have a fixation or some odd infatuation with the talented rock group and also with their catchy rock and roll tune," Dr. Neville commented. "Any other peculiar night fantasies to report at this time?"

"Well, on Wednesday night I had been dreaming that I was driving to New York on the New Jersey Turnpike for no special reason at all and I eventually reached the last toll booth without any money in my pocket or cash in my wallet," Sam uttered in a disconsolate tone of voice. "And no, I didn't have any EZ-Pass transponder attached to my inside windshield either. The macabre-looking toll collector was in the form and dress of the hideous Grim Reaper and the frightful specter was wielding his scythe close to my vulnerable face when I gratefully woke-up from that hideous nightmare, my entire body soaked in a cold sweat."

"I don't think you have a death wish, Sam, and I profess *that* specific belief based on my broad expertise reviewing hundreds of different case studies and then comparing the sum to your exact situation. Now please remember, was the redundant song 'Dream-On' again playing at the turnpike toll booth?"

"Yes, and the sound of the lyrics was very unsettling to say the least," Sam abruptly answered, slightly shivering and squirming. "Very distressing indeed!"

"It could be, Sam, that you're cloaking your deepest thoughts and dreads and subconsciously revealing to me now that you have a distinct fear of dying," the psychiatrist predictably guessed and assessed. "And your morbid Grim Reaper association could very well also mean that you're afraid of living and are concurrently afraid of genuinely expressing your true emotions, always masking *them* with other phony contrived feelings. These problems could have their stem origin way back in your early childhood. And the song 'Dream-On' could be the essential link or thread that your hyperactive mind has chosen to meld together all of your latent anxieties and apprehensions," Dr. Neville cogently explained. "Now then Mr. Dexter, do you have any other pertinent dream recollections in your memory data banks that are worthy of mentioning?"

"There's one more," Sam offered from his subdued and now placid state-of-mind while still mentally hibernating in his classic reclined position. "In this new nightmare I'm describing, I'm lost for hours inside a baffling tall hedge maze quite similar to the one I had once whimsically explored behind the Governor's Mansion in Colonial Williamsburg. Just as I had been confused and disoriented in the department store labyrinth," Sam realized, compared and intelligently expressed, "I couldn't find my way out of the meandering passageways until the irksome song 'Dream-On' finally finished after around three horrible hours. Then rather coincidentally, I had thankfully awakened from my atrocious nightmare."

"Have you ever read the book *Aerosmith* by Sinclair Lewis?" the eclectic-minded multi-faceted doctor asked. "It's one of my favorite fictional works. The main character is a unique fellow named Martin Aerosmith, a dedicated genius in quest of a permanent cure for a certain, deadly bacteria that often causes worldwide plagues and pandemics. At any rate Sam, this marvelous scientist Martin Aerosmith had gathered sufficient facts to author a profound research paper of paramount importance and later he delivers his vital information in a lecture hall presentation that had been given to prominent members of the inept medical establishment of the time. Getting back to my initial premise," Dr. Nevile insisted, "have you ever heard of or read the breakthrough novel *Aerosmith* authored by Sinclair Lewis?"

"No, I'm not at all acquainted with that novel although I have heard of the author," Dexter tersely answered. "I believe he was one of those famous *Depression-era* muckrakers."

"Okay, Sam. In another hour, I'm going to snap you out of your fourth hypnotic trance," the mind doctor casually indicated to his obedient client. "Then, just as you've always done after our past meetings, you'll resume your normal adult life routines for a full seven days and we'll see you again next Monday for our upcoming very essential rendezvous! Now then, let's get on with our fourth interesting interaction."

* * * * * * * * * * * *

176

Session 5

Conscientious Miss Emily Jensen had meticulously finished her record-keeping duties as usual at precisely 7:30 that following Monday evening and the secretary had left the psychiatrist's office soon thereafter. After loyal patient Samuel Dexter had departed the Landis Avenue premises at 9:10 p.m., Dr. Adam Neville walked over to the small refrigerator located in the side room, plunked five ice cubes into a clean glass and then concocted a jigger of vermouth mixed with three generous jiggers of sweet liquor to make a mouth-watering Southern Comfort Manhattan cocktail. Next the tired-but-gratified psychiatrist sat at his desk and concentrated on dictating some exceptional notes into a microphone. The recorded information the mind doctor was about to state would be later entered as a relevant document file into his personal desktop computer.

"I only have about ten more years to become famous in the psychiatry field and finally receive full federal grant funding in order to make my great aspiration come true, my revolutionary contribution to social science," the crazed plotter fancied and said into the microphone. "It is my steadfast goal and desire to become equally as acclaimed as dear old Sigmund Freud himself. My batch of eligible patients is now complete. At last I've accumulated ten good candidates to participate in *my* landmark experimental dream program," Dr. Neville vociferated as he then paused and slowly sipped an ounce of his potent mixed drink. "My psychiatric study will be published in a slue of prominent mental health journals and my valuable literature will be acknowledged and recognized as a major scientific work for many years to come. A vast array of medical experts throughout the world will place absolute credence in my indispensable research study."

The egotistical alcoholic paused for a moment to sip his liquor and then again activated his tape recorder, methodically speaking into the microphone, carefully enunciating each stellar word. "Yes, I've now successfully amassed ten 'Music Dream Study' patients, to all of whom I've diligently played ten different songs for sixty minute durations during each separate two-hour therapy session; of course, the ten individual songs were played on my desktop computer while each subject was under my strict hypnotic control," Dr. Adam Neville proudly articulated before again imbibing an ample swig of his delicious Southern Comfort Manhattan.

"Mrs. Angela Shaner keeps hearing the song 'Dream a Little Dream for Me' by Mama Cass, Mrs. Agnes DeLeo insists that she hears 'Dream Baby' by Roy Orbison, Mr. Vincent Cramer knows all about 'Dream Lover' by Bobby Darin, Ms. Helen Garrison is an expert on 'Dreamin' by Johnny Burnette and Miss Gina Wolfe claims she listens to 'Dream Weaver' by Gary Wright during the hysterical woman's constant nightmares."

After casually glancing inside a readily available oak tag folder, Dr. Neville gulped down another mouthful of his powerful mixed drink before resuming his momentous dictation litany. "And number six on my list is Mrs. Carla Franchetti who simply loves Stevie Nix and Fleetwood Mac's version of 'Dreams,' number seven is Mr. Jason Vaughn, who is enamored with 'Dreaming' by Cliff Richard, number eight Mr. Maurice Dugan truly enjoys the rhythm and beat of 'Dreamtime' by Daryl Hall, number nine Mr. Nigel Pierce finds great merit in the lyrics to 'Dreamer' by Supertramp and now at last my tenth candidate for inclusion into my federally funded program is Mr. Samuel Charles Dexter, who is totally captivated with Aerosmith's outstanding rendition of 'Dream-On.' And all of this preliminary groundwork has been cunningly and fantastically organized and accomplished by little old me, the soon-to-be internationally renowned Dr. Adam Neville, ha, ha, ha, and all of my secret goals have been furtively achieved, even without my very capable secretary Miss Emily Jensen's suspicion or knowledge."

The obsessed psychiatrist ceased his tape-recording oration and then softly placed his microphone upon his very neat and clean side office desk. The half-intoxicated devil-minded doctor again tasted some more of his cold mixed liquor and then in the very midst of his narcissistic catharsis, the fanatic gloated and reminisced for several moments, leaning back in his black swivel chair and then arrogantly smiling at the overhead translucent ceiling light panels. Neville soon self-indulgently contemplated and assessed his own great shrewdness.

'My important study will certainly be the most wonderful and productive achievement of my entire life,' Adam Neville considered and relished. 'I'll be busy touring the whole country and be in demand lecturing at every major university in the United States, and later as my reputation expands,' the maniac further schemed, 'I'll be speaking at colleges all across Europe too. So what if I had mischievously rigged and stacked the deck of cards in my favor! I'm going to win this high jackpot poker game and my good name will be acclaimed and revered throughout the whole-wide world!' the
178

exhilarated madman imagined. 'I only hope that Mr. Sam Dexter and my other nine weak-minded case studies don't go psycho with their numerous dream delusions before my invaluable research project has been consummated and published. Ha, ha, ha! I don't wish to see my ingenious documentation suddenly turn into a tawdry scandalous debacle! Who cares about the fate of my mediocre gullible doltish patients? None of my ten idiotic dream subjects can be allowed to ever ruin my soon-to-be coveted prestige and fame!'

"Ship of Fools"

Philip Greco was born and raised in Hammonton, New Jersey but in the 1970s the elderly gentleman absolutely loved vacationing for a full week every August in sun-kissed Ocean City, Maryland. Phil Greco had memorized every commercial retail business in the inlet's five-block section of the boardwalk starting from South First Street right up to North Division where the Route 50 Bridge over the bay channeled automobile traffic into town. Trimper's Rides, the Red Apple Treats Stand, Dayton's Chicken, Marty's Playland Arcade, Sportland Arcade, Dumser's Ice Cream, The Purple Moose Saloon, Thrashers French Fries, the Alaska Hot Dog Stand, Dollie's Popcorn, Bull on the Beach Roast Beef Sandwiches, the Atlantic Hotel, the Glassblowers Shop, Fisher's Caramel Popcorn, Lombardi's Tower of Pizza, Dealers Choice Poker Game Arcade, the Candy Kitchen Shop, the Psychedelic Shop, The Sea Shell Emporium, The Dutch Bar, Telescope Beach Pictures and the Courtesy Gift Shop all held dear spots in the visiting South Jersey man's heart. And during his annual week-long hiatus Greco loyally patronized all of the mentioned popular boardwalk establishments.

Another Ocean City, Maryland place that Phil Greco was especially fond of was Happy Jack's Pancake House, which in the summer of 1973 was situated on Baltimore Avenue directly behind the landmark Atlantic Hotel. Greco and his Hammonton buddy Anthony Esposito were avid deep-sea fishermen and each summer the two friends would charter a boat out of the bay-side White Marlin Marina, but before each big fish ocean adventure, the New Jersey pals would always eat a hardy breakfast at the famous Happy Jack's Pancake House, which displayed on its four wood-paneled walls two-dimensional ship models that were offered "For Sale" to the public. The creative works were produced by an area artist named Captain James, and one particular post-colonial era warship (mounted on a dark ivory burlap background) immediately caught Philip Greco's attention.

"I really like that black warship hanging on the wall directly above your bald head," Phil sarcastically-but-affectionately told Anthony Esposito. "The vessel looks like it's late eighteenth or early nineteenth century, most probably from the War of 1812 era. And the black strings connecting the three masts really contrast nicely with and complement the dull white background. And Tony," Phil elaborated before gulping down a mouthful of delicious hot coffee,

"I really like the rolled-up canvas sails too! If the price is right, I'm interested in acquiring it!"

Anthony Esposito turned his head and briefly studied the impressive-looking framed battleship rendition on exhibit. "That baby's got seventeen cannons facing us," Phil's friend and confidante counted and announced. "That means the real one that existed way back then carried thirty-four total cannons that could be booming and blasting away at enemy ships."

"I'm going to call that terrific beauty the 'Ship of Fools'," Phil laughed, "and I intend to buy the piece of art and hang it in my den if I can get it for under a hundred and fifty bucks. Let's see the asking price."

Philip Greco did negotiate for and finally purchase Captain James' "masterpiece" for "a Ben Franklin and a Ulysses S. Grant" and three days later the jubilant man transported the treasured item back to Hammonton, New Jersey where the owner proudly displayed the 'conversation piece' on his family den's largest wall.

But in June of 2006, Philip Greco died of a massive heart seizure and his loyal son Gino Greco inherited the "classic and decorative" Ship of Fools, which the beneficiary prominently hung in *his* modest French Street home's family den to specifically honor his father's intense love of the sea.

* * * * * * * * * * * *

Following in his father's footsteps, Gino Greco had graduated from the Philadelphia College of Pharmacy and took great pride in operating the family business trading under the name "The Apothecary Shoppe" on Bellevue Avenue in downtown Hammonton. Keeping with the European-style appellation of the establishment, the owner often referred to himself as "a chemist." And just like his garrulous father, the congenial proprietor was well-respected by virtually everyone he knew in the community and always conducted his "father figure" ownership capacity with both courtesy and integrity, constantly having the welfare of his customers and the dignity of his employees in mind.

"Harry," likeable Gino Greco pleasantly ordered his Apothecary Shoppe manager, "I'd like you to please check all of our inventory in the stock room. An independent pharmacy like this one has to always keep one step ahead of our more prodigious competitors Wal-Mart and Rite Aid Drugs." And then, the "chemist" requested of his counter person, "Jill, since we aren't too busy this morning see if you
182

could restock the over-the-counter patent medicines' shelf. And after refreshing the candy bar selections, remind me to call my wife in a half-hour if you can. My memory is becoming as unreliable as an old sole-less worn-out shoe. I think we need a few more *Snickers*, *Hershey* and *Three Musketeers* bars in those half-empty display boxes. And oh Kathy," the fussy storeowner hollered over to his newly hired cashier, "can you please replenish the soap and deodorant rack next to the alternate cash register?"

At noon on Friday August 13th, 2010 Gino Greco phoned his always on-the-go wife from his Bellevue Avenue pharmacy office to see if Diane was home from her early morning grocery shopping at Bagliani's Market on 12th Street. The wife answered the landline call after the third ring.

"Yes, Gino. I've just finished putting all of the dairy products into the refrigerator," Diane informed. "I've also bought you a half-gallon of your favorite ice cream, *Breyers* vanilla fudge. If you want to know the truth, I really miss Jimmy and Denise helping me. Pretty soon our little urchins are going to be entering those ugly early teen years when their acne-dotted faces look awfully grumpy and then a year later their peevish behavior will become terribly uncooperative most of the time."

"How much longer are the kids staying up in the Poconos with your sister Francine?" the forgetful husband inquired. "Are they coming back to Hammonton tomorrow? What's the name of that kids-oriented resort where they're now hanging out?"

"Jimmy and Denise are coming home to Jersey late Sunday afternoon and if you recall, they're rooming with their young cousins at a nifty place called Great Wolf Lodge up in Tannersville," the wife re-educated her husband. "I understand it's a pretty fantastic resort that's designed to accommodate kids of all ages. Good old Francine must be having a real ball babysitting, er, I meant to say 'chaperoning' four little hellions!"

"Remind me early this coming winter that we have to take an excursion up to Tannersville and do some skiing with our children at Camelback Mountain," Gino suggested. "That's probably the neatest ski mountain in the Poconos. The last time we had spent a weekend up there we all had a blast. And that Tannersville Inn has some really excellent food on their menu. What's the name of that other restaurant that we like?"

"It's the Smugglers Inn located right across the highway from the Tannersville Inn," Diane Greco remembered and informatively answered. "Every hot action place in that town is within a mile of the other sensational attractions. And the newly constructed Mt. Airy Casino Hotel is not too far away from Tannersville either."

"Say, Honey, speaking of casinos, the kids are out of town, right? What do ya' say we' take a thirty-mile ride east to Bally's Casino tonight. If we lose our money too quickly at the green tables and on the slots, we can always stroll the boardwalk and reminisce our first movie theater date we had in Atlantic City."

"Splendid idea, Hubby!" Diane robustly exclaimed over her kitchen phone. "That means I won't have to cook dinner and that'll also give me enough time to do some much-needed housecleaning and a little interior decorating too. The day's jobs will go by much smoother if I know we're going out on the town tonight over in Atlantic City."

"Great, Doll! We'll be leaving Hammonton about five this afternoon," Gino enthusiastically said. "Of course, we'll have to contend with the heavy Friday night Philly' traffic on the Atlantic City Expressway heading down the shore, but I think I'll be able to navigate my Lexus through all of the turmoil and congestion. My EZ-Pass transponder attached to the windshield makes going through the toll plazas almost a pleasure. The Governor's TV ads are right. That useful electronic device is a real time-saving convenience and I'm glad I got it."

"See you around five, Handsome!" Diane verified. "Now, as soon as we hang up, I'm off to complete my basic housekeeping and to then hang a few items on the outside clothesline. As they've said and often repeated for many centuries throughout history, 'A woman's work is never done'!" Click.

* * * * * * * * * * * *

At two that afternoon, a delivery truck dispatched from Frank Mazza Furniture Store pulled into the Greco family's French Street driveway and the elderly driver rang the front doorbell and after the portal was opened, then the company employee gingerly lugged the new mirror (that Diane had secretly purchased) from the foyer, through the hallway and kitchen areas and finally into the house's den. After unwrapping the gilded gold-framed mirror, Mrs. Diane Greco gave her nod of approval and eagerly signed the yellow "Customer's Copy" receipt. She next politely handed the appreciative driver a five-dollar tip.

"Thank you, Mrs. Greco," the furniture store truck/delivery employee said. "In this day and age, every dollar counts!"

"You can spend the money at my husband's pharmacy," Diane giggled. "But better yet, stop and buy yourself a hamburger and a Coke over at Burger King."

"Would you like me to help you hang the mirror?" the suddenly extra-courteous driver volunteered. "I'm quite experienced at it since I do that sort of minor job all the time, especially for good customers like yourself."

"No thanks, Johnny," the woman of the house replied. "I think I can manage the task all by myself. If you remember, my dad was a hard-working ambitious carpenter in town and he was a dependable builder too you know, and from him I learned how to use a hammer and nail at a very young age. Working at odd jobs around the house as a tomboy, well, that sort of activity kept my brothers and me from becoming juvenile delinquents," the woman exaggerated. "Anyway, thanks again Johnny for being so extra careful while carrying that expensive mirror all the way from the front steps into the den. It's a real beauty, isn't it?"

* * * * * * * * * * * *

Diane Greco thought that the out-of-place three-and-a-half decade-old "War of 1812 Battleship" was incompatible with the remainder of her modern den's décor. She felt that the 'obsolete spectacle' had to be removed from the most used room in the residence and then relocated to an empty wall in the upstairs computer room so that the 'eyesore' would be less conspicuous to visiting guests.

'That 'Ship of Fools' as my late father-in-law used to call it is an interesting artifact left over from the early 1970s but it really doesn't match the rest of the den's motif and I think it's much more suitable for the spare room upstairs. Gino and I never did have that third child as we had originally planned when we had built this house. And I don't think that my understanding husband will mind me replacing it with this splendid new gold-framed mirror,' Diane presumed. 'It's not like the all-too-gaudy 'Ship of Fools' room ornament is haunted or cursed or anything like that. Honestly, I'm not throwing Gino's treasured item into the rubbish bin. I'm merely transferring it from the den wall to the upstairs computer room wall. I'm sure my compassionate husband will easily adjust to the new arrangement.'

Mrs. Greco stood and balanced herself on a sturdy wooden kitchen chair and reached-up and removed the two-dimensional out-of-date framed battleship from the den wall. And after descending from her elevated position to the floor's carpet, the wife immediately grabbed onto the recently acquired mirror, stepped up on the chair again and proceeded to skillfully hang the 'Frank Mazza Furniture piece' of merchandise (using the accompanying back wire) onto the old wall hanging clip.

After that simple task had been finished, the on-a-mission wife carried the heavy "Ship of Fools" upstairs and using a spare chair from daughter Denise's bedroom along with an available hammer, wall hook and nail obtained from the hall closet shelf, the wife managed to find a convenient stud in the computer room's designated wall and then very adroitly hung and leveled Gino's beloved Ocean City, Maryland Captain James' Happy Jack's Restaurant memento.

With *that* challenging job being fulfilled, the satisfied wife returned the aforementioned chair to Denise's room, put the hammer back on top of the upstairs hall closet shelf and then slowly descended the thirteen steps downstairs in order to return the borrowed wooden chair from the cozy den back to its normal place in the kitchen nook area.

Upon re-entering the tidy cozy den to admire her exquisite mirror, the wife curiously glanced at a series of old black-and-white pictures positioned in a neat row on top of a corner flat table surface, and upon gazing more intently, Diane Greco was dramatically and literally shocked out of her mind when she noticed that the now-deceased six people that had appeared in the old photograph were presently missing.

'Oh my God! How could *this* possibly be true?' Mrs. Greco alarmingly thought. 'This photo' from the 1950s is supposed to have all of Gino's aunts and uncles in it, but all that is now visible is the beach, the Ocean City Maryland lifeguard stand and the turbulent Atlantic Ocean in the background! Over the years I've looked at this nostalgic picture at least a thousand times,' the astonished wife frightfully realized. 'How arcane, creepy and eerie! Aunt Elena, Uncle Jack, Aunt Vera, Uncle Stan, Aunt Marie and Uncle Joe, all six of them have somehow mysteriously vanished!'

And then, Diane Greco's attention was drawn to another old sentimental 1950s' black-and-white photo' that previously had shown now-deceased cousins from Gino's family standing outside the main entrance to the world-famous Phillip's Restaurant in Ocean City, Maryland. But much to her dismay, only the widely acclaimed Philadelphia Avenue seafood house was represented in the snapshot without any trace of the vacationing six cousins Judy Greco, Anita

186

Greco, Richard Greco, Donald Greco along with married Eleanor Jenkins and Joanne Everitt. Those half-dozen familiar faces had been mysteriously erased.

A third well-preserved black and white '50s Ocean City, Maryland photograph exhibited upon the same flat den table ordinarily featured four family members that upon closer scrutiny, had also strangely been eliminated. In the original framed snapshot, Diane's deceased father-in-law Philip Greco should have been standing in front of the grand old boardwalk Atlantic Hotel with his wife Ruth and his father Antonio Greco along with Gino's younger brother Russell, who years later had horribly died from drowning in the Ocean City, Maryland surf. Russell's untimely death explained why Philip Greco abruptly stopped visiting Ocean City, Maryland every August after the 1974 family tragedy.

'Sixteen family members missing, all of whom are dead and buried in local cemeteries!' Diane fearfully recognized, her frenzied mind entering into a heightened panic-attack state. 'There's only one vital thing I think I must do to reverse this living nightmare! I must run upstairs to the computer room and exchange the 'Ship of Fools' with the mirror I have just received. If I do that superstitious deed without delay, perhaps everything will return back to normal. Most certainly,' the distraught woman thought, 'I don't want to disturb or upset the Powers That Be, especially Death! I must let the poor sixteen dead souls rest in peace and I believe that the Ship of Fools relocation is the key!'

Diane frantically dashed up the familiar thirteen steps, obtained the nondescript chair from daughter Denise's room, rushed and carried the secured object into the spare computer room and then nervously stood upon a den desk, all the while carefully scrutinizing the hanging accursed Ship of Fools.

The result of Diane Greco's frantic labor was emotionally devastating to her. Much to the perspiring woman's horror and terror, the various heads of the sixteen deceased relatives belonging to Gino Greco's ancestral family were now blatantly represented, each with his or her diminished miniature face sticking out of the 1812 battleship's first sixteen cannons that were situated directly below the vessel's starboard-side gunwale railing.

And then, Mrs. Greco screamed loudly and deliriously upon observing that her own head and face had punctured through the remaining seventeenth cannon's opening. While viewing the ghastly phenomenon, the petrified woman's knees buckled, the den desk wobbled and the wife lost her balance.

Still shrieking from her macabre ordeal, Diane Greco fell from her standing position upon the rickety den desk and then swiftly plummeted to the hardwood floor. A minute later the terrified soul stopped breathing. In stark reality, Diane Greco had been literally frightened to death!

* * * * * * * * * * * *

Since Diane Greco had died at a relatively young age, an autopsy had been ordered performed, and according to the subsequent toxicology report, the cause of death was determined to be "trauma to the head from violently impacting with the floor."

The following week, a well-attended but extremely sad Wednesday evening viewing was held for Mrs. Diane Greco at the Carnesale Funeral Home on South Third Street. On Thursday morning a solemn mass for the deceased was celebrated at St. Joseph Catholic Church on North Third. Burial for the aggrieved chemist's wife occurred at high noon at the Greenmount Cemetery on First Road with a reception for family and friends following immediately thereafter at Illianos Restaurant on 12th Street.

When all of the flowers, condolences and traditional funeral distractions were over, a very melancholy and sorrowed Gino Greco sat at his desk in the upstairs computer room staring-at, and studying, the 'Ship of Fools' that *his wife* had moved to its new upstairs location. The somber griever's heart remained inconsolable. The despondent pharmacist was wondering why his spouse had purchased the downstairs den mirror and had transferred the 'family heirloom' to the spare room upstairs without first consulting him.

'I suppose that Diane was just going to surprise me with the newly purchased mirror and in the meantime flaunt her notorious home decorating skills,' the emotionally disheveled chemist regretfully thought. 'Oh well, it's time for me to go and get Jimmy and Denise at my sister-in-law's place. It was nice of her to take the children over to her house for a few hours so that I could gather my wits with a little peace and quiet. Meditation and some basic soul-searching can certainly often be constructive.'

While standing in the upstairs computer room and upon scrutinizing the Ship of Fools more analytically, Gino Greco noticed 'an anomaly' that he thought was very peculiar. He then glanced out the middle window to clear his saddened mind for a moment and then again apprehensively peered at the framed 1812 era string-sailed battleship.

188

The impressive vessel was still mounted on its dull ivory burlap background but oddly enough, Captain James' signature was now on the left-hand-side and not the right where it had always appeared before. And the 'haunted ship' was now reversed in its orientation, the bow pointing in the opposite direction with the seventeen consecutive empty port-side cannons (situated just below the gunwale railing) now facing the appalled ashen-faced viewer.

'The Ship of Fools throughout sea lore legend was reputed to be a legendary ghost vessel,' the very nervous widower recollected from a college professor's literature class lecture. 'I wonder if this cherished Ocean City, Maryland heirloom had anything to do with Diane's untimely accidental death?

"Earth, Water, Air and Fire"

The ancient Greek philosophers believed that the world and its entities consisted of atoms, and those essential tiny particles harmoniously combined to comprise four main observable ingredients: earth, water, air and fire. During medieval times anti-establishment alchemists were aware of various chemical elements and the experimenters vainly and futilely spent their precious time attempting to transform common metals into gold.

In the year 2091 AD, inspired young people throughout America and Europe vehemently rejected the tenets of traditional religion and politicians' propaganda and the callow extremists became "retro" in their antiquated thinking, believing that the pseudo-science of ancient astrology along with primitive zodiac horoscope predictions would provide the fickle youthful adherents with "Divine Guidance." The rebellious and energized advocates stubbornly placed absolute credence in the flimsy theory that such allegiance to the cosmic aspects of the medieval elements of "Earth, Water, Air and Fire" would guarantee the practitioners a rejuvenated spiritual identity and in time, would afford the "New World Alliance" permanent emotional security.

The "cause-oriented", younger generation's, addictive infatuation with astrology eventually represented an imminent existential threat to adult-dominated civilization as the myriad overzealous "Peace and Environmental Confederation" began its clandestine terrorizing of "Evil Western Culture," violently protesting by the tens-of-thousands against American capitalism, against greedy corporate executives, against Wall Street and the New York Stock Exchange, against Christianity, against Hebrew teachings, against the United Nations and last but not least, against their parents' and grandparents' and the adults' time-honored value systems.

Over the span of a mere decade, adult humanity had gradually degenerated into chaos and had become an "endangered species" when the restless "Save the World" demented zealots swiftly transformed into a well-organized subversive army of radical and militant goal-minded petulant antagonistic anarchists.

The four newly developed volatile and rebellious college and high school youth factions' slowly-but-surely gravitated towards four separate activist-involvement/sabotage groups. Those idealistic, aggravated, obstinate insurrectionists that were of the zodiac signs Taurus, Virgo and Capricorn belonged to the ultra-violent Earth

Underground, the Cancer, Scorpio and Pisces rebels generally joined the dangerous Water Underground, the Gemini, Libra and Aquarius discontented adolescents were dedicated to the formidable Air Underground and finally, the Aries, Leo and Sagittarius nihilists eagerly vulcanized into the dreaded Fire Underground. Each of the four separate "Militant Underground Activist Groups" used Internet communications along with pamphlet distributions to recruit new ardent members into their respective insurrectionist "Brotherhoods."

The four revolutionary astrology groups, which were really hybrids that had evolved out of early twenty-first century environmental organizations such as Greenpeace, the Sierra Club and PETA, occasionally coordinated combined attacks on formerly revered historic sites, on previously treasured national monuments and on selected industrial power plants, but for the most part the opposing Earth, Water, Air and Fire "Truth Brigades" plotted and acted independently of one other.

Each devious "Underground" was very active in all fifty states and also in every major "Old World" capital from London to Moscow. Truly, in the year 2094 AD the United States and Europe were more in jeopardy from internal revolt and destruction (from their own restless post-pubescent citizens) than those regions were from insidious foreign invasions or from communist or Arab jihadist missile attacks.

The clandestine Earth Underground units specialized in breeding swarms of African killer bees, huge aggressive wasp and hornet colonies, stimulus-response mobile scorpion nests, poisonous brown recluse and black widow spiders, millions of malaria-carrying mosquitoes, toxic blister beetles, carnivorous ants and a variety of venomous snakes including diamondback rattlers and countless vicious water moccasins.

The relentless Earth Underground used their teeming insects to infest various towns and cities with a coordinated barrage of "surprise blitz attacks." Meanwhile, the toxic snakes, beetles and spiders were indiscriminately deployed to kill or assassinate prominent political leaders and "greedy industrialists." And to make matters even worse, the thousands of Earth Underground laboratories throughout America and Europe were often located in secret urban ghetto basements and others were stealthily concealed in remote country caves and thus, the plethora of makeshift mobile facilities were extremely difficult for the FBI and local law enforcement agencies to discover, quarantine and demolish.

The ultra-dangerous Water Underground members directed their misguided energies into the unscrupulous contaminating and poisoning of various water supplies, reservoirs, and river dams besides tampering with separately owned town and rural wells. Occasionally the ruthless "Water Conservationists" would dynamite a large dam and cause major flood destruction to highly populated river valleys, thus drowning farmers' crops and interrupting and interfering with vital food-chain supplies. And when the fearless "Water Vandals" had available access to sympathizers' boats, the saboteurs would at nighttime cruise out to random oilrigs in the Gulf of Mexico and methodically blow-up the drilling platforms, causing mind-boggling havoc and accompanying ecological devastation besides.

Conversely, the Air Underground "Fiends" used *their* secret biological facilities to furtively develop lethal viruses and bacteria that caused widespread plagues and disease pandemics throughout the major industrial areas of America and Japan. Guided by crazed empathetic power-hungry science professors from leading academic universities, the merciless vernal villains cleverly combined the bird and swine flu strains to form a new deadly virus that immediately terrorized and killed hundreds of thousands of innocent victims, and the implacable thugs had recently perfected a radicalized ecoli bacteria that was beginning to infect already intimidated people in the besieged and beleaguered American Midwestern Plains States.

In terms of destructive potency, the overzealous Fire Underground "Malcontents" movement was equally as deleterious as its three Earth Sign counterpart organizations, the revolution-oriented flame worshipers devoting their destructive efforts to causing horrific infernos, forest blazes and also large factory and office building conflagrations. The warped individuals affiliated with the Fire Underground constituted "the Elite Saboteur Ignition Corps," a cadre of accomplished arsonists and mentally unstable pyromaniacs.

Never before in the annals of history had human civilization been in such dire jeopardy. The four menacing underground movement youth divisions often competed with each other for recognition and for media attention, and each detestable faction was determined to ascend to governmental power once the "Environmental Revolution" had ultimately obliterated the true enemies of the Earth: "the fat bald-headed adult ruling class."

Ironically, all of the man-made catastrophes that were specifically designed to eradicate the "detrimental adult 'Imperialist' population" were, according to rampant Underground propaganda, unselfishly performed to "Save the Planet." The avowed motto shared by the baneful Earth, Water, Air and Fire Undergrounds was remarkably simple and elementary: "Nature is good; man is evil! Evil, exploitation and greed must be eliminated at all costs."

* * * * * * * * * * * *

From his desk inside the White House Oval Office the President of the United States was pressured into signing an executive order and out of sheer necessity appointed a "special think tank committee" composed of representatives from four distinct government departments. The newly formed commission was given a tight deadline of only four weeks to construct a viable counter-intelligence "task force plan" that would neutralize the precarious rise of "the environmental anarchy wave" that was running amuck like "an annihilating pestilence" throughout the country.

Heading and presiding over the newly created secret "strategy panel" was the Pentagon's Major Wayne Bronson. Undercover Secret Agent Valerie Jones of the National Security Service was also assigned to participate in contributing to the confidential inquiry. The FBI chose and sent Agent James Salvo as its representative and complementing the hastily organized elite committee was a competent agent delegated by the CIA, Carmen Martin.

"This discussion group will now come to order," Major Wayne Bronson vociferated to his three distinguished subordinates seated around a long oval conference table located inside a remote subterranean Pentagon meeting room. "As you're all quite aware, we've been entrusted with the enormous responsibility of developing a solid plan to deal with these hordes of plundering environmental marauders that have maliciously initiated a terrible reign of terror throughout the entire United States and the territories belonging to our most trusted allies. Now then," Major Bronson continued his introductory remarks before clearing his throat, "let's hear some of your opinions and assessments of the rebellious youth ecology movement that's heinously sweeping across our all-too-vulnerable nation. Do I hear any constructive suggestions?"

"To be perfectly blunt Major Bronson," advisor Valerie Jones began, "three Senators and five Congressmen have recently been assassinated in just the last two months along with seven governors and fifteen prominent federal judges. Without question, we're mired in a pivotal crisis mode and the vulnerable minds of these young
194

demented maniac/terrorists on the loose have been contaminated and indoctrinated with a hateful ideology," the National Security Agency spokeswoman articulately reviewed. "The roaming young pirates absolutely despise everything that has made America the greatest civilization that mankind has ever known. The belligerent anarchists abhor most everything our nation has ever coveted including the United States Constitution, Christianity and basic free market capitalism, blaming those benign beneficial institutions for all of the world's woes and problems."

"Well Ms. Jones," Major Wayne Bronson peevishly responded, "what the large corporations, the military and the government have been selling, obviously these violent adolescent goons and spiteful thugs aren't buying! What part of the word 'no' don't the reprehensible punks understand? Personally," irritated and frustrated Major Bronson elaborated, "I happen to fault educational psychology for creating this societal menace, a formidable monster that is now completely out of control. When the family philosophy shifted from parent-centered homes to child-centered households and when the public schools adopted a policy of the child-centered curriculum replacing the teacher-centered classroom," Major Bronson opined and elaborated, "well my trusty committee colleagues, that was the classic point of no return that had been reached when the spoiled rebellious immature brats began ruling the country's roosts! Yes, popular family psychology along with mass educational psychology has been the unlikely genesis that has innocently spawned the general environmental insurrection that's presently threatening our time-honored American culture."

"Your comments are true and accurate to a certain extent," agreed Carmen Martin of the CIA. "These rampaging leftist ecology partisans believe strongly in their twisted 'green cause,' but generally speaking, most people that believe in *causes* don't really believe in themselves. These volatile juvenile delinquents lack confidence in their own potential to evolve into dynamic successful individuals functioning inside the boundaries of mainstream society," Agent Martin persuasively communicated. "These dangerous quixotic hooligans want to eradicate the present system and then create a contemporary Utopia, which was proven to be quite impossible in the past with the decline of Marxism and later Communism, both political philosophies being terrible scourges emblematic of the mid-twentieth century. The four hostile Underground groups just don't fathom that Utopia is an individual's personal pursuit where the ambitious citizen finds his or her own

195

happiness through the practice of good old American freedom of speech and free enterprise capitalism," the CIA man maintained. "The ideal Utopian pollution-free society where everyone is happy is merely a false artificial dream that can never be achieved. That irrefutable fact has been often verified by past history."

"Very well stated Agent Martin," Major Wayne Bronson commended. "Yes, very eloquently spoken. The Constitution and the Declaration of Independence afford all Americans equal opportunity for pursuing happiness but those sacred founding documents do not assure the *alluded to* 'happiness' in a phony environmental social paradise where everyone is holding hands and singing 'Cum Bi Yah'. When the state dictates all aspects of a person's life just for the sake of unnecessarily saving Mother Nature from being corrupted by human carelessness and mankind's negligence," Major Bronson grimly emphasized, "then that's the ultimate tipping point in history where the individual's freedom becomes sacrificed and is swiftly surrendered to the authority and discretion of despots. That ugly grotesque circumstance my fellow commission members, which incidentally parallels the evolution of this fanatical toxic Environmental Underground Movement, well, that evil condition is precisely when the birth of tyranny happens. When individual liberties are given up and then raw anarchy persists, totalitarian dictators like Adolph Hitler, Joseph Stalin and most recently the extremely diabolical Mohammed Habash take over and dominate."

FBI Agent James Salvo decided to make a verbal contribution to the first meeting's dialogue. "I think that in order to defeat this wicked burgeoning enemy threat that's positively tearing apart the fabric of our great nation, well, I believe that *we* have to be cunning and use unconventional thinking on this asymmetrical domestic battlefield presently called the United States," the FBI appointee objectively stated. "By *this* statement I mean that *we* have to abandon certain assumed civil privileges such as the domestic terrorists' First Amendment Constitutional Rights and furthermore, we ought to forget about the suspected nihilists' right to habeas corpus. Martial Law should be imposed and all unalienable civil rights ought to be suspended until the rule of law and order is completely restored. The future of America is at stake here and our system cannot be compromised!" FBI Agent James Salvo ardently argued. "This lethal and provocative 'Green Revolution' must be crushed in its infancy if we as patriotic Americans desire for our Republic to survive and thrive into the next century."

"Well, I suppose that national Martial Law could be effectively imposed and enforced," Major Bronson concurred. "Or as a viable alternative, first we could send out military SWAT teams along with Special Forces and Delta Squad units to search-out and sabotage the numerous concealed laboratory nests along with the plentitude of remote warehouse bases that are most frequently utilized by the punk environmental crazies."

"Truthfully, Major. I don't believe that such direct military tactics will work and I think that in the final analysis they'll backfire on the Administration and on the Army," CIA representative Carmen Martin strongly disagreed with the panel chairman. "If you're interested Major Bronson, I have an innovative idea that might be worth exploring."

"And exactly what brainstorming notion is it that you're proposing?" the committee's principal officer enviously asked CIA Agent Carmen Martin.

"Well Major, these four sinister Environmental Underground Groups are all philosophically based on the ancient notions of Earth, Water, Air and Fire, the assumed composition of the world as originally thought by ancient Greek thinkers," Agent Martin generally explained. "The entire principle, or should I say *premise* of the twelve astrological zodiac signs is erroneously founded on those four celestial constellation groupings appearing in the night sky, with each of those four distinct celestial classifications being uniquely constituted by three different Earth signs, by three distinct Water signs, by three separate Air signs and by three unique Fire signs."

"Your description makes perfectly good logical sense," Valerie Jones from the National Security Agency concurred. "The destructive environmental idiots want to send civilization back into the prehistoric Neanderthal era by wiping-out mankind's achievements while endeavoring to salvage the planet through ancient astrology symbolisms. But I still don't exactly fathom how we're going to deal with the four separate zodiac groups."

"Very accurate depiction Ms. Jones," Major Bronson commented, showing his mild dissatisfaction with her attempt at being melodramatic. "But unfortunately Ms. Jones, I'm not in the comedy or soap opera entertainment business. Now please continue with your unique-sounding idea Agent Martin."

The CIA Man was quite willing to expound on his theoretical remarks. "Well Major, I wish to learn more about the enemy's psyche to be able to more effectively study their modus operandi, that is to say, I want to have a week to fully delve into the formerly esoteric field of ancient and medieval astrology as it's currently related to the four basic Greek elements from antiquity and in addition, as it's now fundamentally associated with the four Underground Anarchist Organizations: Earth, Water, Air and Fire," Agent Martin indicated. "Perhaps as a result of my intensive investigations, I'll be able to formulate some kind of intelligent scheme to infiltrate and then counteract the Underground Movement's heinous insurgency campaign. What do you say I give it a shot?"

"You might be on the right course Mr. Martin and I believe that your recommendation is worth a try," Major Wayne Bronson acknowledged. "In retrospect, direct military intervention by our Special Forces might in effect gain the rebellious youth new left-wing supporters to their warped cause. Out of sympathy the ultra-liberal press might even publicly endorse *their* demented antics."

"Could you give me a week to analyze the subject matter?" Agent Martin requested. "I tend to work fast when under a given deadline. I think a full week is all the evaluation time I'll require."

"We'll convene next Tuesday, seven days from today!" the presiding panel member declared. "That'll give you Mr. Martin sufficient time to conduct your cursory investigation. In fact," the Major reminded the rest of the assembled government representatives, "we only have three more weeks to submit a comprehensive report to the White House. Our initial meeting is now officially adjourned and this special ad hoc Presidential Advisory Committee will re-group at this same time and place at 9 a.m. next Tuesday morning."

* * * * * * * * * * * *

A week had elapsed, and inside the subterranean Pentagon conference chamber Major Wayne Bronson convened the second "Goals, Objectives and Methodologies" session of the secretly appointed federal government panel. The all-business chairman called upon Carmen Martin to present his research findings concerning the extremely pernicious Earth, Water, Air and Fire environmental radicals, and *his* intrigued colleagues Valerie Jones and James Salvo were speculating whether the all-too-confident CIA agent's solution would be cost effective and logistically practical to implement.

"First of all, from reading Internet web pages we all know about horoscopes and the zodiac as well as the twelve famous constellation
198

signs," Agent Martin academically began his dissertation. "For example, I'm a Libra and according to superstitious beliefs, Libra is an Air Sign along with Gemini and *Aquarius*."

"Mr. Martin, one would automatically think that 'Aquarius' is a Water Sign," Major Bronson interrupted. "Its root word is associated with words like aquarium, aquanaut, aqua-phobia and aqueduct."

"Well yes, Sir, but technically speaking, Aquarius means 'water-carrier' and not just simply 'water'," knowledgeable and loquacious CIA Agent Carmen Martin clarified. "According to the pseudo-science known as astrology, Air Sign individuals that belong to the classifications Libra, Gemini and Aquarius are supposedly compatible with Fire Sign people connected with Aries, Leo and Sagittarius because in nature, fire needs air to flourish. And an Earth Sign like Taurus, Virgo and Capricorn for example, is believed to be compatible with Water Signs Cancer, Scorpio and Pisces, obviously because Earth and Water go together in nature better than either Earth and Fire or Earth and Air do. Naturally," Agent Martin pontificated, "Fire and Water don't mix or jibe too well. A Leo and a Pisces would be totally incompatible and a Fire Sign Sagittarius, or hunter, would not get along too satisfactorily with an Earth Sign such as a Capricorn or as indicated in ordinary zodiac illustrations, the constellation symbol 'goat'."

"Exactly what is the zodiac?" Major Bronson inquisitively asked. "I meant to say Agent Martin, I know it's the total of the twelve constellations, but does 'zodiac' have any particular scientific application or significance?"

"Imagine in your mind Major the twelve regular astrological constellations of the night sky," Agent Martin said. "Now imagine the path of the sun across the same sky during daytime hours. The twelve celestial constellations of the zodiac occupy in the night sky the narrow band situated on either side of the sun's path during the day. Do I make myself clear?"

"I'm a bit overwhelmed with all of the specific information you've provided us with but I think I've gotten the general gist of what you're attempting to communicate," Valerie Jones of the National Security Agency expressed to CIA Agent Martin. "But I know that I'm an Aries or ram sign, and as you've just pointed out, I'm also a Fire Sign so therefore I would be compatible with an Air Sign like Gemini, Libra or Aquarius but not necessarily harmonious with a Water Sign person like a Cancer, a Scorpio or a Pisces."

"That's quite correct Ms. Jones!" Agent Martin complimented his perceptive committee comrade. "Therefore Valerie, according to your very accurate statement, and assuming that this astrology terminology is valid and correct, which is a stretch to say the least, you as a Fire Sign Aries and me being an Air Sign Libra should probably get along rather well together."

"Mr. Martin, I think I now understand what you're endeavoring to say too," FBI Agent James Salvo comprehended and confirmed. "But Carmen, please tell *us* what this astrology compatibility stuff has to do with disrupting the ever-growing radical youth Underground Environmental Movement, which incidentally I believe is mendaciously modeled after crazy Adolph Hitler's fanatical youth corps."

"Well, Agent Salvo," Carmen Martin assiduously proceeded with disclosing his general thesis, "I suggest that *we* infiltrate the already incompatible Air and Earth groups and have them disagree and fight with one another and then infiltrate the incompatible Fire and Water groups and have them blaming each other for selective sabotage and aggression retaliations caused by *us*. I think that if these numbskull Environmental Youth Undergrounds begin bickering and quarreling, they'll eventually wage war and reek violence amongst themselves and because of their newfound bilateral conflicts, the treacherous youth factions will stop dynamiting dams, power plants and oilrigs and cease spreading diseases, and viruses and last but not least," Agent Martin specified, "they'll also abandon breeding venomous snakes and deadly insects aimed at terrorizing the general population. By acting subversively, *our* Special Forces can surreptitiously destroy the four militant eco-organizations by covertly operating within *their* own ranks."

"Excellent proposition in theory but how could your scheme be realistically accomplished?" Chairman Major Wayne Bronson evaluated and articulated. "Does the federal government have the requisite resources that can be mobilized and subsequently utilized to put your fascinating plan into motion?"

"I have a decent counter-revolutionary idea that just might gel with what Agent Martin has hypothetically advanced," normally reticent FBI Agent James Salvo chimed-in. "The adventurous pioneers that had settled in the American West before and after the Civil War were often outcasts, criminals and basically, the early frontiersmen were the dregs of society who saw an extraordinary opportunity to seize a second lease on life and practice the 'pursuit of happiness' while concurrently exploring a new and exciting Western Wilderness."

"But Mr. Salvo, I'm a trifle bewildered. Can you be more specific? How does your Old West analogy pertain to the diabolical environmental loons we're about to combat?" Major Bronson questioned his 'think tank' team player.

"Well, Major," Agent Salvo expounded. "The government owns millions of acres of land out West and we could furtively hire the down-and-out prisoners that occupy our jails and penitentiaries and offer the idle inmates freedom, giving them pardon from incarceration, and also providing the modern dregs jobs, land and houses in Wyoming, Utah and Nevada in exchange for their cooperation in successfully infiltrating and disrupting the four principal Underground Environmental Divisions, which incidentally are only tolerating one another, but in the future, will be vying for dominance should, Heaven forbid, the core federal government ever topple and fall. Furthermore, Major Bronson," FBI Agent James Salvo continued his sage monologue, "we could also hire the most dreaded motorcycle gangs to assist the prisoners in undermining the lunatic-fringe environmental nutcases from within *their* own ranks. Rewards and incentives could be granted to the bikers too!"

"I see many advantageous possibilities here," Major Bronson marveled and acknowledged. "Our elite Special Forces' units can co-operate with the motivated released prisoners and also with the redneck leather-jacketed bikers. Our newly hired government employees can easily seek-out and destroy a Fire Group's base of operation and then mischievously leave behind some clever clues and evidence, let's say telltale insignias, emblems and paraphernalia from the Water fanatics. And also," Major Bronson enthusiastically conveyed to his astute and captive audience, "the Air Saboteurs' germ research laboratories can be cunningly penetrated by jail-mates and motorcycle gang members and counterfeited Earth Group items could be fortuitously deposited in vital areas after the coordinated raid is enacted. Based on the radicals' suspect astrological beliefs," the panel moderator stated, "the volatile Environmental Anarchists will wind-up battling one another over undefined territorial jurisdictions. *We'll* then be able to soundly defeat the four dastardly astrological divisions internally and not by means of implementing excessive external confrontation or ever having to deploy the execution of huge military combat missions."

"This whole subversive agenda will be administered with cunning discretion!" James Salvo euphorically exclaimed. "Who cares if a couple of hundred thousand lowlife sadistic prisoners and drug-pushing scumbag bikers are killed in the ongoing domestic civil war along with the ultimate destruction of scads of lunatic-fringe Earth, Water, Air and Fire Underground Anarchists!"

"I remember the old joke from several decades ago that was expressed in the telling of a certain exaggerated mathematical equation," Valerie Jones remarked. "Global Warning plus Environmental Expense over U.S. Economy equals American Suffering Squared. That wonderful jest has now become an ugly arithmetical axiom!"

"Then, this illustrious Presidential Advisory Panel will endorse Agent James Salvo's sensational counter-revolutionary plan of action?" CIA problem solver Carmen Martin proposed in the form of a motion. "It does show plenty of imagination!"

"Affirmative! And as the very clever and wise Chinese general Sun Tzu is credited with writing," Major Wayne Bronson summarized and quickly smiled to his very talented 'think tank' ad hoc committee, "First you must know your enemy if you later wish to vanquish him!"

About the Author

Jay Dubya is author' John Wiessner's pen name. John is a retired New Jersey public school teacher, having diligently taught the subject for thirty-four years. John lives in Hammonton, New Jersey.

Counting *Suite 16,* John has written and published forty total books. *Pieces of Eight, Pieces of Eight, Part II, Pieces of Eight, Part III* and *Pieces of Eight, Part IV* all contain short stories and novellas that feature science fiction and paranormal plots and themes. *Nine New Novellas, Nine New Novellas, Part II, Nine New Novellas, Part III, Nine New Novellas, Part IV, One Baker's Dozen, Two Baker's Dozen, Snake Eyes and Boxcars* and *Snake Eyes and Boxcars, Part II* are short story collections all written in the spirit of the *Pieces of Eight* series.

Other Jay Dubya adult-oriented fiction are the works *Black Leather and Blue Denim, A '50s Novel,* and its exciting sequel, *The Great Teen Fruit War, A 1960' Novel. Frat Brats, A '60s Novel* completes the action/adventure trilogy. Jay Dubya also has produced two irreverent Biblical satires, *The Wholly Book of Genesis* and *The Wholly Book of Exodus.* A third satire *Ron Coyote, Man of La Mangia* is a parody on Miguel Cervantes' classic novel, *Don Quixote* published in 1605. *Thirteen Sick Tasteless Classics, TSTC, Part II, TSTC, Part III* and *TSTC, Part IV* are satirical works that each corrupt thirteen classic stories from American and British literature and from Greek mythology. *Fractured Frazzled Folk Fables and Fairy Farces* and *FFFF & FF, Part II* satirize and corrupt famous children's literature stories. *Mauled Maimed Mangled Mutilated Mythology* is another popular adult-oriented satirical/parody work that pokes fun at twenty-one famous classical myths. *O. Henry: Obscenely and Outrageously Obliterated* is another satirical adult rewrite along with *Poe: Pelted, Pounded, Pummeled and Pulverized.* Finally, *Shakespeare: Slammed, Smeared, Savaged and Slaughtered* and *Shakespeare: S, S, S and S. Part II* poke fun at the famous works of the great playwright.

The author has also penned a young adult fantasy trilogy: *Pot of Gold, Enchanta* and *Space Bugs, Earth Invasion. The Eighteen Story Gingerbread House* is a collection of eighteen new children's stories. And last but not least, two non-fiction works are *So Ya' Wanna' Be A Teacher* and *Random Articles and Manuscripts.*

Author Biography

Born in Hammonton, NJ in 1942, John Wiessner had attended St. Joseph School up to and including Grade 5. After his family moved from Hammonton to Levittown, PA in 1954, John attended St. Mark School in Bristol, PA for Grade 6, St. Michael the Archangel School in Levittown for Grades 7 and 8, and then Immaculate Conception School, Levittown, PA for Grade 9. Bishop Egan High School, Levittown PA was John's educational base for Grades 10 and 11, and later in 1960, the aspiring author graduated from Edgewood Regional High, Tansboro, NJ. John then next attended Glassboro State College, where he was an announcer for the school's baseball games and also read the nightly news and sports over WGLS, GSC's radio station.

John Wiessner had been primarily an English teacher in the Hammonton Public School System for 34 years, specializing in the instruction of middle school language arts. Mr. Wiessner was quite active in the Hammonton Education Association, loyally serving in the capacities of Vice-President, then building representative, and finally, teachers' head negotiator for a period of 7 years. During his lengthy teaching career, John had been nominated into "Who's Who among American Teachers" three times. He also was quite active giving professional workshops at schools around South Jersey on the subjects of creative writing and the use of movie videos to motivate students to organize their classroom theme compositions.

In addition, John Wiessner was very active in community service, being a past President of the Hammonton Lions Club, where he also functioned for many years as the club's Tail-Twister, Vice-President and Liontamer. John had been named Hammonton Lion of the Year in 1979 and in 2009 received the prestigious Melvin Jones Fellow Award, the highest honor a Lion can receive.

John also was a successful businessman, starting with being a Philadelphia Bulletin newspaper delivery boy for two-years in the late 1950s in Levittown, Pennsylvania. After his family moved back to New Jersey in 1959, John worked at his grandparents and his parents' farm markets, Square Deal Farm (now Ron's Gardens in Hammonton) and Pete's Farm Market in Elm, respectively. He later managed his wife's parents' farm market, White Horse Farms in Elm for three summers.

Also in a business capacity, for 16 summers starting in 1967 John Wiessner had co-owned Dealers Choice Amusement Arcade on the Ocean City, Maryland boardwalk and also co-owned the New Horizon Tee-Shirt Store for eight summers (1973-'81) on the Rehoboth Beach, Delaware boardwalk. In addition, "Jay Dubya" was a co-owner of Wheel and Deal Amusement Arcade, Missouri Avenue and Boardwalk, Atlantic City. And then, for 18 summers beginning in 1986, John had been the Field Manager in charge of crew-leaders for Atlantic Blueberry Company (the world's largest cultivated blueberry farm), both the Weymouth and Mays Landing Divisions.

After retiring from teaching in 1999, writing under the pen name Jay Dubya (his initials), John Wiessner became the author of 75 books in the genre Action/Adventure Novels, Sci-Fi/Paranormal Story Collections, Adult Satire, Young Adult Fantasy Novels and also Non-Fiction Books. His books exist in hardcover, in paperback and in popular Kindle and Nook e-book formats.

In January of 2022, John Wiessner (Jay Dubya) was nominated into Marquis Who's Who in America, and in April of that same year, was one of nine distinguished Who's Who in America members honored with receiving Lifetime Achievement Awards, all nine sharing a news article of recognition appearing in the Wall Street Journal.

Google: Jay Dubya, books
Google: Walmart, Jay Dubya